THE
UNWANTED

By James McKenna

THE UNWANTED

Lone Cloud Publishing

Unit 1 Betjeman Close, Cowper Road,

Harpenden, Herts AL5 4XH

2013

ISBN 978-0-9569723-5-4

lonecloudpublishing@live.co.uk

This novel is entirely a work of fiction.

The names, characters and incidents portrayed in it are the work of the author's imagination. Any resemblance to actual persons, living or dead, events or localities is entirely coincidental.

A clip catalogue record for this book is available from the British Library

For more crime thrillers by this author, and information about his new books, visit James McKenna's author web page on Amazon or www.crimefiction-jamesmckenna.co.uk.

Other books by this author:

The Unseen
The Uncounted

Coming soon
Global Raider

James McKenna's young readers' book,
The Mind Traveller, the first in a trilogy of action/adventure stories for 9-12 year olds,
will be out in June

CHAPTER 1

A blindfold heightened Justitia's sense of vulnerability, as did the men's silence and their anonymity. She suppressed a shiver but fear remained fused with her thoughts throughout the car journey. An hour later she allowed herself to be led into a building, the clicking of her heels on flagstones was the only sound, the grip on her arm the only indication of another's presence. A door opened and then closed behind. The escort removed his hand leaving silence and darkness to enshroud her. She wondered if they examined her, judged her, as they had judged her over the years she had trained with Universal Youth. During that time they had maintained indoctrination of obedience to their sacred laws, waiting for her acceptance and unquestionable belief in Direct Justice. Self-consciously she straightened, not wishing to show fear. Fear would betray her.

"You may remove your blindfold." The voice was male, cultured and authoritative.

Justitia found herself standing in a single shaft of light, her surroundings left in semi-darkness. She saw five figures seated before her, one perhaps a woman; shadow left the face and gender uncertain. Bigger shadows stood against the wall, large men who stayed still and silent.

"For someone who will dispense justice, I approve of your chosen lodge name."

"The Roman goddess who all recognised," Justitia said. "I wish no one to doubt the nature of my commitment, particularly those who will follow me in our national duty."

"No one doubts you, Justitia. Your background is impeccable, your training excellent and your employment admirably positioned for our purpose. Without question you are an ideal candidate. But you are also a young woman.

5

Entry to the inner chapel demands absolute loyalty and obedience. You will need to exterminate any condemned by the Grand Lodge, those miscreants who violate the decent citizens of this land. Habitual criminals, rapists, paedophiles, terrorists and, more important, those higher up the feral ladder, politicians, bankers and civil servants who betray their high office for self gain, those who dishonour the trust placed in them and follow the path of greed."

"By my hand they will die. I give my life to the sacred duty of this lodge," she replied, watching the speaker lean forward.

"Be aware, Justitia, the condemned may also include any who break our sacred oath of secrecy, men and women you may know. Since the foundation of our order in the times of Roman law, no mercy has been shown to those who betray us."

"I understand and honour my oath," she said, hearing her voice sound crystal clear within the stone walls of the cellar. Because I am chosen, she thought, chosen through the acts committed by my father, chosen for the outrage and vengeance left from the child.

"Justitia, you are about to become a soldier of justice, a warrior at war against the dregs of humanity, criminals and terrorists who, in more enlightened times, would have been hanged. But in these days of political correctness, where the thug has more rights than the victim, your acts of justice may be considered murder."

"I fully understand my legal and moral position," Justitia said, lifting her shoulders to emphasize the point. She felt faith in these people because they in return placed faith in her. They were people of power and influence, people who represented the nation's anger, men and women who adopted means to correct the modern laws they judged as failed. She saw their ranks as a place of liberation where she could stand up for those who lived in fear. A perfect place to hide.

"Assassination requires skill," the voice continued. "The fight for justice may take years. You may be caught and imprisoned but still you will remain irrevocably bound by your oath of secrecy under pain of death. Have you considered what this undertaking places on your young life?"

"Children are violated and the offender is allowed freedom to violate again. Drug dealers become wealthy, burglars repeatedly desecrate our homes. Feral gangs murder, rape and steal. We the people have no protection because criminals' rights are regarded higher then our safety. Islamic terrorists are granted sanctuary and protection while urging the impressionable to turn against this country and kill us. Too many politicians disregard their responsibilities to satisfy their greed. In defence of the people and this Nation, I re-affirm my oath."

"In that case, Justitia, this final test will either break or bind you forever to our code of justice."

She felt a tremor on her skin and prayed it passed unnoticed as a spotlight illuminated an alcove behind. She turned slowly to face her commitment, one that had taken years of preparation. Sweat crept over her skin and the tight knot of her stomach felt clamped by claws.

The prisoner did not appear a miscreant. Middle-aged, with short blond hair he wore glasses and respectable clothes, more a schoolmaster than a criminal. Above the tape that masked his mouth, his eyes protruded under the strain of traumatic terror, his arms and legs were bond, his trousers wet with urine.

"What is his crime?" Justitia said over the man's

increasing muffled protests as two hooded figures pushed him from the alcove and locked him by wooden rails over a trap door set within a wooden floor.

"He sold child pornography of a disturbing nature on the Internet," the voice answered. "Four times he came to trial; four times they set him free due to technicalities. We estimate over forty children have suffered permanent mental and physical damage due to his abuse. Our court has found him guilty. His fate is yours. You may let him go, or you can dispense direct justice. Your decision will reject or accept our laws for the rest of your life."

They know, Justitia thought, that I cannot, will not let him live. Someone who abuses the minds and bodies of children has no place in civilised society. She crossed to the wooden lever protruding from the timber floor, guessing it had only one purpose. This close she could smell his body, smell his fear. She stared at him, assessing the terror that devoured him. His eyes pleaded, begging her to forgive the sinner, knowing she held his life but a moment from extinction as she placed the noose around his neck, allowing sufficient slack for the fatal drop. Satisfied with rope, knot and its position she returned to the front feeling the shaft smooth and round as she clutched the circumference in her strong fingers.

"He is evil," she heard herself say and pressed against the lever, forcing the rounded wood against thighs and stomach until it moved forward. At its far reach the trapdoor cracked wide and her victim fell. The rope jerked beneath his weight, the distinct snap of his neck telling her she had arrived.

"Welcome, Justitia, welcome to Directus Iurisdictio, to the inner chapel, the final and direct administration of justice."

Justitia let go her breath and wiped both hands against

her thighs. "Thank you," she whispered. "I shall not disappoint, I promise you."

CHAPTER 2

"You realise your request may forfeit a man's life?"

"Dramatically put." The Chief of Joint Intelligence smiled without mirth as they passed the statue of Peter Pan in Kensington Gardens. "But the outcome depends on this criminal and Fagan's reaction. You could say we are leaving it to fate." He paused to let a mother pass preceded by two small boys. "He will kill of course?" he said in question. "No point plotting this event if Fagan won't kill."

John Cobbart let go his breath and flexed his jaw. "In defence of the innocent or himself, I think he would. But killing is not listed as a requirement for employment by the Serious Organised Crime Agency."

"Quite," the Chief nodded. "Hence you understand the need for total secrecy. And at this stage that includes Fagan himself."

"I understand the delicacy of the situation. Fagan will only be informed on a need to know basis as events proceed." Cobbart grimaced and clasped hands behind his pin-stripped suit before throwing the question which worried him most. "Considering the unorthodox nature of this operation, I trust the Minister and PM are briefed?"

"I'm not a liberty to say. For your purpose you report all information directly to me." The Chief paused waiting on two joggers to pass. "The Box, MI5, will do the same."

Which means the operation is deniable, Cobbart thought while standing aside.

"If this ever blew up," the Chief continued, "the damage would be considerable. Whitehall is full of busybodies trying to be where they shouldn't and all too ready to prattle should they fall from favour. Therefore at this point only three SIS heads know the scope and complexity of the operation. As for your own man, the shooting will provide cover. His brief would appear on the surface to be solely involved with investigation of the Death Heads, the National Street Security gangs and any active distribution of drugs by them. No one on the other side would ever suspect he had been planted. Who knows, having shot a criminal he might even be approached by Directus Iurisdictio for recruitment."

Cobbart clasped and unclasped his palms, listening to the sound of ducks as they glided on water. Of course, why else would this conversation be held outside with no records of any sort? Those instigating the investigation did not know who the opposition were, did not know who amongst their own ranks were members of DI. He watched the Chief smile and raise his hat to a pretty young nanny in uniform, her tiny charge possibly Arab or Asian. The nanny smiled back.

"So tell me, what exactly is the ultimate objective?" Cobbart asked.

The Chief spread his hands in a gesture of uncertainty. "To disband Directus Iurisdictio, Direct Justice, from the top downwards."

Cobbart could tell the man lied and saw by his eyes he realised as much. "My God, you want control." Cobbart stopped. "You realise the dangers? The laws of Direct Justice are not only unconstitutional, they're medieval."

"John, the human race is medieval. Our so called civilisation is a thin veneer over brutal savagery. Evidence is everywhere. If we were not medieval how do you think an organisation like DI could grow until straddling every class of our society? People are angry. In its present form DI is already saving this country millions. Under proper direction millions would become billions. The Street Security gangs might be predominantly rightwing neo-Nazis but via unofficial but central control they could be a national asset. Only the Death Heads with their radical Islamic teachings and their control by hard East European criminals are a serious threat. Authoritative influence on our nation's will and outlook is eroding; DI is a means to regain Government manipulation. Afterwards, if needed, we eliminate it. But present interest is for the economic good and re-establishment of firm central control over the populace."

"You mean unseen and unrealised control by an alternative political system not accountable to law."

"John, you're been reading and believing too many newspapers. Since the start of history, for the greater good, when has the individual ever been considered? Public relations exercises by politicians expounding the right of freedom and justice are all very commendable. But you and I both know it's a load of bollocks. The populace has always been manipulated by tight monetary indoctrination, all bundled into the illusion of a democracy which allows individual freedom." He raised a finger in a gesture of exclamation. "Let's not bullshit. We must curtail those on the fringes so the inner core is pacified."

Cobbart clenched fists behind his back and stared across the Serpentine to where a group of children played on the grass, their mothers lolling in idle chatter. He felt sweat on his palms. "Now I think you are being dramatic."

"John, like it or not, it's the way civilised humanity works. So, let's put politics aside. All I want from your agent is information. I have others who will do the dirty work."

"And you believe killing this dealer will give Fagan entry to DI ranks?" Cobbart asked.

"St Albans City is one of DI's most active cells. Why do you think it's virtually crime free?"

"What if DI kill Fagan?"

"Why should they? He has legitimate cover investigating the Death Heads for SOCA. These gangs constitute organised crime. Considering the manner in which he will be sent there, I believe DI will not see him as an enemy but as a promising recruit. He's perfectly safe."

"Chief, you know full well if you go undercover as Fagan will, you don't have a team, only someone co-ordinating information received. Amongst the enemy he will stand alone."

"I think not. MI5 is also interested. Quite rightly they fear gangs following extremist Islamic and national policies will lead to unrest. Nationwide there are now reputedly over two hundred gangs from both sectors under a central control by Directus Iurisdictio. Local gangs are virtually disappearing. I repeat, this is organised crime, SOCA's principal business."

Cobbart shook his head. "Alice Sibree only looks after her own. They don't call her the Witch without reason. They will know of Directus Iurisdicio and they will have their own operation." They passed from Long Water to the Serpentine, the breeze rippling the surface to throw sparkled reflections of the afternoon sun. Cobbart kept his gaze on the far bank. "Have you informed Alice Sibree of our intention?" he asked, turning his head.

The man looked uncomfortable. "No, not directly, but she will know, that witch knows everything. I'm almost certain our two operations will eventually link."

"You're asking me to throw Fagan into a nest of vipers."

"John, since taking over this office I have discovered we have more than one agency not spoken of. Fagan will not be alone."

"I don't like it, this is no way to treat a dedicated officer."

"But all for the good of nation, John, all for Queen and country. There's also talk of a knighthood or two."

Sean heard the mobile ring the instant before he entered the clearing. In the deep forest it came as an alien sound, a technical intrusion amidst ancient oaks. The agreement had been adamant, only direct verbal communication, no outside interference, no third parties, no traceable mobile signal, no weapons. Both knew distrust or betrayal might be fatal, which was why Sean pressed his thumb against the safety of the Glock 9mm automatic thrust into the pocket of his parka. Vince Grogan was a dangerous and untrustworthy man.

Stepping from cover the sound of Sean's movement turned Grogan's head. The man had a cell phone to one ear while raising a pistol with his free hand, his eyes and mouth wide, his fear clarifying his intention. Sean dropped to one knee an instant before he saw the muzzle flash and felt the breath of death pass his ear to impact on the tree trunk behind. His response came instinctively and for a second he stayed immobile while aiming. Grogan's gun arm had already levelled for another shot when Sean fired.

The explosive discharge of two weapons simultaneously sent violent sound into the forest and a 9mm bullet through Vince Grogan's head. Sean realigned his wrist from the kickback and took second aim, only to see Grogan dead before he fell.

Sean lowered the pistol, lowered his head, death gave no satisfaction, only a sense of defeat and revulsion. Grogan had been one on a list. Now the list had been shortened, but this was not the way, never would be. The man would spread no more crime, wreck no more lives, but his death simply left a space to be filled by another. The war remained endless.

Sean's mind refocused with the echo of shouts amidst trees as his backup team came running. Simmy arrived first, stopping where foliage gave boundary to the clearing.

"Jesus, guv, you sure took him out," he said, staring at the crumpled body.

"Such is the nature of our game. Shame really, the bastard would have hated prison. What the hell did he think he was doing?" Sean drew an evidence bag from his pocket and carefully deposited his Glock automatic inside. "Here," he said, handing it over. "You'll need that for evidence."

"But you did warn him guv, didn't you?" Simmy asked, accepting the weapon.

"Sure I did, it came by the working end of a gun barrel."

Other team members arrived, Jan, Al and Mike, all keeping their distance as if Sean and the body were carriers of plague. No contamination of the crime scene, Sean thought. These guys were members of the Serious Organised Crime Agency, SOCA, the very best of the best. They knew the drill. They also knew a shot criminal would spread a human rights virus quicker than plague. Sean realised they feared for their own contamination.

"Grogan's dead. For reasons unknown he decided on a shoot out rather than constructive dialogue," Sean said to the silent team. "Secure the area, call Forensics and the local boys. Time to do the paperwork."

"Bad business, Sean," John Cobbart said, not looking up. "The politically correct smell blood. The media already have a headline story of how gun-happy police shot an innocent and unarmed walker."

Sean stayed silent, easing his long frame in the chair while staring at his boss. Cobbart wore his usual crumpled suit, his office a shambles of files and papers, an untidy image behind which lurked a shrewd and calculating mind. Sean gave respect to the man, he even liked him, but never quite trusted him. "We're not police," he said finally. "We're the Serious Organised Crime Agency dealing with serious villains."

Cobbart raised a hand in helpless gesture. "Our problems came with the shooting after 7/7. Now the media blackens every person in the force as a gun-happy killer."

"Something we live with," Sean said, clenching fingers on the arm of his chair. "But it doesn't change the fact our op went seriously wrong. Grogan wanted to pass info on his rival Bently and the emergence of his Dead Head gangs, so why try to kill me? His mobile rang moments before I reached the clearing. It was agreed neither of us would carry a traceable mobile. Someone spooked him, someone changed the scene."

Again Cobbart shifted papers on the desk, still avoiding eye contact. "So your statement said, and I believe you. But you realise truth has nothing to do with an outsider's biased interpretation of events. For some, the fact you carried a weapon was an act of premeditated murder. The civil rights and PC brigades are banging their bibles. You think they care about truth, about reality?"

"The guy had a weapon, he fired it."

"Maybe he was scared, maybe he wanted to surrender.

His pistol went off by accident."

"For Christ's sake, John, to hell with the PC loose heads. You don't surrender a weapon by aiming and firing at a target, me."

"Sean," Cobbart finally looked at him. "I'm on you side. I know you fired in defence. So will others. But the shit which comes out in court has only to do with proof governed by politics. It has nothing to do with truth."

Sean clenched a large boned knuckled hand into the palm of the other. Drawing breath through teeth he suppressed a shudder over what threatened to explode inside of him. "The truth, if wanted, is that Grogan was a wholesale drug-dealer. For profit he ruined thousands of lives."

Again Cobbart moved papers on his desktop, sliding sheets with an index finger. Again he lowered his eyes. "You want to know how some papers describe him? A loving family man; a wealthy entrepreneur who gave to charity. The police hounded him for years without getting a single criminal conviction. The enquiry will be told he was lured into a trap and murdered by a member of the Serious Organised Crime Agency because that was the only way they could deal with him."

"That's total bollocks." Sean sat back seeing the full gravity of what might arise.

"But it's what we face."

"What of the truth? He fired first."

"The truth, Sean, is that you're in the shit."

"For doing my job. You set up that meeting, John. Grogan had information vital to our investigation, proof, he said, that Calvin Bently had a national gang of Easties called the Death Heads. I gather criminal intelligence, that's how we put these guys away." Teeth clenched he watched Cobbart shift in his chair, sensing the man's unease and the tension now coiled between them. "Someone put the frighteners on Grogan," Sean continued. "We need to know who. We need to check that mobile."

Cobbart continued toying with the papers before him.

"Can we go off record?" Cobbart stared up at him.

"If that's what it takes for truth."

"The truth is, we're both sitting in shit, but shit not of our making. It's a quagmire of political deceit between the police hierarchy and the political untouchables in the Home Office. We can't check Grogan's mobile because Grogan's mobile was never found."

"But I heard it, saw it."

"You were the only one who did. Until I read your statement and report I never knew of any mobile. There is no mention of a mobile in the scene of crime report. Do you realise the complication? It means evidence was removed by one of the crime scene officers, or you are wrong."

"I distinctly heard and saw a mobile."

"Tell that to the enquiry."

Sean saw the dark clouds gather. "Someone fucked our operation, breeched SOCA security."

Cobbart nodded. " The thing is, did Bently learn of the meeting?"

Sean continued to stare in silence. He knew Cobbart as

devious, scheming and manipulative. He was also Sean's principal lifeline. It was time to listen with care.

"It's my belief," Cobbart continued. "That whoever called his mobile told him you were Bently's hit man."

"So who did you tell of this meeting?" Sean asked.

"I had to clear it from above, inform St Albans station we had an armed team in the area. Like it or not, others are involved. Bently was not the only one connected to the Death Heads. They're national. MI5, the Joint Intelligence Board and God knows who else are all lurking in the shadows." Again Cobbart raised his hands. "Someone is meddling."

"So who else wanted Grogan dead other than Bently?"

"Perhaps someone higher up the criminal ladder. Someone is organising the Death Heads, infiltrating local territory and gangs, then taking them over."

"Is that why MI5, K branch is involved? Did they set this up?" Sean asked.

"Alice Sibree might be called the Wicked Witch, but MI5 wouldn't risk your life to have you take out a drug baron. Like it or not, in shooting Grogan you've been thrown into the middle but that also gives an ideal opportunity for you to start SOCA's own investigation at St Albans. We need to know who is killing who and why. Is Bently alone or is he part of an organised criminal syndicate out for control of the British drugs trade? A lot is at stake including whether you and I remain in SOCA. Some will argue that in shooting Grogan you opened the door for Bently to expand his territory."

Sean let the significance of Cobbart's words sink in. The police had been his life since leaving school. From Hendon

College, through the ranks to CID, the National Crime Squad and finally Grade One, Senior Investigator in the Serious Organised Crime Agency. The job had broken his marriage, taken away his children and dominated his life. "I ain't going to stand for this," he said feeling the web of injustice tighten over his body. "Just what the fuck's going on?"

"For both our sakes I need you to find out. Calvin Bently is suddenly centre stage. Alice Sibree of MI5 is also watching through K branch."

"Bently must have spooked Grogan," Sean said. "So I take the team and go after him."

Cobbart shook his head. "We don't have time for the formal route. There's more at play here than meets the eye. It's my belief there are hidden players and none of them are on our side."

"So what's the game plan?"

"To play by different rules. You go covert. Enquiries against both Grogan and Bently are still carried out by St Albans CID. They have the files, but within their ranks will be other knowledge never recorded. You go there as a lone operator from SOCA seeking info, evidence for SOCA's defence at the enquiry but also looking into the Death Heads while offering any assistance required. If there are more murders, involve yourself. Then by whatever official or unofficial means necessary, you find out who is really culling the street dealers. Someone within Hertfordshire Constabulary removed Grogan's mobile. St Albans has a high success rate in crime reduction, in fact the best, but then it would have if every mainstream criminal had been exterminated. Something there is not right. Trust no one."

"Do we have any allies in this?"

"Alice Sibree. Like her or not, she is on our side and she does have players in the field. I have a briefing with the Chief Constable and Minister tomorrow. They'll encourage co-operation, but ultimately will only be looking to have clean hands. I'll be honest, Sean, if you accept, you'll be going into the snake pit. There is more to this than spilling feral blood."

Sean examined the man's expression and his eyes, realising he had not been told the whole truth. "Do I have a choice?"

"No." Cobbart stood and reached out his hand. "You're the best there is, Sean, and more than myself will be relying on you. I'll do what I can to cover your back. Start immediately, and for God's sake watch out."

CHAPTER 3

Justitia focused her mind allowing the concentration of conviction to infuse with righteous indignation. This man had raped and to violate one sister was to violate all. He had no place upon this earth. Jogging to the park in the morning sunshine she felt far from the reality of her surroundings, more a warrior going into battle, all energy concentrated for the ordeal ahead. Now the climax of the operation was imminent she chose as always to act alone. During the past years, since joining Directus Iurisdictio, she had deliberately never asked for help in the final act of execution, preferring each kill to demonstrate her commitment. In consequence she accepted the danger, accepted her plans might go wrong, accepted the fear which knotted in her stomach. On learning of his crime she had personally requested this drug-dealing rapist be added to her list, knowing in so doing she must act with speed while he was free from prison. Within months, crime would have returned him inside where execution became more difficult and undertaken by others. For what he had done she wanted this animal for herself.

Weekday morning the park held few people, ideal for her victim who preyed on young mothers with pushchairs and toddlers. Her breath laboured as she ascended the hill following the path from open parkland into woods. Traffic noise became muted and shadow cast her into a grey isolated world. In her head the coursing of blood mingled with the harsh intake of her breath and the rhythmic slap of her running shoes. Sweat glistened over her skin, soaking her vest and the elasticated waist of her running shorts. She saw no one ahead, not even a dog walker and found her spirit in being the warrior knight increasingly clawed by fear.

The tarmac curved for three hundred metres and she had covered half before he came into view. He had positioned himself perfectly, taking maximum advantage of the sweeping path and surrounding trees. No one could see them. In the centre of the city park she was alone with a serial rapist.

He was running on the spot in an absurd manner, almost slow motion, watching as she approached. She was conscious of her bounce and the minuscule cover of her outfit. Revulsion over what he intended pitted her stomach, but she also felt a deeper conflicting sensuality which coiled in mind and body. In a moment she had passed him, then in dread heard him fall in behind. Involuntarily her pace quickened. She could sense his presence closing in on her, sensed his eyes on her movement, her body and her legs. Then he drew alongside and began to overtake. Next moment his arm went around her neck. She screamed, hearing the squeal of her own voice as if it was someone else. Swung into the bushes, the momentum crashed them both through bracken and branches until she fell on wet earth.

Instantly he came on top of her, his hands everywhere. Her vest went up while she grappled to save her shorts. Her scream stifled by his hand, she tried to shift his fingers now clamped over her face but in so doing left her lower body defenceless. The next moment she reached back, desperately scrabbling in her pocket for what it contained before her shorts were ripped away. She could feel her exposure, see his teeth and smell his breath. He used one hand to clamp her jaw, the other to assault her. When she thrust upwards she capitulated to her predominant senses and watched the shock of pain spread over his face. Her sisters were avenged.

From the moment he left the flat and slotted himself into the car, Sean sensed he was being followed. He figured it maybe primeval instinct or training but any close proximity of a malevolent presence always brought a feeling of unease. He shifted lanes, altered speed, but in the morning rush hour the motorway was packed with aggressive traffic. In the end he noted six vehicles which might have been following and memorised their make and colour. In between times he mused how his security could have been compromised. Only SOCA and those close knew his address. If his sanctuary became known to any of the opposition he would need to move out, not that the flat amounted to much, but until now it had at least provided a refuge. School fees for two teenaged daughters ate most of his salary and the financial bribery of his ex-wife for unhindered access to them, ate most of the rest. He loved the girls and believed they loved him back. They gave life a purpose. Victoria Lawless lived in Maida Vale very close to his Camden flat. She also gave life a purpose. MI5 kept her busy as SOCA kept him busy but like the bachelor pad, he felt each provided the other a refuge when needed. In normal times Camden was fine. SOCA's Head Office stood in Pimlico and operations were primarily in London. But St Albans was a pain. Too close yet too far. In rush hour the journey lasted ninety minutes, three wasted hours a day. He had suffered it for two weeks along with the whole of Herts Constabulary treating him like a leper. Still, the tea lady once smiled at him. Acceptance came slow out in the sticks. More important he had to find a room, lodgings, somewhere to stay within the operational area where he could think, work and hopefully stay safe.

Guiding his aged Mercedes off the motorway he glanced again in his rear mirror. Two of the suspect cars followed, a blue Vauxhall and a red Mondeo, both lagging well behind. They stayed until once more he pushed into heavy traffic near St Albans city centre. The towering 11th century abbey gave the city some sense of ancient history but though relatively free of crime, dark spots still marred its middle class surface, mostly fed by drugs. Two weeks after start of operation he had only uncovered what he already knew; that Grogan's patch was up for grabs, with Bently and the Death Heads taking over. Members of the Hertfordshire Constabulary had been polite, professional but decidedly distant. He knew they didn't trust him and who could blame them? To them he represented the gung-ho SOCA agent looking for dirt on their home turf. He'd feel the same in their position. But somewhere amongst their ranks hid one or more bent coppers. Sean figured conventional policing would achieve little in the timescale available, better, he felt, to rattle the silence and see who dropped out of the darkness, who got irritated and edgy, who made a mistake or gave the wrong reaction. He just hoped the result did not come at high velocity via one of Bently's Death Heads. Bent coppers might squeal in the sunlight, but to stay in the shadow they'd sell their souls. As he drove he began to wonder if the one he hunted had tipped off the opposition to follow him home, turning the hunter into the hunted.

Sean manoeuvred his Mercedes to see what he could of the following two cars and mentally noted their registrations. Then he phoned Heidi, his admin assistant at SOCA headquarters in Pimlico.

"I possibly have someone tailing," he told her over the mobile and gave registrations, make and colour of both vehicles.

"Leave it with me, boss," Heidi answered in her soft cherub voice.

Sean imagined her chubby presence, her radiant smile. He considered her the best in the business. Someone who got the job done, the only member of his team he had been allowed to retain, even then her time was shared with other operations.

"Cheers," he said, and cut the call while watching his rear-view mirror. For the first time he managed a clear sighting of the red Mondeo's occupants. Two males, shaven heads, lean faces; they could have been a couple of thugs or a couple of policemen, they certainly had the hard look of the professional. The blare of his mobile from the hands-free socket interrupted concentration. Chief Superintendent Hackett, head of St Alban's District spoke over the cell phone, his voice clipped and to the point.

"I've an emergency," Hackett told him. "I'm stretched and need your help in a new investigation."

"If it's to do with Grogan, it's why I'm here."

Hackett went silent, his breathing hesitant before he answered. "Some idiot let Frank Routt out of prison and he's gone missing. Area priority is to find him."

"Missing persons are not my speciality. Bently and Grogan are."

"Routt used to work as Bently's enforcer. He's an animal whose whole life is wrapped in violent brutality. I'm not asking your help to find him, I want you to look into a murder I believe he's just committed in Verulamium Park."

"How do you know it's him?" Sean manoeuvred the car to a side road and stopped.

"Has all his trade marks. The guy stabbed and gutted was an ex-dealer for Bently, probably fiddled Bently's payment. Routt is like an automated killing machine, even the Death Heads would run. Look Fagan, all my guys are tied up. I've already got a detective sergeant who does most of our pleb killings down there, but I'd like your opinion. Go find out what's happening will you." Hackett switched off.

To Sean's knowledge, Hackett had one of the country's best records for reducing crime, fifty percent in four years. That made him a clever and shrewd operator who knew the system, best to give him some leeway. He tapped fingers on the wheel. Street level crime invariably provided a fast track to involvement with the locals, and lower ranks often knew more than those above.

He left his Mercedes at the back of Verulamium Park, locking the doors while watching the red Ford Mondeo drive by. Neither occupant took interest in him but their proximity was too much of a coincidence. These guys were professionals.

The sense of a malevolent presence did not ease as Sean walked the last few hundred yards across open grass and climbed towards trees and the crime scene tape.

Forensics were there, stalking through the undergrowth in their blue overalls, others picked painstakingly over ground near the path. A tent shielded the corpse and surrounding bushes. Beyond the trees he saw uniformed police dotting the grasslands in their yellow coats, unwinding yet more tape to keep away dog walkers, curious mothers with pushchairs and passing joggers.

One person stood alone, her arms folded. Tall and slender with black hair coiled to a bun, she turned on his approach, her eyes large, dark and questioning.

"Sean Fagan," he said, showing his ID.

"I'm Sergeant Robson. Chief said you were coming. A top man from SOCA, you going to solve this?"

He guessed her of Asian mix. A mix resulting in delicate features and a honey complexion. Her arms remained folded until he offered his hand.

"Not me, but together you and I might."

She clasped his fingers with her own, her grip slight and non-committal.

"That depends on whom listens to whom, sir."

"I'm not police, I'm SOCA, so call me Sean. What's your first name?" he asked, watching her large brown eyes narrow.

"Anjali, sir. So who's going to be up front, write the report and do the briefing?"

"You take the glory. I'm just a back shadow helping if needed. My interest is any connection to Bently or Grogan."

"When out of jail the victim worked for Bently. All the hard-boils here sold for Grogan or Bently. And not just in St Albans, both groups worked areas from Cambridge, Luton, Stevenage, right into Watford and North London."

"That I know, but brief me on this guy."

"The corpse used to be Wayne Finck, a violent druggy, thief and rapist. They released him three weeks ago. On first evidence it appears he attacked another woman, save it didn't go as expected. She fought back." Sean watched a smirk of satisfaction touch her lips.

"So you don't think it was Routt?"

She shuddered and shook her head. "Routt is not human, he wouldn't have cut the guy's genitalia off, he would have ripped it off. Besides, this guy wasn't gay, or female. Routt stood trial for beating a woman to death with a six pound club hammer. Slime bag lawyers got him off. Didn't the boss tell you, that's why you're helping because every single person in the station will be looking for the brute.

One week, two weeks and Routt will kill again. Not good for statistics."

"And what's your opinion?" he asked.

"I'm a sergeant, sir, I do as I'm told." She turned away and called to one of the forensic team. "Can we go in?"

"Just stay within the guide lines. Doc Kielly's in the tent," someone answered.

"So who's Finck?" Sean said to Anjali and lifted the tape so she might pass beneath. They walked across grass between markers.

"A habitual and aggressive criminal. Eighteen months ago I helped in his arrest. He served only half his sentence, probably let out on the whim of some psychiatrist from a prison with no room to keep him."

"Ours is not to reason why," Sean quoted, glancing to her, seeing lips compress.

"Maybe, but we still have a duty to protect the public. I live close by and regularly jog through this park. I recognised Finck ten days ago. He was lurking around, just standing about, looking for another victim I guess. I informed the boss who told the park police who said thanks, but they didn't have resources for dedicated surveillance. They were too busy watching for paedophiles and litter louts, and Finck broke no laws."

Both stopped by the tent and drew on white coverall suits before Sean lifted the flap allowing Anjali to enter. The tent covered as much ground as the trees allowed, including the surrounding bushes. Anjali gave a wave of recognition to Dr Kielly who knelt by the corpse with an assistant. Sean stopped before an internal tape preventing further advance into air permeated by the victim's exposed viscera.

Anjali shrugged. "I knew this guy. I had to do something so I approached a girlfriend on the local rag. We made up a photofit and put it in the paper suggesting a rapist was stalking the pathways. Next day the park was empty," she said, face smug.

"Very community-spirited but was it wise?"

"Definitely. The courts don't protect us so women need to adopt alternative measures."

Sean glanced at her and saw an expression reflecting her words. "But your actions also emptied the park, ideal for a rapist, or for someone who on discovering Finck was here, came to kill him. A past victim maybe."

She screwed her nose a little. "Finck never took the help offered by Social Services, never accepted advice or opportunities to change. He was a lost cause." She sniffed. "Maybe providence gave him early release so he could receive the justice he deserved."

"Maybe." Sean glanced to her then across to Kielly. "Anything for us?"

"At this stage just educated guesswork. The autopsy will give more substantial facts." Kielly straightened up from her work, hand on back, rising from a knee stool she may have used when tending her garden. Mid-fifties, solid and bespectacled, Sean felt she had the quaintness of one attending the Women's Institute rather than a murder investigation. But she was also the person who wrote Grogan's crime scene report. Unless someone had removed the mobile before her arrival, she was a prime suspect. The corpse lay on its back partly supported and propped by crushed bracken. His T-shirt sagged to one side with the disembowelled contents of his stomach, while his shorts were askew around his thighs to reveal a mutilated groin.

"You think he attacked someone, or someone attacked him?" Sean asked.

"There was definitely a struggle, then both went down on the ground. Knee marks suggest he finished astride. We've found fibres of pink polyester cotton, also a torn length of elasticised lace probably from female underwear. Most interesting discovery is a wad of tightly wrapped tissue paper with a central channel that possibly held a short blade. Also strands of long black hair snagged by bracken. Definitely not from the corpse. But this place is open to the public. They could be from anyone."

"But his killer was probably female and not one of the Death Head gang?"

She gave a sharp grimace. "By assumption rather than fact, yes. Finck was a convicted sex offender and first evidence points to his victim being a woman, one who turned the tables. That person stabbed him in the side, then up under the ribcage which caused him to roll off and try to crawl backwards allowing the killer to eviscerate him. The final strike was under the groin, the blade ripped upwards to sever the genitalia. His shorts must have already been down which indicates what he intended before the victim retaliated. Unless the Death Heads have female members, this guy was killed by one angry woman. He died from blood loss but the autopsy will show all." Kielly knelt back to her work, going first to one knee then two.

"I can see why Hackett figured Routt did this," Sean said to Anjali. "The guy wasn't murdered, he was butchered." Sean lifted the flap and they returned outside, striped off their white coverall suits and shoes then placed them back on the pile.

"Never thought the DH, sorry, Death Heads, might have female members but it's possible, would certainly wrap it up as gang warfare," Anjali said.

"Would a DH member cut off male genitalia then gut the victim to make it look like Routt's work?" Sean asked.

"DH or lone female jogger. Someone brutal or someone with cold anger," she said and raised a hand in question. "Not all the Death Heads have Islamic leanings, many from Chechnya and such are just gangsters. But I'd say this one was definitely female."

"Or someone playing at female to blur the facts. Someone who carried a short bladed knife sheathed in tissues, realising if they got into a struggle it would do less damage to themselves than a long bladed knife. How many joggers carry knives?"

"Possibly one determined to run and also to defend herself if attacked. Unlike Routt, this guy won't be coming back. I can't feel sorry about that."

"Feel as you want, but there are still two options, defensive retaliation or premeditated murder."

"You should know, like carrying an automatic pistol just in case," she said, looking to him, her expression clear.

"Point taken. But I know the circumstances of that particular incident, and it's not as you suggest."

"Then 'til we find the circumstances of this incident we should reserve our judgement, sir." She stopped before him. She didn't quite smile but it was the nearest to one since they had met.

"Can we be friends?" he asked.

"Certainly, sir."

"Sean."

"OK, Sir Sean. It's my morning break, care to join me?"

They walked slowly downhill and found a coffee shop near the abbey entrance. Inside Sean sensed her relax a little. He could smell the faint essence of her perfume and felt the ambiance of her personality. Anjali, he decided, had something special.

"Tell me more about Finck," he said, matter of fact, keeping the conversation on business.

"Serious low-life feral," she answered. "He had five convictions for burglary with another forty-three taken into consideration. Two for aggravated burglary and rape, one for rape while on probation and six for possession and selling of Class A drugs. And that count is only when he got caught. Yet still they let him out. It's no wonder the population get angry. His big mistake was working for Bently instead of Grogan. That's why the Chief thinks it's Routt." She sipped her coffee and looked across the tables amidst the clatter of coffee cups and the hiss of espresso machines.

"But you think someone else was angry enough to kill him," he said and watched her expression. "Are you angry too?"

"Angry over the harm he caused for bestial gratification, angry over the injustice of it all for victims while the politically correct crusade for his criminal rights. I'm quite pleased he's dead though." She put down her cup and looked across at him. "You glad you killed Grogan?"

"No, I wanted him on trial and in prison."

"Killing him did no good. Bently and the DH will take his place."

"I know that, it's why I'm interested in Bently, why I'm here."

"You won't get Calvin Bently so easily, the man's a shrewd and careful operator. He administers crime but never participates. He has the DH, sorry, Death Heads, to do that."

"So tell me what you think," Sean said, trying gentle encouragement.

She shrugged. "It's my belief Bently's a front man for someone hiding in the shadows. Someone supplying drugs to build a street army not unlike the right-wing gangs of Street Security. Using Bently he's killed off Grogan's men to enlarge his territory. It's also my belief Bently's bumping off his own indigenous guys and replacing them with the Death Heads. They're named that on account of their black T-shirts and skull head logo. Some members are radical extremists who impose Sharia law in their territories. Others are a mixture of Brit and East European hoodies. If it was a member of the Death Heads who killed Finck it's like they're swatting flies who are a nuisance. Finck was one of the last half dozen of the indigenous dealers. Bently's street sales have now spread to every city. If radical and fundamental Islam takes hold of the DH then Britain has a much greater problem than drugs."

"You think a member of the DH is your target?" Sean asked, conscious of her eyes, warm, deep, but somehow hurt. "Because if that's how Finck went down it kind of complicates the rape theory."

Folded arms resting on the table she looked back at him as she pursed her lips. "Maybe a female member of DH went there knowing Finck would try to rape her. Bently's heavily into trafficking, men for drug pushing, women for prostitution."

"So possibly one of Bently's women killed Finck, maybe the DH do have female members."

She shrugged again. "At this point I'm sticking with a rape victim, female DH or not."

"Why?"

"Woman's intuition and male enforcers don't normally wear elastic knicker lace." She checked her watch. "Coffee break over. I have to return to crime scene."

"Can we meet for another discussion? I'd like to hear more about your intuition," he said.

"You're the only one who does." She stood. "You really going to help on the Finck enquiry?"

"I've been asked to provide relevant info from my own operations. Happy to oblige if we can swap."

"Interesting." She allowed him to open the coffee shop door and walked out into sunshine. "I still don't understand why the Chief wants your involvement. You're into serious organised crime, what interest is a minor thug?"

"Because the Death Heads are serious organised crime. Perhaps Hackett's looking for an outside opinion. Let's meet again and discuss it. Care for a drink this evening?" he asked, following her down steps and walking beside her towards his car.

"I don't drink," she said, looking at him, judging the man not the colleague, sizing his physical shape and attractions. He'd been called good looking, even though his young daughter accused him of having a big nose. Under the woman's scrutiny it felt enormous.

"A mineral water then?"

"I'm busy tonight. I train local kids at Universal Youth; netball, all very girly."

He nodded. "Admirable work. Tell me, being local, do you know of any rooms or flats on a short lease?"

"You'll get nothing in St Albans without a hefty deposit and a minimum of six months commitment at premium rate. You want to stay, try Travel Lodge or ask Bertha on the front desk, if anyone knows, she will. Bertha knows everything."

Sean nodded, glancing at her profile, thinking her features too soft and delicate for the hard grit of her job. But that, he figured, was being sexist.

"Finck's murder has all the marks of a gangland killing," he said. "Mutilation to spread brute fear, but it's too neat. A hatchet man would do just that, not use a short bladed knife. I think you're right, maybe we do have a female, but one who would have us think otherwise and one very skilled in what she does."

"A female assassin." Anjali glanced at him with doubtful eyes.

"The Death Heads are organised crime and organised crime has killers of both genders."

CHAPTER 4

Sean entered a busy St Albans police station around lunchtime. A few uniformed constables kept sentinel watch, the Routt emergency allowing a more macho attitude in front of anyone suspected of being Press. Those officers lurking in back corridors were predominantly plain-clothed with a few senior uniformed figures amongst them. Whatever the situation, Sean figured, no one had yet found a solution. His mobile rang and for a moment Sean listened to a hollow tinny echo which distorted the words.

"They will not let you interfere," a mechanical voice sounded. *"Go now or you will die."*

"Hello." Sean frowned. "Who's that?" The line went dead. He stared bewildered until Detective Inspector Dan Reece crossed over to him, the man's hamburger rolls of bulging flesh contained by the stretched cloth of his buttoned suit. "Bloody nutcase," Sean muttered.

"Are those bastards still out there?" Reece asked, sneaking a side-glance from the window. "I hate journalists, they create a bullshit story then look for some poor jerk to hang it on." He drew back from the glass "It's not our fault the stupid sods let Routt go free."

"Put out a general warning."

"And cause panic? The Press will crucify us. Routt hates women and the hacks would really stir it. Myself and a few got him ten years for aggravated burglary. He beat a woman to death in her own home. When we found him it took six of our guys to hold him down. He put two in hospital. Now after five years they've let the animal lose and didn't warn us."

"So go take the glory, tell the Press you'll put him away

again."

"If we knew where he was. The first thing he did was pull his tag off. Tagging Routt," Reece shook his head. "These probation guys are too stupid. I tell you, blokes here are shitting themselves. Routt's violence is driven by grudge, especially for the police and courts. That's from the judge downwards. Routt is a psycho with a long memory. They should have suffocated him at birth. Ain't no one in the station going to put their name in a press report where Routt can read it."

Sean looked from the windows to the huddled reporters. "Bit more than a Saturday night punch-up then. OK, so bait a trap and draw him out. You got big capable guys here, and if you're worried, shoot him."

"You want to shoot him for us, you've had the practice." Reece pushed out a blubbery lip. "It's OK for SOCA, you guys hide behind secrecy. We get to play it hands on, full political correctness. On top of that it's quite likely the bait would end with an axe in his head."

Sean ignored the jibe, but it ended polite conversation. "Well, I guess every neighbourhood has one. Good luck with the hunt." He crossed to the station front desk.

Sergeant Bertha Smith lurked behind the counter with bull square shoulders and cropped hair. "Chief wants to see you," she said.

Sean nodded and signed the entry book. "Anjali Robson told me you might know of a short-term place I can rent, six, eight weeks."

Bertha rested ham fists on the counter. "No chance."

Sean left the desk, phoned Hackett's secretary and received the okay to visit.

Hackett's office gleamed, no files, no papers on neat Spartan furniture that blended with the thin bespectacled man who sat straight-backed behind a shiny desk. He reminded Sean of a stone lizard.

"Sorry to interrupt your day," Hackett said, not offering his hand. "What news on Finck?"

"First evidence indicates he was stabbed in self-defence by one of his rape victims, but a victim determined Finck never came back."

"Not Routt, pity. But we'll keep him firmly in the picture. Coupled with our manhunt it should produce good publicity for police dedication. So, another victim of the Death Heads gangs. I'll get Robson to wrap it."

"She, or he, killed someone. What about the perpetrator?" Sean frowned over the man's dismissal.

"If it was Routt great, if it's some helpless woman defending her honour I doubt she'll come forward. Truth is, low-life gets low budget. I need resources spent on finding Routt and other important matters. Having Finck out the way is useful mind, no more wasted police time."

"Murder is murder," Sean said.

"Save in Finck's case it seems self-defence."

"We won't know if it's never investigated. It could be a female Death Head."

"They don't use females. Don't worry, we'll make the usual show, appeal for witnesses. Thanks for your assistance on that one. Hope you don't mind but I mentioned your name regarding suspicions that Routt is still killing for drug barons. It means he might come out the woodwork looking for you. It makes you a kind of bait but you're a big guy, I'm sure you could handle any confrontation. Now to business." He pressed narrow shoulders against the back of his chair and continued without pause. "I've only just completed reading your report on the Grogan shooting. Do you intend to accuse any on my staff of removing this elusive mobile?" He stared at Sean.

"Should I?" Sean stared back, deciding verbal retaliation would produce little. If Hackett had given Sean's name to the Press, that basically made Sean Routt's next victim. How to remove a threat by use of an unwitting, if violent, third party.

"My staff are the very best, each with total integrity plus dedication to duty." Hackett nodded agreement with himself.

"I don't doubt it," Sean said, realising his exclusion from such praise. In return he found something about Hackett unreal. Not a person to trust.

"You killed a man and now excuse your action by insinuating a member of my staff removed evidence. If I had known that, I would not have allowed you inside this station."

Sean saw the opportunity to ensnare and picked his words with care. "I'm not looking for a member of your staff, sir, I'm looking for a member of Bently's criminal organisation. The person who called Grogan on his mobile had knowledge of my operation via leakage, deliberate or otherwise, from internal or external agencies. The only person who can tell me that source is Bently. He's the person I want."

"Do you have enough to arrest Bently?" Hackett asked, eyes fixed on Sean.

"We have a serious file. His current organisation covers areas from the Home Counties right down into Watford and

North London. And by use of the Death Heads his sales are spreading nationwide. People trafficking, drugs, prostitution, alcohol and tobacco smuggling, he's high on the list. Of course, we'll only charge him with one offence, then he'll do a deal to save himself from the others. He'll certainly tell us if any member of any agency accepted a payoff." Sean watched the surrounds of Hackett's eyes marginally narrow, his thin lips compressed as if to prevent the darting of his tongue.

"Due to my efforts and dedicated staff, the crime rate in St Albans and Hertfordshire has decreased annually by ten percent, and in particular to drug related crime. Burglary, violence, robbery, muggings, street stabbings, rape, my methods are highly valued. If we can talk purposefully, Mr Fagan, if this missing mobile should materialise, I want my team to arrest Bently and deal with any conduits that might exist to other crimes. By that I mean the organised East European gangs known as the Death Heads. I want my team under my guidance to maintain their excellent record and enhance the standing of all those involved with the operation."

Sean deliberately extended his pause before answering, throwing more bait into the trap. "As you know, sir, SOCA prefers to stay in the shadows and doesn't encourage publicity. Our job is to gather intelligence, not make arrests. That is for others. However, the mobile from Grogan's crime scene will need to be found. Whether it became lost by administrative neglect or criminal interference from outside is for your own department to resolve, but the service providers' record of mobile calls goes to SOCA." He stared hard at Hackett then produced what he hope was a cynical smile and flippant tone. "Such a pity Grogan did not live to tell us, so sad."

Chief Superintendent Hackett leant back and laced his fingers. "I do believe we are talking the same language, Mr

Fagan," he said, and spread his thin lips into a smile. "I shall make internal enquiries regarding this mobile. In return I would appreciate your full dossier on Bently and his gang of so called Death Heads."

"I'll speak with John Cobbart. I'm sure he would be delighted to arrange cross-departmental assistance and information," Sean said, knowing Cobbart would never agree, save to exploit Hackett's lust for glory. When it came to police politics, Cobbart stood supreme.

"How did you get on with Sergeant Robson?" Hackett asked, as if the previous conversation had been settled and closed.

"She appears able and competent."

"Excellent. She's a clever girl, has an OU degree and is studying for her inspectorate. I'll allocate her to assist your enquiries."

To spy and report back, Sean thought and nodded. "Most helpful, sir, thank you."

"Glad we've been able to have this little chat." Hackett stood and offered his hand. "I'll have logistics allocate you a room. Welcome to St Albans and Hertfordshire Constabulary, Mr Fagan."

Out in the corridor Sean wiped his hand on the sleeve of his jacket. When Cobbart warned he entered a snake pit, he had meant it.

Having secured a name to print, the journalists had gone, leaving the reception empty save for a few dossers plus a hysterical dog owner holding an empty lead and collar. Sean headed for the nearest pub and lunch.

In the saloon bar a huddle of plain-clothed detectives

muttered over their beers. Sean chose the public bar, bought a sandwich, a glass of Guinness and hitched himself onto a stool. He couldn't believe his luck that Hackett had been so gullible. Any information Sean passed from SOCA would be pre-vetted by Cobbart; and Cobbart gave nothing, save maybe to the old boys club in return for favours. Anjali, on the other hand could prove a gold mine. Beneath her professional exterior he had sensed angry disenchantment. If he gained her trust she might tell of things only whispered behind hands. Halfway into the sandwich his mobile range and Heidi's soft voice spoke into his ear.

"You got company," she told him. "Both the red Mondeo and the blue Vauxhall are registered to the Home Office and that's as far as any info goes."

"So, is it MI5 or who?"

"Who, more like it. MI5 don't normally use cars that old. Can't help beyond that boss."

"So the question is, do I have watchdogs or guardian angels? Someone above is taking this seriously. Dig out all you can on a couple of local yobs, Wayne Finck and Frank Routt. Both violent head-bangers, both been in the nick. Leave it on my email."

"Will do, boss."

Sean switched off and immediately rang John Cobbart.

"You having me tailed?" Sean asked.

"No."

"Then someone on high is."

"Clearly there is more involved than we first realised. Be very careful, Sean."

"Hackett wants info on Bently."

"Hackett wants glory and clean hands. The man's an arsehole, leave him to me."

"Cheers, boss," Sean said hearing Cobbart switch off. He finished his Guinness and crossed the road to the station, all the time watching traffic and pedestrians. All seemed normal save for a solitary figure who, by height and lack of movement, stood out from others. Dressed in flat cap, wax jacket and cords he stared at Sean with intent immobile concentration. For moments he stared back then turned away. When he glanced again the solitary figure had gone. He collected a laptop from the Mercedes and entered the building. Sergeant Bertha Smith beckoned him, even smiled.

"Room 17, upstairs." She handed him a key. "Courtesy of the boss. It's yours for the duration. And also," she scribbled a phone number on a slip, "you want a room, Dolores is a friend of mine."

"Thanks Bertha." Sean tried a return smile. "I owe you."

"It's Berty," she said and slapped a collection box in front of him. "You want to donate to Universal Youth? We help young kids and ex-cons, training, sport, employment opportunities."

"Yeah, heard of them, they're OK." Sean fished out his wallet and extracted a five-pound note before seeing her stoic face. He returned the fiver and extracted twenty. She nodded.

"Much appreciated." She tucked the box out of sight.

On the first floor he found door 17 and tried the key. Inside one desk, two chairs and a filing cabinet left enough room to shuffle. A small window looked towards the abbey. He plugged his encrypted laptop into the station's power and downloaded the info Heidi had sent regarding the two villains.

Wayne Finck had been in and out of custody since childhood. He appeared to use rape as a macho chat-up line and burglary as a means of support. Sean understood Anjali's anger. Prison had no effect and the judicial system alternated between caging him and letting him loose on the public.

Frank Routt came over as a cunning and violent psychopath. A homophobic misogynist bent on some kind of vengeance against society, particularly anyone who restrained him, be it judge, policeman or an unfortunate who stepped in his path.

Sean drummed fingers on the desk in absent thought. Three years of local statistics showed no sudden increase in local gang related murders, only a steady evaporation of feral criminals through accidents or disappearance. Hackett seemed to put any resulting drop in crime down to his organisation's abilities and only occasionally to gang warfare between dealers. Or did something lay hidden in the paperwork? He picked up his mobile, toyed with it for a moment then called Heidi.

"Got a mission for you," he told her.

"I don't work past midnight," she said. "I got my cats to love and cherish."

"Would I ask such a thing?" He imagined her standing hand on hip, her rosy face set in grim determination not to falter. "All I want are names, addresses, crimes, current whereabouts or death of all known street dealers and habitual criminals in the Bently and Grogan areas over the last five years." He paused, listening to her silence.

"Sean Fagan, you said you loved me."

"I do. It's just that right now you're more useful at a computer and the National Criminal Database than cooking a meal or lying on a bed."

"And you wonder why women have cats instead of men. You've asked for a week's work."

"That's OK, I don't need it 'til tomorrow," he said. "Heidi, you're an angel. Speak to you soon." He switched off before she answered. Luck had been pushed to the limit.

The phone number Sergeant Smith provided rang for just seconds before a curt, female voice answered.

"I'm Sean Fagan," he said. "Bertha Smith tells me you have rooms to let."

"Recommended by Berty," the voice paused. "OK, if you come down now before I go out I'll show you." She gave an address in the old quarter of St Michael's Manor.

The house looked as if built in Dickens' time and stood in a terrace of similar properties. A short full-chested woman opened the 19th century door, her clothes 1940s in appearance.

"I'm Dolores Fairbright," she said, offering a firm hand.

"Fagan, Sean Fagan."

"How appropriate." She beckoned him in. "I'll show you the rooms. We share the kitchen." She led him down the panelled corridor to stairs. An antique drawing room opened to the left and a kitchen at the far end. The decor and fittings all appeared original.

"It's incredible," Sean said. "How do you keep it authentic?"

"Simple, just leave it alone. Save for plumbing and electricity, the house remains as built. My father put in hot water and two bathrooms with period fittings. Be warned, you'll need bed socks. It gets cold at night."

Sean followed the sway of her hips upwards and past more accommodation on the first floor landing, finally arriving in the attic and two small rooms.

"Used to be the servants quarters." She opened both doors. One was laid out as a diner cum dayroom; the other contained a bed. "You have your own small en suite bathroom." She pointed to an inner door. "So, for how long?" she asked.

"Six, ten weeks," he answered, ducking his head below sloping rafters.

"Including sheets and towels, two hundred pounds a week, cash." She stretched lips to an expectant smile. "Plus one week in advance."

Sean nodded and held his hand out to agree the deal. "From tomorrow." She smiled properly for him then, her narrow face suddenly warm. He guessed her early forties with an agility and speed on the stairs that clearly indicated fitness. She extracted three keys from her pocket.

"Front door and key for each room. There's a microwave in the kitchen, it's my one luxury. The only house rules are, you don't smoke, you keep out of my quarters and out of my knickers, including my daughter's." She put her head to one side. "Policemen think they have a God given right."

"I'm Serious Organised Crime Agency. I'm not police."

"In that case, I'll trust you for the rent until tomorrow." She brushed past and headed for the stairs. "You'll need a resident's parking permit or you won't get a place within a mile. Of course, that will cost you money in the tin."

"Tin?" Sean queried, following her to the kitchen.

"Universal Youth, I'm area accountant. We do youth clubs, sports centres, rehabilitation, single mothers, counselling, general help to lift our youngsters to a higher level." She opened a drawer then turned to him holding tin and her own permit. "Forty quid," she said. "Otherwise you won't get to park. Don't worry about the registration, I know the warden. Yours will arrive in two days."

Sean fished in his wallet and extracted the money.

"Anything to help the under-privileged." He dropped notes into the tin.

"Oh we certainly do that, Mr Fagan, we certainly do that."

Sean bought a vindaloo on the way home. Darkness prevented him from checking if he was followed. The Edwardian mansion block in Camden Town had been divided into numerous dwellings then mortgaged out at great expense to the occupants. Sean parked round the back, locked the Mercedes and looked up to where a kitchen light showed through drawn curtains in his own flat. Only one other person had a key. He went up the internal staircase two steps at a time, then paused by the entrance, listening closely before inserting the key. The door made no sound as it opened.

Victoria Lawless lay on the chaise langue and dropped a magazine before removing small oval spectacles from her delicate shaped nose. She swung long legs to the floor and rose on high stiletto heels, her black hair hung loose and full, her figure draped in a fitted dress that clung to every curve with no evidence she wore anything beneath.

"Do you always crash in like that?" she asked, walking across to touch his lips with her own. "And what is this disgusting mess?" She removed the brown carrier from his hand and disdainfully deposited it into the kitchen bin.

"My dinner," Sean said and closed the door behind him.

She turned and folded her arms, her head to one side. "Well, I've bought you a nice salmon steak with sauté potatoes and fresh salad. Much more nourishing."

"What are you doing in my flat?"

"What a silly question." She returned with the slinking glide of a confident predator and pushed his coat from shoulder and arms. "What you should really ask is, before or after dinner?"

Sean's reply was muted by her lips over his.

"Both," he whispered finally.

CHAPTER 5

Dawn crept over Camden with the noise of traffic. Sean found the space beside him empty and saw the silhouette of Victoria's figure emerging from the bathroom wrapped in a towel.

"You're early." He opened both eyes.

"MI5 put in a full day."

"Two cars with Home Office registrations followed me yesterday," he said, watching the movements of her trim figure. "You know why?"

"You live a dangerous life. Some angel is probably watching over you."

"Making sure I turn the right way, uncovering only what is wanted, leaving what some would prefer to remain unseen."

"Precisely, standard MI5 procedure." She stood near the bed and pulled the towel off to dry her legs. "At the moment we need you to help uncover who is really organising the Death Heads."

"You drive a blue Vauxhall at work?" he asked.

"You saw me. I thought you'd be looking for my BM. I thought an old car might fool you."

"So what does the Witch want?"

"Co-operation between our enquiries. The Death Heads now have gangs from Glasgow to Brighton. Our worry is drug dealing might start funding terrorism."

"Co-operation, that's a new word for the Witch. I tell

you, but you don't tell me."

"As it happens, it is I who have the information, not you. So you better just be nice to me." She wrapped the towel beneath her arms and crossed to the fridge. Returning with a glass of orange juice she stood poised above him.

"I'm always nice to you." He stretched out a hand but she stepped back.

"For the Death Head gangs to reach their current force it means they have a central organisation with financial control."

"Organised crime, my world." Sean let his fingers play with the towel's edge.

"And that's where it gets interesting and where MI5, K Branch looks closer. First, who is central control? Not Bently, he doesn't have the muscle or the logistic ability."

"So he's number two."

"That's what I need you to find out, and more important, who is number one? We have our suspicions but you're in a better position to gain positive info." She leant away so the towel hung a fraction beyond his fingertips.

"You got any suspects?"

"The son of an Afghan warlord currently living near St Albans. His father has close ties with NATO due to him mustering tribes to fight on their side, all for money of course."

Sean shrugged, one finger still hopefully exploring the air. "Money rules. The only way out of that country is to buy our way out."

"Because he's an ally, it's maybe why NATO turns a blind eye to his other activities. He's also one of the biggest producers and shippers of heroin worldwide. In the UK he wholesales out to the Death Head gangs as sole supplier."

"Go on." Sean moved his hand away.

"I want a return first. What do you know about Directus Iurisdictio?"

"Never heard of them, Latin isn't it?"

"Direct Justice. So," she placed a finger beneath her chin. "Cobbart is not so clever as he thinks. Or maybe he hasn't briefed you yet."

"He said I entered a snake pit. But so far I've seen no activity."

For a moment she stared down at him as if undecided then twisted her legs and sat, her expression so serious he thought it inadvisable to slide his hand along her thigh.

"Our knowledge of DI is limited. They're very secretive and extremely dangerous. But the Witch believes there are connections between them, the Death Heads and Universal Youth from where the Street Security gangs emerged, and the fact St Alban's is relatively crime free."

"Well done the police."

"Yeah." She suppressed a smirk. "And the main reason for that is because local habitual criminals have simply disappeared, like someone waved a magic wand. Hackett believes he's the greatest crime fighter since Superman. Truth is, most habitual criminals started falling from high windows, were stabbed, run over, committed suicide, simply disappeared or decided to reform by joining the SS, Street Security."

"Reform? Those idiots consider themselves hard men."

"Try herding a gang into a cellar then cutting the leader up with a chainsaw. Surprising how the others conform, particularly when national socialism appeals to the criminal mind. The same is happening throughout our major cities, except now it's not the SS who are gaining street control but also the Death Heads, predominantly in our Muslim communities."

"So have we got good gangs and bad gangs?" He rested fingers on her knee.

"With the SS, more like a bunch of neo-Nazi thugs. Worrying thing is, some neighbourhoods and communities have welcomed them. The SS show zero tolerance to violent gangs, hoodies, or any who are a public nuisance. In Muslim communities the Death Heads help the vulnerable, police the streets and now impose Shari law."

"But they sell drugs, for Christ's sake."

"They're very secretive about it and law abiding local communities do not see that side of them. They see good, religious young men, not gangsters. Whereas the SS portray themselves as strong, righteous individuals ready to defend street, village, town and nation. Any local gang or dealer who gets in the way they remove. Some police forces unofficially even co-operate with them."

"If they have central control, then both groups have a weakness. Remove that and they collapse," Sean said, shifting his fingers along her skin to the towel edge.

"Exactly our intention," she said, staring at the far wall. "Except the guy we suspect of controlling the Death Heads is politically untouchable. The perfect immigrant, highly educated in a British public school, then university; a wealthy philanthropic Conservative who, amongst other things, supports Universal Youth. He built their St Albans sports centre. He's polite, charismatic and a perfect gentleman. We have never been able to pin anything near him. He uses third party people like Bently to do his dirty work."

"Are you putting out a challenge?" He edged his fingers beneath the towel. "MI5 can't get evidence against him so they want SOCA to help."

She looked down and smiled. "Not SOCA. You, Sean Fagan. Somehow there is a connection between Directus Iurisdictio and the Death Heads. The Witch believes that link is in St Albans. And you, my love, are now perfectly placed."

He moved fingers to his ultimate goal and shook his head before suddenly realising the implication. "You pair of bitches." He snatched his hand away. "It was you who stole that mobile."

"Not me." She moved his fingers back and preened with innocent eyes. "Look to Alice Sibree, the Witch, she's the Boss. I'm only here to hold your hand and look after your every need."

"Bloody MI5 set me up. Did you phone Grogan as I entered the woods, tell him I was someone else?"

"Oh Sean, don't be cruel to me." She pressed her thighs on his hand. "That was DI or Bently. We simply took advantage of the situation to set up Operation Deep Cut. DI were about to take Grogan out anyway."

"Just who are DI?" He pulled his hand away.

"Directus Iurisdictio. They're very powerful, dangerous and fully operational," she said, reaching to put his hand back on her legs. "I can help, I promise. Please let me, I need you."

"What you need is a damn good spanking."

She pouted. "If it makes you happy."

"Victoria, you're impossible." He swung both legs from the bed and stood. "What happen to Grogan's mobile?"

"It got stolen. Which makes you appear to have coldly shot a serious criminal. And it's our belief some may just see that as the perfect qualification for entry into Directus Iurisdictio."

"And I thought the black arts a myth." He grabbed a dressing gown then lowered his face until staring eyeball to eyeball. "OK, if you're capable, this time try telling me the truth."

"You're not alone, you ever heard of the Combined Agency Taskforce, or CAT, for short?"

"No, and I don't want to."

"They've heard of you. Think of them as a counter-terrorist group. They're unknown outside of the SIS because they don't exist, least not officially. They were set up during the IRA troubles and believe me, they are as secret and deadly as DI. In fact destruction of DI and the Death Heads is now their main concern."

"So what have they got to do with me?" He stood back, wishing any sense of love he felt was really lust, wishing her somewhere else, not staring up at him with big soft eyes.

"Sean, I hate to tell you but I think you're now a member, seconded to them for the duration of current operations."

"What the hell do you mean?" he shouted, "current operations, I got my own operation."

"Sean, darling, not so loud, you'll wake the neighbours." She stood and placed a hand on his chest. "I'm only trying to help, ask Cobbart."

"How about someone asking me?" He turned away, heading for the kitchen, grinding teeth as he filled the kettle.

"Sean, you're perfectly placed," she said from the doorway. "Cobbart will give you a full briefing. Operation Deep Cut has been on-going for the past four weeks. All I know is that it's big and it affects the nation. You had to be drawn in this way. DI have too many eyes and ears. Everything is below surface, everything."

"For Christ's sake, Victoria. I may no longer be married, but I do have a life, I got kids."

"That's how we need it, everything appearing as normal everyday existence. We fight as they do, from behind our own shadows."

"Shit."

"I'd feel the same."

"So just how dangerous is this operation?" He walked back to her.

"Triple A. You armed?"

"You kidding? I just shot a man. Not even Cobbart would issue a weapons permit."

She kissed him and smoothed his chest as if settling feathers. "Off record, I'll see what I can do."

"My God, you love me so much?" he said, shaking clenched fists. "Victoria, how do I go undercover? Everyone in St Albans nick knows exactly who I am and what I'm after."

"That's exactly as it should be. Perfect. That is your cover. Because they think you're after a mobile and the Death Heads. They wouldn't dream your real target is DI. Simply hint you shot Grogan deliberately and would like to do more. Let them come to you. Only remember, the danger is real and immediate." She pouted lips. "Do you want me to get dressed?"

Sean sat by the window watching early morning turn to a blue-clouded sky, his mind churning, he wondered what caldron of evil he had been manoeuvred into. He'd give Cobbart hell for all the good it would do. Victoria had been the messenger, he couldn't blame her, but now she had gone he cursed the love he knew lay beneath his lust. Victoria, sweet, seductive, devious Victoria, a true apprentice of the Witch. At 0900 hours he rang Cobbart at SOCA HQ in Pimlico. Cobbart just better have a good explanation. His secretary informed he had a prior engagement which kept him away from the office. Sean just bet he did, more so when the man refused to answer his mobile. But he couldn't hide forever. Some time he would need to give a full briefing.

Half an hour later Sean drove up the motorway, a small case on the car's back seat, the red Mondeo reflected in his rear-view mirror. Sooner or later he knew he would need to deal with these guys. It would help if he knew whose side they were on. His phone rang and he slotted it into hands-free. No one spoke, a hollow crackle sounding followed by a metallic voice.

"Remove yourself or die. You have been warned. If you remain, in

forty-eight hours you will be dead." The voice stopped.

Sean grabbed the mobile but the caller had gone. He checked the number, then with one eye on the road, one on the iPhone, he emailed it to Heidi with the message *Please check.*

Semi darkness in the church crypt cast shadow over the faces gathered around the table. Silence grew intense until the Lord High Justice for Directus Iurisdictio's St Albans lodge tapped his gravel on the wooden surface.

"Ladies and gentlemen, I have called this extraordinary meeting of our Inner Chamber due to an emergency requiring immediate attention. The London Grand Chamber has received information from a reliable source in Whitehall that a spy is at work amongst us. Chief Superintendent Hackett, please rise."

"Not me, my lord." Hackett stood knocking over his chair. "By our most sacred oath I swear it is not me."

"Calm yourself, sir. I never accused you. The individual concerned is currently outside our ranks. His name is Fagan, Sean Fagan from the Serious Organised Crime Agency. He has been classified a serious threat to our security, to our national and sacred cause. The Grand Chamber has sanctioned his immediate removal."

"No, my lord, I ask you to reconsider. He is a Government official." Hackett looked round the table. "He shot a criminal in cold blood, he believes as we do."

"All a ploy to fool us, to gain our trust. This order is from Directus Iurisdictio's Grand Master after consideration by the central Grand Chamber. Justitia, I charge you with this task. Use whatever assistance you require."

Hackett leant hands on the table. "But, my lord, Fagan is not dishonourable nor a criminal. Please time to recruit him to our cause and beliefs."

"Alas, Superintendent, we cannot take that chance and I question your judgement on the issue. It has taken since the second world war to rebuild Directus Iurisdictio to its former glory and strength. Faced with the ongoing threat of Islamic extremists it is imperative for this nation to have a firm and responsible judicial system. A system not bogged down by abuse of human rights or the over zealous politically correct. Some of us have to stand up and be counted which is why DI exists and why we cannot jeopardise its security in anyway. Fagan must be removed. We have no choice in this matter. Planning for his execution will start immediately. The Inner Chamber has requested this judgement be expedited with immediate effect."

CHAPTER 6

Con Priestly tapped keys on his laptop and sent a message into the private chat room under the pseudonym of Cool Luke.

I nicked this stuff from the high street but Martha won't let me keep it. You want, it's yours, cheap.

How cheap? Chrissy replied.

5 quid.

I ain't got 5.

A snog then, maybe a feel.

Piss off.

He thought quickly then typed again.

I got 10 DVDs, the latest. 15 CDs including the new Puppy Boys release. Pink trainers size 3, designer jeans to match and sunglasses. A big snog and a look at what you got.

Poss, but I bring my friend, Paula.

Deal. Meet 2 o'clock. There's a derelict house waiting for builders end of London Road, you get in round back.

No way. I'll still be at school, dung-head. So will you. I'll nip out lunchtime, 1 o'clock, OK?

He waited. After three weeks coaxing the girl to trust him he did not want to lose her. At one o'clock other kids would be around, mothers on the school run, people he could do without. He had visited the area where she lived a dozen times. He knew where he wanted her. Sweat glistened on his puffy cheeks and trickled into the stubble of his chin. This was an opportunity to have two of them and the thought made him tremble.

School sucks, he typed. *If you're scared, I'll do the deal with someone else.*

Chrissy's reply came within seconds.

I'm scared of nothing, but I ain't going to no house. Meet you Faulkners Wood, Harpenden, other side of the golf course, the back of our school. There's a car park and a path leading to the common. We'll be halfway along, and you better not try nothing.

Priestly closed his trap. *And you better not be some soppy little kid*, he typed.

I'm same as you, 12. So, what's for Paula?

Depends what she'll do.

You must be real fat and ugly to give stuff for a snog and grope.

I'm Cool Luke, the cream. How do I know you're coming?

Ya don't. See ya.

"More than you think," he whispered. "And yeah, I am fat and ugly." He waited but when the box stayed empty he signed off and disconnected the laptop from the Internet before placing it back inside the case beneath his bed. The hostel corridor outside his room remained silent. He knew most residents would still be boozed up, lying in bed before going out to shoplift or hang around the high street. He was panting when he moved. Images of Chrissy's limbs clouded his mind in fantasy and the very thought of her young body groped by his fingers made him secrete in his pants. And there would be two. He had never handled two girls before. Realising the challenge he placed packaging tape, mask and latex gloves into a bag.

Jenkins, the day warden, sat at his desk and Priestly adopted an expression of submission to pacify the man's aggression.

"Can't you sleep" Jenkins said, in mockery.

"Got a job interview," Priestly told him, and dutifully signed the departure book.

"Back six-thirty sharp," Jenkins instructed, glancing momentarily from his television. "Let's see your tag."

"Certainly, Mr Jenkins." Priestly lifted his trouser leg to reveal the electronic device that monitored his entry into forbidden areas. Priestly kept his eyes down and his tone insipid but outside in the street he straightened and walked with a purposeful stride. The indifference of his wardens gave him open licence. He knew no one cared what time he came back, no one cared where he went or what he did providing the books were dutifully signed and the paperwork done.

Sitting on the train to Harpenden he again allowed his mind to fill with fantasy over what he intended. If caught he reckoned on three years in prison, four at most, which mean he would be out in two. One year per girl, one year per body. He had never had two girls at once, that would be a challenge, but worth the risk.

He pulled up his hood so as to hide his face and hurried round the golf course perimeter to the common, careful the few walkers he saw always remained at a distance. Sweat began to creep from the folds of his skin and he held his groin in anticipation. If they did not want to be touched they wouldn't come, he assured himself. Children were so greedy, and he was only trading.

In the hope of added surprise he entered the wood from the opposite direction she had instructed and immediately saw a girl's bicycle half hidden in bushes.

She was trying to fool him, he thought. But instead he would fool her. In shadow of trees he removed a bunny rabbit mask and latex gloves, pulling them on before continuing along the path. Centre of the woods he stopped and listened, hearing first silence, then the far distant hum of traffic.

"Chrissy," he called. "I've got the DVDs."

"I'm hiding." The voice came from his left, definitely female, but not with the childish tones he had expected.

Moving away from the path he edged between shrubbery towards a tangle of brambles. "That you, Chrissy? I've got the stuff. Cool Luke sent me, he got caught bunking out of school so I came instead."

"I'm here, don't want anyone to see me."

"You two alone?" He unzipped his jacket, unzipped his trousers and moved closer to the voice until finding the way blocked by a trench central to an enclave of bushes. "Luke said I was to give it personally as you were his friend. Where are you?"

"Here," the voice said from behind.

He turned and gagged in surprise when confronted by a figure in cloak and Halloween mask. "Who are you? Are you Chrissy?"

"No, Justitia."

His instant reaction was to reach for her mask, grabbing for her neck with his other hand, but instead it was hit by a lump of lead piping. He heard the crack of his fingers breaking and snatched back in pain. The second blow struck his head and defused the light, blurring it with patches of darkness. His legs buckled as the third blow struck beneath his jaw, forcing his teeth upwards to sever his tongue and reduce his cry to chocking gurgles. Then the blows landed on his groin, again and again, the pain excruciating. He fell backwards, half in and half out of the trench, gasping in agony until blackness smothered him.

Consciousness partly returned and he sensed the smell of wet earth and fungi pressed against his nostrils. The bones of arms and legs felt like jelly, the joints shattered and useless, the pain unbearable. Earth landed on his cheeks making him conscious of something sharp and metallic against his teeth. He looked up into the face of an angel as she shovelled soil into his broken mouth. Only then did he realise she was burying him alive.

Sean waited in the bright fluorescent glare of the autopsy room seeing the corpse of Wayne Finck as unreal, akin to a fashionable exhibit in a conceptual art gallery. His waxed and sallow skin resembled that of a plucked chicken, yellowed where the pathologist's instruments had exposed internal organs for examination, a deep purple where gravity had collected blood at the underside of the body. Sean was relieved a glass partition shielded him from chemicals and corpse. He hated the smell of death, of offal and formaldehyde.

Dr Kielly spoke with the pathologist then stripped off gloves and mask before entering the observation room.

"Much as expected," she said. "Damage from drug and alcohol abuse, but otherwise a reasonable healthy specimen for his age. He drowned when blood entered his lungs. Six wounds from a short, one hundred-millimetre blade, probably a kitchen knife. The first entered above the pelvis slicing the small intestine, the second pierced the upper abdomen. These are consistent with defensive strikes from the victim as Finck sat over her. Then he must have rolled off because the third and forth strikes were delivered with much greater force and skilful precision. These went between the ribcage and pierced the lungs. The fifth thrust virtually sliced off his genitals, the last disgorged his intestines. He died approximately fifteen minutes later. The pathologist's report will be more comprehensive, but in a nutshell, that's what she has given us."

"Was there evidence of a third person on the ground?" Sean asked.

"The body was only metres from the path. Dead and new bracken trampled throughout the area. Contamination by the park wardens doesn't help and prints of other trainers are visible. Yes, there could have been more people. But not necessarily when the incident took place."

"So possibly a lone woman, possibly two plus."

"Or men, or both. Sorry not to be more helpful."

"What of the hair sample?" he asked, following her to a side office where photos of body and area were pinned to the wall.

"Lab report indicates female, black, strong growth from a healthy scalp regularly washed, traces of salt from sweat so she could have been a jogger. At some time it had also been dyed. But no evidence it belonged to Finck's victim. I'd say from the position and indentation in the bracken that it probably did. The same time, it could have been from any passing female."

"Young or old?" Sean asked.

"Late twenties, early thirties, no older. We're still

analysing fibres found. The elasticised lace might reveal DNA, but then we are only assuming this evidence came from the woman." She opened a filing cabinet and searched through folders.

"Did he ejaculate?" Sean asked.

"No visible deposits. Neither did he penetrate. So, no body fluid from him."

"Pity," he said absently.

"I doubt his victim thought that." She offered a sharp, tense smile.

"I meant ..."

"I know what you meant. However this might interest you more." She removed an evidence bag. Inside lay a small silver brooch in the shape of a skull. "This was found under the body." She passed the envelope. "A Death Head brooch, possibly worn by either gender, but more likely female."

"Very careless of them."

"Or were we meant to find it?"

"So they're claiming responsibility?"

She shrugged, returned the bag to the drawer, still flicking through files as she talked. "Or someone's trying to shift responsibility. If Finck sold drugs the DH would see him as competition."

Sean took a chance. "What about DI?" he asked, watching her eyes.

Her expression stayed stoic, then she hinted at a frown and shook her head. "That's a new one to me," she said.

"But then I don't have the resources of SOCA."

"At the moment, neither do I," he said, thinking she had lied.

"What does DI stand for?" she asked, her expression still bland.

"Directus Iurisdictio, Direct Justice. I wonder if they planted the brooch."

"That's for you to find out, Mr Fagan." She raised eyebrows in dismissal. "I know what Chief Hackett will decide. Another gangland killing by the Death Heads. Have you been in here?" she asked, indicating the files.

"No."

"Someone has, the hair sample is missing."

Back in his office Sean shuffled between wall and furniture and sat at the desk, his encrypted laptop before him. For moments he stayed in contemplation, wondering which route to take. Victoria and her boss had turned his whole initial operation inside out. Important though they were, Bently and Grogan now became side players, pawns in a much larger game, as he himself had become a pawn. Operation Deep Cut had swallowed all. He fished out his mobile and pressed for Heidi.

"You're not my favourite man," she answered. "You realise how many petty criminals you've asked me to tab?"

"I'll make life easy. Give only those dead or missing."

"Fine," she said, "because that's most of them." He heard her clicking keys. "OK, in your immediate vicinity, of the forty-four records I've dealt with, eighteen are dead, five are in prison, four are disabled," she clicked more keys. "Five are still on the street and fifteen are missing, whereabouts unknown."

"What's the average age?"

"Eighteen to ..." she paused. "Oldest is fifty."

"That's a very high proportion of dead criminals."

"Well, that's what the records list. They must be careless in Hertfordshire."

"Send me just those you've already tabbed, forget the rest. I've something new. Find all you can on Universal Youth, structure, headquarters, president, chairman etc."

"They're global," Heidi said. "Even recognised by the United Nations. You want the UK branch or head office? That's in America."

"Stick with UK for now, particularly St Alban's branch, they could be mixed up in something. Also, anything on Directus Iurisdictio, Direct Justice. They're a closed and secret order associated with the main charity."

"OK boss," she said, drawing out the phrase as if uncertain.

No, not Heidi, Sean thought. She wouldn't belong, not with her rosy cheeks and sweet dimpled smile.

"The mobile number you asked me to check belongs to a phone reported stolen in London. The original owner was African who has since gone home."

"Cheers Heidi, speak to you later," he said and switched off thinking someone out in the fog was warning him, or trying to frighten him. Someone who didn't want him investigating. Or maybe someone with a conscious. He booted up his laptop and looked through the lists she had sent.

All named were habitual criminals, most in their twenties, thirties or forties. Offences covered drug dealing, violence and burglary, some aggravated. Others were child traffickers, habitual rapists, muggers, the general scum of low life. Half of their adolescent and adult years had been spent in prison. For the remaining time they had constantly inflicted their sick lifestyle on the public.

Eighteen dead, he thought. That's a careless amount of people for the criminal fraternity to lose. Four disabled, fifteen missing, five still on the street. He wondered if Finck had been one of those five.

His thoughts were interrupted by a knock and Anjali eased in beside the desk.

"Chief sent me to assist," she said, knuckles on her hips. She wore a trouser suit that shaped and flattered the figure beneath and an expression that defied assertion of any male attitudes.

"If we can be professional friends, that's fine." Sean pointedly looked her over. "But if you're going to be a pain in the arse you can fuck off."

For seconds she stared in silence.

"I like men who talk straight." She held out her hand. "So what's the brief?"

Sean clasped her fingers, found a firmness that wasn't there yesterday and waved her to the second chair. "For you it's finding out who killed Finck. I got my own set of problems."

"Share them." She leant elbows on the desk and clasped hands.

Trust, Sean thought, just whom the hell do I trust? "Little by little," he said. "I believe my enquiry and Finck's murder maybe connected. I want to eliminate or involve the woman who stabbed him. Be she a Death Head member or not we need to find her."

"I've already appealed for witnesses, she must have been covered in blood. But I doubt anyone will show. In all honesty, unless we get a positive break, we won't find her. Soon as the Chief hears about this Death Head brooch he'll assume they're collectively responsible for removing another one of the local opposition."

"True about the blood, but if the murder was premeditated our killer may have had a clean tracksuit hidden nearby. On the other hand, if she was a helpless victim she may want to speak out."

Anjali shook her head. "She'll be terrified. If a woman is sexually assaulted she doesn't murder her assailant, she defends herself."

"But he never penetrated."

"He ripped her underwear, rifled her body. St Albans is an old-fashioned shire city, very Christian, very conservative. It also has its fair share of Muslim and Hindu families, respectable, law abiding citizens who hold family honour sacred. Most women from our community would be deeply humiliated, even ashamed of being sexually assaulted. If our lady is an innocent jogger she'll want to hide, not have herself publicized by a court case. If she's one of the Death Heads, she'll still tell no one."

"Point taken," Sean nodded. "So we start at the obvious and work up. Interview the park wardens. Find out if they know of regular joggers, someone they saw that morning, someone who has not come back."

Anjali nodded and scribbled on her pad.

"Also we need to interview past rape victims. Any who, through the news article, knew he hung out in the park."

"I can only think of two women, one more likely to seek vengeance than the other. I worked on both cases. It's all on the database. Want me to set up interviews?"

"Please. We need to remember the last three stab wounds were not to stop any attack. Finck was already on his back. The last three were to kill and mutilate him."

"You're thinking like a politically correct male." Anjali shook her head. "If it had been me, not only would I have killed the bastard, I would have stuffed his severed gentiles down his throat. That swine would never have come back, not on me or any other woman." She stood to leave. "I'll work from the communal office, there's more room." She edged past him, her thigh brushing his arm.

"Phone when you have interview times." He looked up at her, looked up to her big brown eyes looking down, not moving his arm as her other leg brushed by.

"Tell me," she said. "Why is a big shot SOCA man taking interest in a hick town murder? You really think Bently is involved?"

"I think whoever did this killing may not be as innocent as she seems."

Anjali wrinkled her nose but made no comment, the pause interrupted when her mobile rang. Sean watched her lips stretch in a tight grimace. "OK," she said. "I'm on my way, Chief. No I don't need help, Doc Kielly doesn't like too many cluttering the scene." She switched off. "Got to go, someone walking their dog had it dig up a body. Looks like a missing paedophile. Dark Angel again. I'll be in touch," she said.

"You want me along?"

She shook her head and gave a half smile. "'S, OK, I'm a big girl."

Sean watched her departure trying not to admit her attraction. Not so much big, he thought, as very shapely. He went back to his computer and the Police National Crime Register. He figured somewhere within lay secrets.

At 13:00 hours Sean broke for lunch. He avoided the pub and settled for a sandwich in the canteen. The place was a hive of uniforms, plain clothed and admin staff, all talking amidst the clatter of cutlery and plates. He saw only one possible table and walked across.

"Mind if I join you?" he asked Detective Inspector Dan Reece who was stuffing pie, beans and chips into his rotund body.

"Be my guest," Reece said while chewing. "I'm in celebratory mood, whacked a crack dealer this morning. Caught him in the act," he paused. "I hear Finck got his balls cut off and his guts ripped out. That's good for the community. Nasty bit of shit."

"You familiar with him?" Sean sat.

"I arrested him three times. What's your interest?"

"He used to work for Bently. Just checking for connections to my own enquiry."

"You going to shoot Bently like you did Grogan then?"

Sean allowed a knowing smile. "You know anyone who might want Finck dead?"

"Everybody, like I said, he was shit. Take my advice, do the paperwork and put it down to Dark Angel via the Death Heads. The same will happen with this child molester they found on the common."

"How do you mean?" Sean bit into his sandwich.

"Last five years, maybe twenty or so of our city's low life citizens have met premature death. All explained, all accounted for, at least to the satisfaction of the coroners. It was nicknamed the Dark Angel Syndrome and shrugged off as coincidence. Certainly no one has considered it worth the money to investigate."

"You think there are connections?"

"None that would warrant serious enquiry. These arseholes died in accordance with their lifestyle. They OD'd, crashed cars, fell out of windows, choked on their own vomit, not to mention the majority who simply disappeared. Good riddance."

"What about the Death Head gangs removing opposition?"

"All bullshit to save money. Gangs stab or shoot each other and Hackett won't spend money on shitheads, that's why he sends in Robocop Robson. No, these arseholes died courtesy of their stupidity. Now," he waved his fork, "rumour has it you can help us nail Bently. So, you got anything to help, let's have it."

"SOCA info relating to Bently indicates he has grubby hands everywhere," Sean said.

"From here to London. He's the bloke we want." Reece mash chips between his teeth. "Dodgy pubs and bars, strip clubs, massage parlours, porn. But drugs and trafficking are his big business. We've been trying to pin the bastard for years. We should do what SOCA does and shoot the sods," he paused. "How're you getting on with Robocop?"

Sean wiped fingers on a napkin. "Anjali? She's fine, a good detective."

"She's has experience, I'll warrant. But she comes up with more guesswork than fact, even if she is proved right, detection needs hard evidence. Plus she's got female attitude," Reece said as he chewed. "Be warned by one who knows. A good-looking assembly, but don't tell her what you think of it."

"I'll stay indifferent," Sean said and sipped coffee. "Did she work for you?"

"Until six months ago. In her time she's worked on every team. She helped me put Finck away, helped me put most of the crap away. You're right, she is a good detective, but she ruins it with her dyke attitude."

"That I don't swallow, and if she is gay, so what?"

Reece shrugged, glared at his last few chips then went for the kill. With mouth full he clattered knife and fork onto an empty plate and rubbed a hand over his distended stomach. "Some of our gentlemen girls think she is, not to mention our lady boys, and they should know. It takes one to know one. I assume you're briefed on her association with Routt?"

"No. Only what you told me. He's homophobic, misogynous and hates policemen."

"She fits the full bill. Rumour has it she's also Judge

Osborne's daughter, or more precisely, one of his little bastards. Osborne sentenced Routt." Reece blew out his cheeks. "Routt's an animal. I wouldn't want that bastard after me."

"Lucky he's not. After a term in prison he'll be rampant. Christ knows what he'd do to you." Sean watched the man's face, pleased with the effect of his words. He left the canteen with his mind half on Anjali's safety from Routt and half on Dark Angel. Of one thing he was sure, more could be gleaned from canteen gossip than from records.

Back in his box room Sean sat and allowed all to churn through his mind. Why had Dark Angel not raised Hackett's suspicion? Anything unexplained had simply been accredited to the Death Heads and disputes between Grogan and Bently. To Sean it seemed inconceivable that no one cared. Low life was low life, but they were still human. Directus Iurisdictio began to look more plausible. He switched on the laptop and flicked through the first forty on Heidi's list. All were social misfits with few having missed the annual crime club photograph. But with eighteen dead via accident or misfortune and fifteen missing, the frame would have gradually grown very empty. It certainly seemed providence had intervened to save the taxpayers a fortune in prison and legal fees. Perhaps they did have a dark angel amongst the leafy lanes of St Albans, a member of Directus Iurisdictio whose victims were society's miscreants. That left Sean wondering who would be next. Again he tapped keys looking for addresses and not surprisingly found that on release from prison most had been temporarily housed by the rehabilitation branch of Universal Youth. Victoria's story began to feel uncomfortably real. Next step was to make contact, to encourage Directus Iurisdictio forward by using less subtle hints regarding his shooting of Grogan. Also to identify the occupants of the Mondeo and where he stood on the risk scale. Maybe then he would find out who was making cranky phone calls. Anjali knocked and put her head round the door.

"I got Finck's rape victims lined up, but if you want to interview both today, we need to move now."

Sean closed the laptop, locked it in the metal filing cabinet and grabbed his coat. "We'll take your car," he told her, then to show interest. "Anything from the new crime scene?"

"A guy called Priestly, child molester. He was beaten senseless then buried alive with a DH badge in his mouth. This was nothing to do with drugs so I think the badge was to avert suspicion or give DH a better image with the Press as vigilantes. Problem is, because they profess to be Islamic, the Chief is worrying about upsetting race relations. Can't have a woman questioning men so he's handed the whole thing over to Reece." She shook her head.

"Been talking to Reece," he said when they were finally driving. "That man's got a problem."

"Too much fat between the ears." She wrinkled her nose.

"He said you helped on his investigations, said you were a good detective."

He watched her lips spread in a muted laugh.

"Strange, he usually calls me a dyke. He's the most prejudiced rat face I know. He hates me because I'm part Asian, because I'm a woman, because I work hard at my job, but mainly because I speak my mind."

"What about Dark Angel? Priestly demise sounds more like her work."

"Dark Angel is one of the subjects on which I speak my mind. No one listens though." She glanced at him, eyebrows raised as if seeking his comment.

"I'll listen," he said.

Anjali pulled into a council estate and parked the car.

"Will you? Well first, angels don't have gender." She opened the door. "This is where Sandra Drabble lives, one of Finck's victims."

Sean watched Sandra Drabble nervously twiddle a child's bib in her fingers. She was over plump, pink faced with dark hair pulled by an elastic band to the nape of her neck. Sean found the flat overbearingly hot, which was perhaps why Ms Drabble wore a skimpy vest that revealed a bulbous ring of stomach and a tattoo on one shoulder. For the rest she wore tracksuit bottoms with pink flip-flops. Sean guessed her age no more than eighteen, too young to have mothered children.

Her own mother sat like a rotund frog with an open mouth. No sign of the kids other than scattered plastic toys.

"It is necessary in all police investigations, Ms Drabble, to eliminate from the enquiry any person who might be on the fringe of our concern," Sean said, choosing his words with care.

"She ain't a suspect," her mother said and returned to a motionless glare.

"I agree, madam but I just need to know if Ms Drabble had seen Mr Finck since his release from prison."

"No," the daughter said.

"Do you know anyone who has?"

"No."

"Were you in the park on Monday morning?"

"No, I was minding me kids."

"Do you go jogging at all?"

"Jogging?" She wrinkled her face. "No."

"Has any family member or any friend had dealings with Wayne Finck since his attack on you?"

"Of course, his parents live on this estate. That's why rehab gave him a flat over on the Cottonmill estate. I have to manage with child maintenance and the Social, but he gets a flat in the best place. Justice, my arse."

"No consideration for us," the mother said and snapped her jaw shut.

"St Albans is small. Did any acquaintance see him with someone they recognised?" Sean asked.

"No, except Davy."

"Who's Davy?"

"The father of my youngest. He's been seeing me now and then. He was there when that bastard raped me. We'd been clubbing and he got me drunk, then he raped me in the street. Did it in front of all me mates. I was just fourteen. I didn't know what was happening. They were laughing. No one cared, still don't."

"No support," her mother said.

"You think Davy may have taken revenge for you?"

"No. They were in prison together. Most of the time they were mates. Davy just got out. He came here, but he was on drugs so I didn't give him nothing."

"You say they were mates sometimes. Did they fall out occasionally?"

"Of course, they were always fighting. Over drugs mainly. He deserved what he got. Wayne was a nasty little bastard."

"I would have stabbed him for what he did to our Sandra," the mother said.

"Can we have Davy's surname? Just so we can eliminate him from our enquiries."

"Wallis," Sandra said. "Davy Wallis."

"You know this Wallis?" Sean asked, as he and Anjali walked back to the car.

"The usual pavement scum. He's spent more time in prison than out. I arrested him four times myself. You do the paperwork, put him away, wait 'til he comes out and re-offends, then start all over again. It keeps us employed."

"That's a very pessimistic view."

"Maybe, but unfortunately, it's also true. I think I should carry out the next interview. Gosling can be very edgy over men, especially policemen."

"If you advise, that's fine, but don't spare her."

Sean considered Mrs Gosling and Ms Drabble from two different planets. Mrs Gosling was mid-thirties, of healthy build and dressed in a well-cut business suit. Her husband sat close looking solid and sullen, occasionally crunching his knuckles as if to give warning of limitation.

"Anything to help," Mrs Gosling said. "But my experience was traumatic and I do not wish to dwell on it. Please be brief."

"Have you, your husband, family or any associate made contact with Finck since the incident?" Anjali asked.

"No, and I never would, ever."

"That's as well. He's dead."

"Good," her husband said.

Sean watched Mrs Gosling's eyes. No surprise, just a slight twitch of eyebrows.

"I admit that news gives me a sense of satisfaction," she said. "He visited our old house twice. Once to steal, once for me. In my mind was the dread he might visit a third time. That's why we moved. Understand the trauma put upon us that week. They came to burgle; they intruded into my personal belongings, my clothes, intimate possessions, private letters, papers and diaries. They stole irreplaceable gifts, jewellery my mother left, my father's war medals. They stole a silver framed photo of me when I was eighteen. I think that is whom they expected when they came back."

She clasped hands and lowered her head. Her hair was jet black, tied and pinned from her face save for a few strands that had escaped during the day's activities. It was the kind of hair, Sean thought, which a woman casts about her home and workplace or while revenging herself on a rapist.

"We have every sympathy," Anjali said in a hushed voice. "As a woman I can imagine the trauma of such an invasion."

"Only a woman could realise." She gave Anjali a tight smile. "The police did nothing. To them I was a case number. It was a question of sorting the paperwork. Would you believe, after the first break-in they even knew who the two men were? But they could not be arrested due to lack of irrefutable evidence. Off record, a constable told me there was a technical hitch the defence could use that made it financially unfeasible to bring charges. So they left them at large, and four days later they came back, only this time I was at home and this time one of them deposited irrefutable evidence of his visit inside my body."

"Enough." The husband stood.

Mrs Gosling raised her hand and waved him down. "No, it never goes away, so I face it."

"You refer to two intruders, Mrs Gosling," Sean said. "But the police have evidence on record of only one."

"There were two. They were ripping at my clothes, forcing me down, one raped me from behind, the other watching while holding my neck." She shook her head, clasping and unclasping her fingers in her lap. "Everything was a haze and I was hysterical. I finally passed out. When I awoke, when they had gone, except for the pain, it seemed unreal. How could that ever happen? The police said one, they convicted one. Finck said there was no other. Who am I to say different?"

"Right, that's it." The husband was on his feet again.

Sean stood also. "Do you ever go to Verulamium Park?" he asked.

"No, if I walk, I always go where other people will be."

"You look fit, Mr Gosling, do you jog?"

"Yes, and now I also do martial arts. They should have put him away for life, then he wouldn't have been murdered or some other poor women raped."

Sean handed Mrs Gosling his card. "In case you recall anything else. Sometimes events are so dark people lock them away, they don't want to remember. But occasionally they do."

"What's the point? If I had seen an opportunity I would have stabbed him myself." She took the card, turning it back and front. "I thought SOCA chased organised crime," she said. "Is my rape so serious?"

"Very serious, Mrs Gosling. Tell me, do you know of Universal Youth?"

"Yes, we're both members, both helpers. They're big around here. I train in their gym."

"It's a civilised way of hitting back," the husband said. "Why do you ask?"

"Just wondered if Finck had been a member."

"Scum like that. Never."

Sean offered his hand on departure and felt anger in the other man's grip.

CHAPTER 7

"So why the reference to UY?" Anjali asked on their return to the car. "I belong, quite a few guys at the stations do. And yes, through UY I remotely know the Goslings."

Drizzle fell and dampened the late evening air. He felt St Albans getting to be very cosy with UY members seemingly everywhere. That made it decision time, to trust her or not. Even in the rain she looked good. He thought of Victoria and remembered one of her frequent warnings as she lay on the bed, seductive, beguiling, enticing. You're such a pushover for a pretty face, she would tell him and stretch like a silken cat. But not all were like Victoria. Many a pretty face belonged to a straight forward, public spirited woman with concerns for her community.

"During my enquiries the name cropped up a few times," he finally said in answer to her question. "I also note they occasionally give temporary housing to newly released cons, including Finck."

She shrugged. "You should join. If you help out you get to use their gym, saves a lot of money." She opened the car with her remote key and Sean bunched his long solid frame in beside her.

"You help?" he asked.

"Sure. I run the girls netball. We're St Albans champs. If you belong to a lodge or chapter, there're plenty of social events." She put the car in gear and drew out into the road. "Seriously, why don't you join? The lodge is short of guys at the moment."

"Somehow I don't think I'd fit into the netball team."

She laughed, the first time he had hear her laugh. It changed her whole ambience and made her even more

83

appealing.

"How about boxing, martial arts, rugby, outdoor survival, football? At our lodge, that's St Albans, we have social activities both for adults and children. They're very organised."

"I was told they have a similar structure to the Masons," Sean said, matter of fact.

"Similar in that they use the term lodge, but I don't think they're secretive. There are other lodges higher up, but they're more political."

"Like Directus Iurisdictio?" Sean said.

She stayed silent a moment. "Never heard of that one. What's their line?"

Clever or honest, Sean thought. "Don't know," he said. "Their name came up on file, probably not important."

"No, probably not." She checked her watch. "Eighteen thirty hours, my shift is over. If you don't want me this evening I'm going to UY now." She glanced at him then back to the road. "Unless you care to come along. We got the best rap dancers this side of London."

"Seeing as UY already cost me money, why not?"

"Great." She threw a smile. "We're always looking for new recruits. Only a tenner to join."

"But on condition you come for a drink with me afterwards," he said.

"Ha." She made the sound an expression of non-committal, one that meant either way.

Along the Harpenden road and past the fire station,

Anjali turned into a car park that would have out spaced most supermarkets. Central to the plot stood a state of the art multi-purpose hall that no council could ever afford.

"They got money." Sean stepped out of the car the same time as a red Mondeo pulled in and parked on the far side.

"Courtesy of Rashid Bayat, a wealthy Asian entrepreneur with serious connections to Middle East oil. He is a prime example of the British Muslim who stands up for his adopted country," Anjali said, leading him to the main entrance. "The great thing about Universal Youth is, they welcome all religions, but teach none."

Sean glanced over his shoulder to the Mondeo and saw one of the occupants emerge. Shaven headed, lean and hard, he produced a mobile and began to talk, staring over as if wanting Sean to realise his presence. Sean felt the old grip of unease and wondered if the guy had a metallic voice.

Anjali led him through reception and into the main hall. He calculated at least six activities in progress, kids of all ages being encouraged by trainers and helpers, the noise a cacophony of rubber soles squeaking on wood, bouncing balls and the excited shouts of young enthusiasts. Somewhere in the background he heard the thump, thump of techno music.

Anjali tapped his shoulder.

"You'll recognise some faces. A lot of guys from the station give time here." She pointed to where Bertha Smith encouraged kids over a vaulting horse.

"Is it always this busy?"

"Never stops. Chief Hackett may think he's responsible for the fall in crime rate, but I can tell you now, it's due to the efforts of UY. These kids are in here having fun instead of prowling the streets in gangs and dealing drugs. They're given a purpose and pride."

"Sounds good." Sean nodded agreement.

"I have to change for my class. You want to watch, you go back through reception and up the stairs to the surrounding seats. There's a bar somewhere, but you have to be a member. See you in just over an hour." She waved to a group of fourteen-year-old girls bouncing a ball and ran across, they in turn eyed Sean as if an alien from planet Mars threatened their leader. Sean retreated, the bar sounded interesting.

Reception was bustled with groups milling in and out. A sign pointing to the bar clearly stated Members Only. Sean hesitated.

"Mr Fagan," a female voice called. "I do believe you are considering alcohol which gives the opportunity to extract more money from you." Dolores Fairbright stood behind the reception counter, her hands clasped, her breasts prominent beneath a tailored blouse. "It's a members only bar."

"So what will it cost me?" he asked.

"Social member, £10 subscription per year." She produced a form and turned towards him holding out a pen. "You'll need to be seconded, but I'll do that, and I'm sure Anjali won't mind her name attached."

Sean filled out the form, put in the address of a SOCA drop box and pushed the paper back towards her. "How about full membership?" he said. "Maybe one of the lodges?"

"£10," Dolores held out her hand. "Full membership is

more complex. You can join as a helper or trainer, but you'll need to be vetted, insured and qualified. Membership of an inner lodge is by invitation only. It depends what you have to offer and what you can afford. Some lodges cost serious money with connections to serious places. I'll give you our introductory pamphlet."

"The bar will do for now," Sean said, pocketing the brochure, then looking to her outstretched hand before finding his wallet. "£10," he said and paid her. In return she pinned a badge to his lapel.

Crossing the foyer he glanced over the many posters advertising different activities. The mothers and toddlers club, pre-school activities, nurseries, single mother job search, pensioners club and re-employment training. Universal Youth clearly gave help across the community. The big society had arrived. So had one occupant from the Mondeo who sat by a far wall. Time to stir waves, Sean thought and walked up to the bar.

Typical sports and social club he figured. Trophies round the wall, the décor modern but utilitarian, the money spent elsewhere. A dozen people turned their heads when he entered. The men were solid enough for rugby players, the women young and athletic, others, older couples looked down on the main hall from the observation windows. Moving to the bar Sean recognised a few faces from the station, beefy guys huddled with their beers, whispering.

"Pint of Guinness, please," Sean asked the steward.

"No problem." The man glanced at his lapel badge and started to pour.

While waiting on the stout to settle Sean crossed to the window. Now in tracksuit, a whistle in her mouth, Anjali rushed amongst her girls who pounded and threw the ball with vigorous speed.

"New member?" a voice spoke beside him. Sean looked to a man booted and tweedy, his shirt checked, his tie paisley, his face somewhere past sixty. He offered his hand. "Richard Cranby, club president."

"Fagan, Sean Fagan." Sean shook hands and felt a firm grip. "I'm a friend of Anjali Robson and Dolores Fairbright."

"Then you come highly recommended. They're two of our bright young things, both very active."

"You have a great place here," Sean said, hoping to dig info.

"One of twenty throughout the UK, all donated by big companies and entrepreneurial wealth, both here and overseas. If we save our youth, guide them in the right direction, educate them, show them justice and strength, then we save our nation, and by embracing all nations, we save the world."

"Is that UY's philosophy?" Sean asked, surprised when the steward courteously brought over his Guinness.

"Have that on me," Cranby said and nodded to the steward. "And in answer, yes, universally so. We build schools in Africa, feed the hungry, rehabilitate criminals, help the old, the sick and the desperate."

"All commendable." Sean raised his glass.

"My pleasure. Tell me, what do you do Mr Fagan?"

Sean hesitated. "I'm a civil servant."

"Interesting. Which branch?"

"Removal."

"And what exactly do you remove, Mr Fagan?"

Sean sipped his Guinness realising the price of his pint was interrogation.

"Tiresome people," he said, hoping the hint would be taken.

"You must excuse my questions, but the police are a bunch of chatterboxes. Your fame precedes you, old boy. I'm merely try to establish if you are in fact who I think you are."

"And who's that, Mr Cranby?"

"The man reported in the papers as having shot that gangster, Vince Grogan."

"I'm not at liberty to discuss such matters."

"Enough said. I trust we can talk again, Mr Fagan. Do excuse me, and welcome to Universal Youth." He turned to leave.

Testing, testing, Sean thought and felt it worth taking a risk.

"Do you know of Directus Iurisdictio?" he asked.

Cranby stopped mid-stride. "I believe it's one of our lodges. Different charitable arms have different lodges. For example those combating poverty or providing healthcare and education have their lodges. Others dealing with rehabilitation of criminals, housing, skills training, life correction, well, they have theirs. Such I believe is Directus Iurisdictio. They're a closed lodge, very secretive, most lodges are. I have always considered intrigue and mystery part of the attraction. Some just love it." He paused and raised an eyebrow. "And what is your interest, Mr Fagan?"

"Direct Justice," Sean said, watching Cranby for a reaction. "The kind Vince Grogan received."

"Timely so, and by your very own hand." Cranby nodded. "Until another time, Mr Fagan," he said, and walked away.

Sean sipped at his Guinness and turned back to the window knowing if the snake pit existed, he'd just thrown himself in. Cobbart had a lot of explaining to do.

Looking to the floor below he found the heavy from the Mondeo staring back at him with open intimidation. Time, he thought, to swot the guy. Anjali still played ball with her girls, blowing her whistle on some point of order before resuming the game. Sean finished his drink and put down the glass considering his best course of action. No violence, no playing at policeman, too many of the real ones were present. But he figured they could at least be useful.

His thoughts were interrupted by the entrance of a tall, statuesque woman who brushed through the swing doors like she belonged. Sean drew breath and felt the onset of base instinct, more so when she strode purposefully towards him. Her printed voile dress caressed each curve and indentation of her body, every movement creating a flowing sensuality, captivating male eyes and narrowing those of women. With long black hair held back by an Alice band she advanced with the prowling grace of one who has it, and knows it.

"Sean." She held out her hand. "I'm Charlotte Osborne, Anjali's half sister. She told me you were up here alone and considering membership."

"She was right. I trust you've come to persuade me."

He clasped her soft hand, receiving the scent of her perfume and the pure ambiance of her feminine vitality. "She never mentioned a sister."

"Same father, different house, different mother. The sign of modern times I fear. John Osborne, our father, was a founding member of Universal Youth. I'm a senior committee member."

Sean guessed her early thirties, a touch older than Anjali. Judge John Osborne had clearly been a busy man.

"So," she clasped hands. "How can I extract your money for the benefit of our organisation?"

Sean felt his instinctive suggestion might not be well received, so said instead, "Afraid I have two teenaged daughters and a hungry ex-wife. Spare cash is in copper coins only."

She laughed, natural and easy and Sean let his smile join with hers.

"Another sign of modern times," he added.

"No worries, a fine bodied man like yourself can help in many other ways. A lot of kids out there need a good role model. Let me show you around." She linked his arm and by chance or design gave the softness of her breast against him in the process.

Sean felt immediate capitulation, but in his mind he visualised Victoria shaking her head. Such a pushover for a pretty face, her words came clearly to his memory. "You make an offer I can't refuse," he said, allowing himself led through doors to a long galley circumnavigating the hall.

"Anjali said you are a colleague from the Smoke. Tell me, what brings a high shot from London to respectable St

Albans?"

Second interrogation, Sean thought, this time via the soft approach. "Grogan, you heard of him?"

"Oh yes." She nodded. "And Bently. I find temporary accommodation for many ex-offenders. You'd be surprised what we learn. Show these guys a little kindness and they cry their hearts out. I probably know more about county crime and gangs than the police do."

"You housed Finck?" he asked.

"Him and others. But like Grogan, I hear he's one less trouble on the street. This is our coffee shop," she said, stopping before doors. "I could write a book on the heartache poured out in there. Abused wives, pregnant girls, lonely kids, druggies, alcoholics, ex-cons, I hear it all. Someone who listens can make all the difference." She led him on pointing as they proceeded. "Here we have admin offices, plus rooms for education and playgroups."

"UY must save Social Services a fortune," Sean said, truly impressed.

"Not that they appreciate it. If we save a young criminal or homeless drug addict it's credited to Government policy, not our efforts. Most of this district's funds come courtesy of Rashid. Rashid Bayat, he's an Afghan. His father is a great supporter of NATO and our troops."

"I'd like to meet him."

"If you join you will, though he's a busy man."

"Such are politics and business."

At the far end of the hall he stopped by the balcony rails feeling the cessation of movement momentarily reconnect her breast with his arm. He noted it stayed there. He saw no sign of Anjali or her girls, which meant they had probably gone to change. Time to take action.

"I think you got a problem," he said to her, nodding in the direction of his trailing hard man, who fortunately at that moment stood ogling a line of schoolgirls in gymnastic leotards. "The guy down there looking your girls over, the one in the green jacket who appears like an unattached Rottweiler, I think I know him. He sells drugs to kids, one of the Death Heads."

"What." Charlotte let go his arm and took out a mobile.

"Wait, I might be wrong. He always works with another guy, a shaven headed thug who drives a red Mondeo. If there's one in the car park I advise you get both off the premises with a warning. If there's no accomplice, then I'm mistaken."

Charlotte's face became creased with concern as she punched numbers and talked rapidly into the mobile. "Don't worry," she said. "We have trained security guys big enough to put fear into King Kong."

"Don't hurt them."

"Would we do that?" She shook her head in mockery. "But we look after our kids. Grogan and Bently made their fortunes corrupting kids like the ones here."

"You know of Bently?" He spoke while continuing their way around the balcony.

"I've talked to a lot of young people who were trapped by that man. His dealers sell them drugs while they're still school kids. In result they turned to burglary and shoplifting to pay for their habit. Then via his street enforcers they sell for him back to school kids. It's a vicious circle and Bently grows rich on it. He also has a lot of prostitutes out there, most of them Easties, desperate girls without money, passports or work permits. One of our properties is a refuge for them."

"Pity he couldn't go the same way as Grogan," Sean said and waited.

"That takes guys like yourself." She stopped him, breast definitely against arm as she nodded to the hall below. "They must have found his accomplice outside," she said, as a group of outsized brawlers entered the hall to surreptitiously encircle the guy tailing Sean, easing him out through the door.

"Professionally done," Sean said impressed.

"Some of these guys look after top politicians. They know how to handle the intruders and we don't want any radical DH thugs in here."

He judged the intimate pressure of her body as an invitation. Time, he thought, to take more chances. "What about National Street Security, the SS as they are called? Is that a coincidence or to suit their fascist image?"

"Some media have simply used the abbreviation in an effort to create sensationalism. They confused love of country and military bearing with National Socialism. Truth is, they're more a band of rightwing boy scouts. They help old ladies across the road, chase off yobs and break up estate gangs. Many of them join the police or army."

Sean nodded. "And what about Directus Iurisdictio?" he asked. "I hear they also deal with the unwanted?"

She made a small noise in the back of her throat. "Way out of my league," she said. "They're not here. They're one of the old moneyed, London lodges. I know they run private schools for our most promising but other than that they're very hush, hush. I don't think they even let women in. Boys stuff you know."

They descended steps and out onto the main floor of the hall at the same time Anjali appeared from a far door, chatting amicably with her girls and dressed once more for the street.

"Perfect timing," Charlotte said, and walked to meet her halfway.

Having started down the path, Sean saw no advantage in stopping. These two were the key into Universal Youth and beyond.

"You two ladies care for a drink?" he asked.

"We don't drink," Anjali said. "Besides, we're babysitting each other in case Routt comes calling."

"If you're that worried, you need protection. I'll call Hackett and get some uniforms outside your house."

"That would be a dead giveaway." Charlotte shook her head. "He'd know our exact location."

"You have to understand," Anjali continued. "Our father sentenced Routt and Routt doesn't forget. Added to that he's misogynous and he hates police. Kind of puts us top of the list."

"Then you definitely need protection."

"You think guys here wouldn't be leaping to our side if we asked? One request and we'd have the whole rugby team encircling our bed." Charlotte shook her head and laughed.

"You get our drift," Anjali finished. "We turned

Hackett's offer down, it's not necessary. We have our own protection and defence and the best is, Routt hasn't a clue where we stay. But I'll compromise on the drinks, I'll give you a lift back to the high street. Stay for one then come back for Charlotte."

"If you're sure." Sean offered Charlotte his hand and again felt the firm embrace of her fingers.

Outside in the car park he saw no sign of the Mondeo. He eased into Anjali's car and watched as she sat beside him.

"Hear you tumbled one of Bently's Death Head pushers," she said, starting the car and moving it out onto the road.

"Glad to be of use," he said, looking at her profile. For the first time he saw similarity with Charlotte's facial structure.

"One of the reasons I'm a policewoman is to nail such pigs. You want to visit one of Bently's pubs? See how he operates?"

"Sure."

Anjali parked off the high street so they walked through cobbled allies to the main area of evening activity. Groups of youngsters milled on the pavement, girls in skirts too short and overgrown boys already hyper on their first three lagers. A few uniformed cops kept discreet watch while squad cars cruised the kerbs. The evening's entertainment had clearly begun. Anjali thrust hands in pockets and walked beside him. Twice he noticed two or more youths wearing black T-shirts with SS insignia on the front.

"Thursday night is pay night for some, so they're going to spend while they got it," she said. "Can't count the times I walked this street in uniform. Most of the kids are decent, some of them stupid, but basically just out for fun. Once they're steamed up on strong beer they chase the girls, who either want to be caught or suddenly realise they're showing too much flesh. That's when the rows begin. But what turns it to madness is beer combined with drugs. Idiots go crazy, out come the knives while the girls start screaming over sexual assaults. Members of Street Security sometimes step in or report to our guys. They in turn keep it contained and arrest the loonies, but violence still happens. You ready for this?" she said and led him into a huge corner pub. A doorman watched them enter, glancing over Sean as if he were trouble, the wrong man in the wrong place.

The vast bar area was more a sound box of loud, incomprehensible pop music than a pub, busy enough for anyone to remain unnoticed while giving space enough to watch. He bought a Guinness and a mineral water, then crossed to where Anjali had found two high stools and table amidst the blaze of electronic vibration.

"No wonder you don't drink in pubs," he shouted over the noise. "It's horrendous."

She nodded, shouting back close to his ear. "It belongs to Calvin Bently, one of his drug outlets. In two hours it will be jammed solid with heaving youngsters. If you're a street detective, this is the place you get your info. The guy on the door will have already warned the bar we're cops. He'll be an Eastie. It all looks good for the council's health and safety, but he's really there to ensure no other dealer gets in. Only Bently's stuff is sold here, and then in private."

He watched as a girl sauntered by, her long legs stretching all the way up to a minuscule wraparound skirt.

"She's one of the drug squad," Anjali said, her arms folded as if reading his masculine thoughts. "We have undercover girls who regularly trawl the high street for intelligence. The bouncers don't realise. I used to be one of them, dressed like a Goth with red streaks in my hair. She's the reason Reece caught his crack-dealer. Did he tell you about her?"

Sean shook his head.

"He wouldn't."

"Forget Reece. I want to know about Dark Angel."

She stared back with solemn brown eyes. "Want to hear my theory?"

Sean nodded.

"When Routt went inside, his place as street enforcer was taken by a sadistic head banger called Salem Kadyrov, an asylum seeker from Chechnya. Like Routt he kills people for Saturday night fun but he does it more subtly like throwing his victim off a roof or out a window. My bet, those who disappeared or found violent ends met Salem. He's Dark Angel. Every death was investigated, paperwork done but nothing proven. Perhaps as Superintendent Hackett thinks, they are all coincidental. Most victims of Dark Angel pushed drugs for Grogan or Bently. Grogan and his men are wiped out, but in the past years Bently's been changing his street boys for Easties. Head-bangers mainly from Romania, Bulgaria, Ukraine and Chechnya, but also some Brits, including radical Muslims, the hardcore Death Heads. That's where his girls come from too. By virtue of Bently's betrayal of them, his old dealers become a threat so Salem systematically removes them. The real fun will be when Salem and Routt meet up, and hopefully that will be soon. So," she raised a hand, "that's my theory on Dark Angel but no one listens."

For Sean the downside of her beliefs was obvious. "Without proof it's speculation and without an investigation it will always remains so."

She nodded. "Hence we go nowhere."

Sean stayed quiet a moment. "So who killed Finck, Routt, Salem or some rape victim?"

"On reflection, my guess, Salem used a female agent. Routt will be otherwise engaged looking to find Charlotte and myself."

"So not a helpless rape victim?"

She looked at him and shrugged. "Our investigation is low budget. Lowlife, low budget. And Finck was scum."

Sean watched a cluster of legs go by followed by a huddle of boys.

"Those girls are Easties, trafficked in from the old Soviet Union. You can tell because their faces have hardened under the duress of controlled lives. They circulate in all of Bently's clubs and pubs from Watford out to Luton and Stevenage. They attract the men; the men spend money, which attracts the local girls, that attracts more men. Then his dealers go round selling them drugs. Bently makes millions from the exploitation of women." She finished her drink. "I have to go."

"Will you drop me at the station, I need to pick up a bag. I'm staying with Dolores Fairbright. You know her?"

"Dolores." Anjali dropped her head to one side and raised brows. "A formidable lady," she said. "But watch out for Berty, she gets jealous."

"Bertha, from the front desk?"

"When Berty Smith is fired up with jealousy over

Dolores, she'd scare the life out of Routt and Salem together."

Wallis walked the wet pavement uttering animalist grunts from the back of his throat. Rage consumed his mind over the humiliation of being forced to return home by the 8pm curfew. The tag on his ankle ticked away time. If it showed him on the street after curfew the police would revoke his early release licence. Having only sold forty pounds worth of crack to a couple of school kid dealers, he was well short of his target. That bastard Salem would be round knocking on the door.

"Shit." He kicked a car as he passed. School kids had no money, late night was the time to sell. He grunted again, jerking his head as he did so, hunching shoulders below his hood. "Fuck you bastard," Wallis shouted to no one as he walked the opposite pavement to his hostel, kicking another car as he passed. He checked traffic on the road and sauntered across, hood up, shoulders hunched.

The black four by four that pulled from the kerb accelerated fast. Wallis stopped to let it pass but the vehicle swung in on him, clipping his hip so he fell face up. Screaming disbelief, he tried to sit, hearing the squeal of brakes before the driver slammed into reverse and in a spin of smoking tyres flew back towards him. The rear bumper smashed down on his head and his eyes watched the vehicle pass over him, watched until a front wheel twisted its course, ripping away his face to ride up over his skull.

CHAPTER 8

Sean's watch read 9 pm when Anjali dropped him at the station. A squad car pulled out with blue light flashing, foot hard down as it headed for some incident. Sean checked reception and found it occupied by a lone desk sergeant diligently bent over books and laptop, clearly studying for an upgrade in rank.

"No messages for Fagan?" Sean asked.

"No boss."

Sean went back to his car. No messages meant Hackett was staying off his shoulder. He had to assume Anjali reported back, unless of course she was genuinely on Sean's side. That cheered him. Night bag in hand he headed to the high street where roads led down to Dolores. No point taking the Mercedes, he needed something to eat and that meant somewhere to park. While walking the pavement his mobile rang. The metallic voice spoke again.

"This is your last warning. Get out now before they kill you. They know why you are here. Leave or die."

He checked the number. The same. He shrugged, someone trying to frighten him off, warn him, or serious about killing him? He recalled the large solitary figure in the wax jacket and for the first time wished he was armed.

At the bank he used plastic to get money from an ATM, then bought a chicken vindaloo from an Indian takeaway. Pubs and high street had grown busy with groups of young men and women out on the prowl, searching for fun and the elusive partner that would make their life. Occasionally he saw members of Street Security in black T-shirts and berets watching out for trouble, reporting over mobiles to whoever led that evening's patrols. A few drunks clustered in aimless groups, held subdued by the restraining presence of SS patrols. Three girls in skirts and tops which barely existed argued noisily over a boy who leant against railings, waiting with impatience for the winner.

Youth was youth, Sean thought, and no matter what laws existed they would make the same mistakes made by their fathers and grandfathers. Grandma had danced naked in the 1960s while granddad freaked out on LSD, both gyrating to rock and roll. Such remained a fact of history which repeated itself in different modes through a continuous cycle. Those who thought they could subdue the high street with a form of prohibition by increasing the tax on alcohol, lived in committee rooms not the real world. The likes of Bently would make a fortune by brewing and selling illegal spirits.

Sean turned off the high street and headed down hill into the residential area of St Michael's Manor. The pavements were empty here, the cars packed tight against the kerb, the dark shadow of the abbey rising against the night sky. With no traffic Sean stayed in the centre of the road, tense and uneasy, more so when he found the red Mondeo outside Dolores's house.

He figured a chicken vindaloo not much of a defensive weapon but he saw confrontation as the only option. He transferred the takeaway and night bag to his left hand and turned casually to the enemy. The Rottweiler stepped out of the car, his colleague from the other side. He was built like a rolled ball of muscle, shaven head, no neck, shoulders and arms curved round a barrelled chest.

"I suppose you thought that little stunt funny?" the Rottweiler said.

"Shouldn't leach over young girls. So you got a problem?" Sean stood his ground, vindaloo and bag clutched in his ham fist. If blood was spilt he was determined both men contributed their quota.

Rottweiler stopped out of fist range, the muscle ball behind him. "You're the one with the problem mate, not us. You're the one stirring Directus Iurisdictio, and if they go for you and we ain't around, then you're dead."

When neither man made a move Sean began to wonder if he had misread the situation. "Why you following me?" he asked, looking between them

"Orders."

"Whose?"

"If you don't know, you'd better find out. Ask the birdie." Rottweiler moved back towards the car, his colleague following.

Sean opened his clenched fist, his breath passing over lips in relief. At least for now there would be no battered bodies in the street, no one giving Dolores's neighbourhood a bad name. He remained staring while the Mondeo started, moving aside only when the car pulled out and drove away.

Not the opposition, he thought. Not Direct Justice either, or they would never have been pushed out of the hall. "Ask the birdie," he repeated and drew out his mobile as he turned to the house. Victoria's voice came as a soft caress.

"Sean, are you missing me?"

"Victoria, have you got two meatball minders on my tail?"

"Not mine, my lovely. I trust you with other women."

"So who?"

"If I had to guess I'd say they're the Combined Agency Taskforce. Hard heads mainly, police, paras, ex Unit 14 and the DET, SAS, Boat Service, intelligence. They were formed during the IRA troubles, never officially recognised and on record don't exist. I'm told it's best not to upset them."

"I think I may have."

"Oh darling, don't let them hurt that lovely body of yours. I'll never find another like it."

Sean reached the house and fished in his pocket for keys. "You around this weekend?"

"Only if you ask me nicely."

"Care for dinner on Saturday?"

"My place, seven-thirty sharp. And if you're very sweet to me, I might even give you a present, might even tell you secrets. You should be seeing the picture by now," she said, and hung up.

Sean unlocked the door, pushed it wide and stepped into the hall. At the far end Sergeant Bertha Smith stood in the kitchen doorway, Dolores behind her, tucking in a blouse.

"Mr Fagan," she said. "It's so late we thought you weren't coming." She eased past Bertha. Both had the flush of guilt on their faces. As if to gain composure Dolores sniffed and looked disapprovingly at the vindaloo. "I don't encourage Indian takeaways into this house, Mr Fagan. The smell does so permeate."

"Rent and parking." Sean held out two hundred and forty pounds drawn from the ATM.

She smiled briefly, accepted the cash and stroked it as she might a pet. "However, on this one occasion I'll make an exception."

"So kind of you." He looked at the solid menace of Bertha and remembered Anjali's warning. "I won't keep you," he said. "I've had a hard day."

He edged by and headed for the stairs as the two women passed back towards the kitchen. Before turning on the next landing he glanced down between the railings Bertha's hand was firmly clamped to the back of Dolores's skirt, gently propelling her towards whatever was intended.

He found a single knife, fork, spoon and plate in the table drawer, a glass in the bathroom. He spread his dishes from the bag and after some thought phoned Heidi. She didn't answer and he didn't blame her, instead he got voicemail.

"Heidi, my sweet, I have another assignment for you. Salem Kadyrov, an asylum seeker from Chechnya. I need all the info you can get. He's a sadistic murderer and works for Bently. Also Rashid Bayat, wealthy Afghan businessman with oil connections. As Afghanistan doesn't have any oil I suspect his interests really lie elsewhere, probably in the Afghan poppy fields. Also I need the lodge structure of Universal Youth, particularly a lodge called Directus Iurisdictio, Direct Justice." He paused. "Hope your cats are treating you well." He switched off. Always best to stay on the right side of Heidi, she was mistress of the intelligence world.

Stretched on his bed Sean listened to rain pattering on the slate roof above his head, cursing his neglect to buy any drink and wishing sleep would solve the problem. Instead his mobile rang.

"Fagan, Hackett here."

Sean pushed up on the bed. The man's voice quivered on the edge of fear, possibly panic.

"We've had another road kill. Third this month. This thing is getting out of hand, like there's no tomorrow. This is not what we agreed."

"Road kill?" Sean flopped back on the pillow. "What's that, dog or cat?"

"Don't fuck with me, Fagan. Cobbart said we could talk, that he'd arrange with MI5 for a way out ... I..."

"OK, just checking. No problem. Let's meet," Sean said, moving back on to one elbow and checking his watch.

"I've sent Robson." Hackett went off on a tangent. "She'll put it down to a hit and run by Salem. But Salem is being followed, he's in Luton and Routt doesn't do cars. It has to be Justitia."

Sean sat and swung both legs to the floor, choosing his words as he bluffed and remembered Victoria's warning. The danger is real and immediate. "Justitia," he repeated. "OK, let's meet, now."

"No." The voice rose an octave. "We may be watched. We need a chance meeting. This Saturday Timpton village has a fete. Universal Youth will give a gymnastic display, I'll be expected to take my wife and grandchildren. The vicar has an oyster and champagne bar in his garden, meet me there two-thirty. What could be more innocent, more safe with wife and grandchildren."

"You sure?"

"Perfectly."

"OK." Sean heard him switch off and sat for a moment mobile in hand. Vicar's garden party, village fete, he thought. That also solved the problem of a pre-arranged meeting with his daughters. After a moment he texted Cobbart.

Have contact and possible source. Need meeting ASAP.

He waited two minutes before the reply came.

My office 0900.

Sneaky sod, Sean thought, I'll give him shit.

CHAPTER 9

Sean rose early, showered and dressed then went quietly down the stairs. No sound or movement came from Dolores' quarters, no grunt or snore from Berty. Sean released the chain and eased open the front door. The face which looked in at him squealed, eyes wide, shoulders hunching in fright.

"Jesus." Sean stepped back himself, staring at the young woman who stood with key poised in hand.

"Who are you?" Both said simultaneously.

"Fagan, I live here."

"I live here too. I'm Dolly's daughter," she said in a still startled but low soft voice.

"I'm the new lodger. Sorry love, but I'm on an early start."

"I'm on a late finish and I ain't nobody's love. The name's Sammy, short for Samantha." For moments she stood with chest out and eyebrows raised in some kind of youthful defiance. Sean gave his trust me smile and saw her shoulders relax. They were on the same side. He figured her around the twenty mark, her hair short and punkish. Her face held a boyish ambiance beneath elaborate makeup which, he reckoned, placed her somewhere around the Gothic camp. A black micro web dress provided partial cover to her lean body and high black boots to her lower legs. A silver chain and skull hung around her neck and an elaborate flower tattoo snaked round her left arm.

"Good party?" he asked.

"Techno rave. You should go sometime."

"The Death Heads are not my style." He nodded to the skull.

"Not mine either, but skulls are currently fashionable. My girlfriend bought it in the market." She eased past him and down the corridor to the kitchen.

Girlfriend, Sean thought. Like mother, like daughter. Satisfied she spoke the truth he closed the door and started at a brisk walk towards to the station. The same young desk sergeant sat studiously over his laptop and notebooks, looking up only when Sean pressed the security buzzer.

"You had a hit and run last night, what street?" Sean asked him.

"Crabbie, off London Road. Some dip head from the hostel, probably pissed or high."

"Hostel, what sort of hostel?"

"Rehab. On of them charity places for ex-junkies and cons. Waste of space. Still, it's in a good location, dangerous spot that. In the past year three idiots got themselves knocked down. Got known as Road Kill Alley."

Sean headed his Mercedes towards London and Pimlico. No sign of the red Mondeo, though it could be they had changed cars. If so they were being careful. At 0900 hours precisely Sean knocked on Cobbart's door.

"No bullshit, boss. This time tell me the truth."

Dressed in his normal crumpled pinstripe suit, Cobbart nodded and indicated the chair before his desk.

"I apologise if I seem to have misled you, please let me

explain and at the same time please understand the national security risk. What has Victoria told you?"

"Only MI5 waffle around the great conspiracy theory, secret societies who kill people. She left the rest to you," Sean said, easing his long body into the chair, his legs stretched, his elbows resting on the arms. "Victoria, bless her, is a protégé of the Witch. Anything I hear from those honey lips I reserve until I've found proof."

"Wise man. So here it is, and Sean," Cobbart lifted a finger, "What I tell you is absolutely in confidence and between no others. No doubt Victoria told you of Directus Iurisdictio?"

"According to her they are powerful, ultra-secretive, rich, worldwide and well established in this country."

"All true. Directus Iurisdictio started in Roman times, were adopted by the Knights Templar and since the 18th century have loosely based their structure on the Masonic movement. Though hidden in the background, it is believed they helped Hitler and the Nazis rise to power. After the war they totally reorganised themselves with a new front called Universal Youth." Cobbart raised his hands. "No one would question the good that movement has done. They are a charitable organisation recognised by virtually all countries."

"That no one can deny," Sean said. "But Universal Youth and Street Security have similar soundings to Hitler's Youth and the SS."

"And not a coincidence, which is one of our fears. The old Directus Iurisdictio has always simmered in the shadows. Fifty odd years ago they re-established themselves in Britain, mainly amongst the middle and upper classes and those who aspire to them. Their big attraction is a network of mutual help, all wrapped in total secrecy. The inner chamber of Directus Iurisdictio, Direct Justice, has become the ultimate club for the chosen few. Their objective is to protect the nation and its people from injustice, corruption, exploitation, dishonour and greed. Their motto 'All who labour and provide will be rewarded'."

"Sounds like some kind of Masonic boy's club." Sean shrugged. "Some people like secrecy and class keeps it select."

Cobbart gave a sour smile. "The next line reads "But perish all those who deny their country, justice, protection and glory.""

"Glory has connotations to rightwing bigotry."

Again Cobbart shrugged. "For some maybe, but only in certain ideologies. Their ranks in this country and others are made of brethren from all colours, race and creeds. And this is the difficult bit, they honestly believe they are a force for good against evil."

"So, besides Universal Youth, what do they do?"

"Kill people. Mainly habitual criminals and terrorists. The unwanted. But of late they have turned their attention to dishonest bankers, politicians and at least one of our tax fiddling lords."

"You telling me these guys have their own justice system?" Sean watched Cobbart nod.

"You recall Philip Carver, the Minister for Health?"

"The guy who fiddled his parliamentary expenses? He got killed in a boat accident."

"Except it wasn't an accident. Accused of fraud he saw

his life in ruins so went to the Witch telling her he was an inner core member of DI. A Grand Master no less. She offered him immunity from prosecution and a peerage if he spilled the beans. With guaranteed protection from the SIS he agreed, but the guy was terrified, literally shitting himself. The Box arranged he took a holiday in Greece where one of their operatives pretending to be an assistant would debrief him. Unfortunately DI got there first and ran him down with a speedboat. The Greek police dismissed it as another tiresome accident by a drunken tourist. For DI it gave a clear statement that no matter how high your ranking, betray their code of secrecy and you're dead. To us it proved DI had infiltrated the Civil Service to a depth which gave them access to the SIS. The Government can no longer trust their internal system, which is why they looked outside to us. Or more correctly, under a set of contrived circumstances, to you."

"Me, you've got to be joking."

"Unfortunately not We have a situation which can only be handled with the utmost secrecy. In the last two years DI have increased their sphere of judgement to include suspect Islamic terrorists, preachers of Jihad and difficult asylum seekers. Those the Government cannot remove due to the so called Court of Human Rights. Now we suspect non-members of DI, certain elements within Government's dark circles may be giving DI co-operation."

Sean slumped back in the chair. "Come on, this is England not some mafia state."

"You think not? Since the early seventies the DI have been quietly removing hardened criminals without causing serious problems. They've remained undetected for so long because those in power have chosen not to investigate, either because they themselves are inner core members of DI, or considered DI beneficial to the populace. And if you don't investigate you have the perfect excuse to remain ignorant of the whole thing, or like many, dismiss all as a great conspiracy theory. Remember, the seventies was a difficult time with union dominance and police corruption. The middle class revolted and DI grasped the opportunity to expand. They quietly sanitised the community while embedding themselves in police, army, civil service, the professions, the politicians and working class backbone of this country."

"They're in mainstream politics?" Sean questioned and saw a black chasm opening.

"All parties, at all levels, we don't know who. One of our problems is membership of DI is highly select and for life. They don't talk, they don't leave. Any who break or threaten to break the rules are terminated. Hence their closed and secret ranks."

"Ominous."

"Which makes both myself and the Witch believe our internal security is now compromised. This is Britain tearing itself apart over liberal excess, greed and rightwing retaliation. I am not at liberty to say more. But you realise the implications. We have an alternative judicial system at the heart of Government and Nation. So far DI have prevented more terrorist attacks than police and MI5 combined. No trials, no human rights to hide behind, no questions. You realise the benefits to politicians, taxpayers and country."

"I realise what that does to the heart of a civilised nation whose judicial system is supposedly the very best."

"Worse. DI's net has spread to the dark underside of politics. By Machiavellian manipulation they are engineering sex scandals, fraud and character assassination."

"That's normal."

"And murder. Murder at Cabinet level." He raised his eyebrows. "Can you imagine this country's international reputation if it came out Government was involved in a vigilante medieval judicial system of execution? Sean, this is the most serious operation SOCA or MI5 have ever faced."

Sean controlled his breath knowing Cobbart's words allowed him no way out. "So what's the game plan?"

"DI operate on a lodge or chapel system. Each lodge has one or more cells. The controllers of DI don't use electronic communication so it's nearly impossible to eavesdrop. But we estimate maybe forty, fifty lodges scattered throughout the country, certainly in all principal cities. Each chapel comprises a lodge master who controls one or more assassins plus others for intelligence gathering. However, assassins sometimes have their own dedicated assistants, usually trainees who work in a tight knit group with no idea of higher members' identities. It's possible a cell may comprise of say twenty members with half not knowing who the other half are or their function within the cell structure. Each cell remains independent with no communication or knowledge of another cell. The Lodge Master of each reports to the Grand Chapel of Masters, who in turn have an executive lodge. On those members we have absolutely no info of who or where."

Sean pulled up his legs and covered face with hands. "How many on this operation? I mean do I have a team?"

Cobbart looked at him, looked to the floor and laced his fingers. "I report direct to the Witch and the Minister, but due to the sensitive nature of this operation and our lack of knowledge regarding DI's infiltration of any agency, at this moment, so far as SOCA is concerned, we have only one operative, you. At this end there will be myself and Heidi."

"You're fucking kidding me." Sean sat upright. "You throw me in the shit, then hit me with a shovel."

"Listen to me," Cobbart pointed, his eyes wide. "I'm in the shit too. There is only one way to destroy DI and that is from within, cell by cell. We fight secrecy with undercover secrecy. We live our normal lives and work our way inside till able to crumble the interior. For God's sake man, do you think I'm happy about it?" He sat back and clasped hands to his waistcoat. "If it's any consolation, I believe we are part of a much wider operation nationwide, but no one above is saying. Our objective is to gain information and names. With controlling DI members so highly placed, threat of their individual exposure should start to make cracks."

"You want me to penetrate the cell in St Albans and report back?"

"In a nutshell, yes. Live your normal life, investigate Bently and his Death Heads or whatever Hackett desires. See your daughters, go to the pub, be normal. You shot Grogan so let DI come and recruit you. All you have to do is tread with caution."

"Our business is to gather information on organised crime."

"This is organised murder. And we need to gather information."

Sean laughed, feeling total despair at the nightmare spread before him. "And just who do I trust with this information?"

"That's our trouble Sean, we don't know. It's not so much going undercover as going under subterfuge. We are watching, and in return may also be watched from cabinet minister to street cleaner. Out in the field you trust no one. Use that canny judgement of yours. On the home side you have myself, Heidi and Victoria."

"And who do I submit my reports to?"

"Either myself or Victoria. You see her frequently so continue to do the same, be normal. She'll be your handler." Cobbart stared from the window but could not help the side pull of a smile. Sean knew exactly what his thoughts hovered on.

"Hallelujah, live a normal life with Victoria."

"Or whoever you choose. This operation is purely to gather information and the closer you are to source the better. Sean, you won't be alone."

No, you'll be back here in the office, he thought, but said. "Victoria mentioned the Combined Agency Taskforce, or CAT. Who or what are they?"

"Out of my league." Cobbart shrugged. "But I'm told they're active backup in case you need it."

"You're never alone with a CAT," Sean said in a futile attempt to make light of his knowledge.

"Just track Bently and the Death Heads. Arrest him if possible."

"So that's what a road kill is." Sean looked to his boss and tried a smile. "Removal of the unwanted."

CHAPTER 10

During the return drive to St Albans Sean sensed clouds of anger ready to swallow him. Lies, deceit and Machiavellian manipulation had left him a pawn kicked around by faceless bureaucrats sitting at some SIS committee meeting. With concern only for themselves, they had sacrificed him to Operations Deep Cut but with no say and no control in the field of play. They allowed him no way to identify the opposition or the home side. So just who the hell did he trust without getting his head blown off?

"Fuck it." He banged palm against steering wheel then clamped his teeth, realising rage solved nothing. The only way out lay in playing the game his way. He needed to put out feelers via a web of intrigue which placed himself centre as both predator and bait. But of one thing he felt certain, there would be no rules of engagement. This was kill or be killed. All he had to do was stand in the open with a smile on his face.

On the home side he could be sure of Victoria, Cobbart and Heidi, with Victoria designated as his handler. For the first time that morning he found a smile. If it was necessary for someone to handle him, he knew of no better person than Victoria. Anjali? Certainly well connected which made her either a deadly, if good looking adversary, or possibly a fast route into DI's activities. He knew it was essential to gain her trust and get close, very close. That left Hackett. Sean wrinkled his nose remembering his phone call. The man had sounded troubled and anxious to talk, be it over the Death Heads, Directus Iurisdictio or his own career prospects Sean felt unsure, probably the latter. But he had at least been partly briefed by Cobbart, which meant the man trusted him. Sean felt less sure. Still, he saw no harm in meeting at Timpton village fete, plus it gave a rare opportunity to mix family life and business. What gathering could be safer than a good old English village fete? Sean glanced from motorway to his mobile and punched in numbers before plugging the phone into hands-free.

"Yeees," his ex-wife's bored and lethargic voice sounded over the speakers.

"I'll pick up the girls 11 am tomorrow. I'm taking them to a fete," Sean said, imagining her sitting plump and open mouthed, an iPod and packet of biscuits before her.

"Make it 10.30, I wanna play golf."

"No problem," he said and switched off, shaking his head. Golf seemed the only activity she and Bradley thought of. Why in hell did I ever marry her? Because you were both young, stupid and she was pregnant, he answered himself in thought. Again he pressed buttons on the mobile and waited thirty seconds before she answered. Her voice came over soft and warm with only a touch of business tone. Had she looked to see who called her? Or did he just fantasize that the voice held promise?

"Hi Anjali," he replied. "Want to help? I'm going after witnesses to last night's hit and run, my guess it's Dark Angel."

"Already done that, been knocking on doors all morning. I have three witnesses who swear they saw a young woman driving, two who say they saw a man. It's lunchtime now. I'll be there again 14.30 hours."

Sean checked his watch. "OK, meet you 14.30 in Crabbie Road."

"Roger that," she said and went.

Sean parked at the station and headed for The Cricketers pub. The usual plain clothed squad huddled in the saloon. Sean found a stool in the public bar and ordered Guinness and a sandwich. A few builders with plaster and cement flecked clothes watched football on the television. Half a dozen old boys occupied their allotted seats, all mumbling their usual discontent. Sean drank and ate in silence, musing over how far he should push Anjali regarding DI without raising her suspicions. He figured her sister the best source of info, but sisters could be close and secretive. He wanted his approach to seem natural. If they did know anything he preferred they volunteered their information as they manoeuvred to draw him in, to recruit him or at least introduce him to those with connections.

When he parked in Crabbie Road she stood talking to a constable but then waved and crossed over. The trouser suit she wore looked even more male orientated than the one worn yesterday, tight fitting over hips and bust which gave clear detail of the figure beneath.

"Most residents were questioned last night," she said walking beside him onto the estate. "The people here are a mix of police-friendly and resentful. There're also a few at work."

"Any you missed overlooking the crime scene?" he asked.

"None," Anjali said. "The constable called on the flat directly opposite and said the old boy inside was gaga. The three flats on either side saw nothing. The witnesses I have are all from the floor above. I suggest we continue there."

"The old boy was more likely to have been at home and definitely with a better view. Let's sound him again. You know some of these old boys are not so daft as they appear."

Anjali shrugged and led him to flat 16. The man who answered their knock peered out and scrutinised Sean with deep suspicion, the door latch firmly chained. He had sparse grey hair and facial skin resembling a dried onion.

"Sorry to disturb you, sir." Sean showed his ID. "I'm making further enquiries into the death of a young man killed outside your flat."

"This used to be a good estate. Now the council let anyone in. He was a yob."

"You saw him?"

"I got night vision. I saw him, I see everything. Not many people can see in the dark."

Sean maintained his best public relations smile. "So, no one ever asked if you saw the hit and run?"

"No. When I told the copper I got night vision he walked off."

Sean had sympathy with the constable. "But did you see the incident?"

"Course I did. I'm Community Watch. No one else looks out for us, no one listens to us. They just tax and rob us."

"And what did you see, sir?"

"Saw him park across the road on the corner."

"What type of car?"

"One of them big things that nobody really needs. She drove straight over him, reversed, then back over him again. Popped his head and flattened it like a pancake. She didn't like him, that's for sure."

Sean maintained his smile. "Him or her, did you see a man or woman?"

"Course I saw him, I got night vision."

"Do you mind showing me where you were standing when this occurred?"

"What, let you in so you can beat me up and rob me? Never."

"I assure you, sir, I have only your safety and well-being at heart. Could you give me your name, sir?"

"Reg Arnold. I'm eighty-four, but I still got night vision."

"Would you let this police lady in and give her a statement of what you saw?"

He peered at Anjali. "I'll have to get me glasses."

"But you did see the driver of the vehicle?"

"I saw her clear as day." He thrust his head forward on a tortoise neck.

"So it was a woman driver?"

"Well if it wasn't a woman it was a man," he said. "I can't see without my glasses. Maud would know, she never misses a trick."

"Is Maud here now, sir?"

"No, Maud died three years ago. I could have told them all this when they first came, but no one listened. They used to call me Cats Eyes Reg."

"We'll listen, sir, I promise we'll listen very closely."

Reg Arnold considered carefully, then disappeared from sight. Moments later he returned wearing his glasses. Still with the door chained he observed Anjali with critical eyes.

"So you found her then?"

"Found who, Mr Arnold?"

"The woman who runs over yobs in her four by four."

"This is Sergeant Robson, she works with me. She's my colleague, not the suspect," Sean said, his mind clouding.

"May we come in, Mr Arnold?" Anjali asked in a sweet angelic voice.

Arnold unlatched the chain and stood aside to watch her pass before following her down the hall to a sitting room unchanged since the 1950s. The central heating pumped stifling heat while the air smelt of yesterday's cabbage and wet dog.

"I stood here," he said and passed to a window looking straight onto the crime scene. "She came round that corner like the clappers, hit him, reversed, then went over him again. His head popped like an exploding melon, I heard it, even in here."

"Were you wearing your glasses at the time, Mr Arnold?" Anjali smiled for him.

"Of course, I always wear my glasses after seven. How else can I see in the dark?"

"Perhaps you could make a statement? Just tell the way you saw it," she said.

"Tell it yourself, you were there doing it."

Sean watched Anjali momentarily close her eyes, then smile again. "You saw someone like me, Mr Arnold, I wasn't there. Shall we sit?"

He indicated a low, threadbare settee and sat on a dining chair opposite, occasionally looking to Sean as if for confirmation.

Anjali wrote the old boy's tale in a small, precise script, her eyes never moving from the page. Leaning before the window, Sean listened and tried not to imagine Anjali behind the wheel as he concentrated on her profile. Could she be Dark Angel, Justitia? Or was the old boy simply confused? None of which, he realised, helped the credibility of Reg as a witness. Any defence lawyer would tear him to pieces.

When they finished, Anjali passed her pad across and watched as Reg added a spidery signature.

"And you think this woman looks like me?" she asked.

"Definitely. I got night vision, I can see in the dark."

Back outside Sean breathed in the cool clean air.

"OK," she said. "He's identified me as the killer. Do you believe him?"

"No, because first he said it was a male, then a female and you're definitely and unmistakably a woman. I think he just wanted to add a face so chose yours. If Charlotte had been here he would have chosen her."

"Charlotte, you're joking?" She gave a false laugh. "Little Miss Prim and Proper, the choir girl. Charlotte is head candidate for the yummy maids of England. The four by four murder vehicle might have suited her. But it was evening, so she'd be wearing a designer dress, with designer heels. I don't really see her hunting down yobs in St Albans. Foxes and deer maybe between charitable work and the vicar's garden party. In fact, you might as well blame the vicar and his wife as blame Charlotte."

Both stopped by her car. "OK," he said. "But that still leaves a suspect with similar features to yourself, male or female."

"So you want to do more witness interviews?"

No, I want to look inside your head, he thought, and checked his watch. "If a girl drove the car, it could be the same girl who stabbed Finck."

"You mean a female Death Head?" she asked.

"Possibly."

"I got stuff on my laptop at home, you want to look it over?"

"OK, let the constable do the other witnesses. Let's see what you have." He opened the car door. "You lead, I'll follow."

"OK, but from the look in your eyes I must remind you this is police time, plus I'm a very modest and proper girl."

Stumped, he drew breath to reply, only to see the car door close, leaving him to hurry back to the Mercedes. To read a thought which had briefly fluttered across his expression made her pretty cute. He also had to admit such thoughts now bubbled without restriction. For this reason normal powers of observation were seriously distracted and he drove straight past the scruffy black builders' van parked outside the tape. His mind fixed on images of Anjali's figure and her red Corsa in front, he strove for a return to reality and the best way of extracting whatever information she had on DI. He had to know if she was a member or an investigating officer with more knowledge than most. The old boy had identified her as a killer, except the old boy suffered identity confusion. The possibility remained, however, that he might have seen Anjali as her half sister

Charlotte. Or just seen her as a face on which he could hang his jumbled imagination. Sean ground his teeth, he needed to know her sister better. In fact, he needed to know both women better because each might open a conduit into Directus Iurisdictio. But there lay dangerous ground in more ways than one.

Keeping the black van well behind the Mercedes, Routt hoped the latter stayed with the red Corsa. He hissed harsh breath over the frustration he had suffered for five years while his anger fermented into black hatred and lust for brutal revenge. A savage emotion of blind rage tore apart his mind and gave deep pleasure. Now he wanted that pleasure realised in vicious and bloody mutilation of those Judge John Osborne had appeared to love. Internet access in jail allowed him to meticulously research the Register of Births, Deaths and Marriages. The bastard Osborne had fathered one illegitimate girl.

Routt had considered killing all, but the boys were too spread apart and did not offer the satisfaction he found in killing women. Men just died with a few squeals, but women offered pleasurable hours. Better still, the illegitimate daughter, Anjali Robson had been a favourite, as much so as his legitimate daughter Charlotte. Osborne had regularly visited both, right up to the time of his death in the car crash. Pity the girlfriend had died with him, Routt would have enjoyed her death as he would have enjoyed the death of Osborne's legal wife, now long departed. The best he had achieved came in desecrating their graves, defecating and urinating over the headstones. But it still left two women to make up for his disappointment.

His immediate problem lay in finding their residence. Neither home had been listed in any documents, but the papers had given Robson as a crime scene officer. All he had to do was turn up after a crime and wait, as he had waited near the police station for sight of Fagan. The papers described him as the big shot detective who swore to put Routt back behind bars. Routt wiped his hand across wet lips thinking if he went behind bars again it would be for triple murder, Fagan, Robson and Charlotte Osborne.

Now he had two of them he had simply to follow until he found where they lived, then he would make plans. He figured decapitation best for Fagan but he wanted something special for the girls, preferably together so they could hear each other scream.

Salem watched the black van pull away then followed in a Toyota pickup.

"How you know this bastard be here?" he asked the girl beside him, the scars across his lips causing the words to rasp in guttural menace.

"Logical deduction. Berty said Routt would be after Anjali, Anjali is a crime scene officer. Routt would know that from the papers so he'd come looking, then follow her. She in turn will lead him to Charlotte Osborne. He'd have them both."

"So you think you are clever little bitch?"

"Should have been a detective, but instead I joined the Death Heads. So, after this you make me a gang leader, introduce me to the Boss?"

"You joke." Salem glanced to the slight figure beside him. "You never meet big Boss, and Mr Bently never make you gang leader. To be gang leader you need control of men. Need plenty muscle."

"You'd be surprised who I can control. And you don't need muscle, you need brain."

"Don't worry." He squeezed her thigh. "You get Routt lonely place where I can kill him, you get big bonus. Maybe I even fuck you. You fail, I personally cut your cunt out."

"Charming." Samantha sank further into her seat so at first glance it appeared a child sat beside the towering Chechen. "You going to kill him yourself then? That will be fun for you."

"Big Boss say kill him. Mr Bently say kill him. Routt is now enemy. Salem will cut his balls off. You get him quiet place, leave rest to me."

"My pleasure." She smiled with little sharp teeth thinking this was finally her big break, to hit three targets simultaneously.

Routt watched the red Vauxhall Corsa pull into the driveway of a large mock Tudor house in St Albans' leafy suburbs. After driving straight past he parked several hundred metres away before climbing over the van's bench seat to crouch at the rear windows. Field glasses in hand he searched across the house then to the figure locking the Mercedes and following the woman inside. Now Routt knew where she lived he had only to wait before she led him to the other bitch. Fagan, he decided, could be killed at leisure, but for maximum pleasure the two women would need careful planning.

Forever conscious of searching police he scanned back along the road. Four cars and a pickup dotted the kerb between driveways. He did not recall the pickup and when he adjusted his focus on the cab's interior he allowed his breath to escape in a venomous hiss The scarred lips and pock marked face left little doubt. It was his hated rival, one described to him so many times with fear and loathing by fellow prisoners, Salem. Routt curled his fist and almost crashed out of the van determined on an immediate kill. Except Salem might have a gun. He sank back on his knees. Better to wait, he thought, waiting always produced unexpected opportunities. There appeared a child or small woman beside him. He would kill that first, then Salem later.

CHAPTER 11

"Nice house," Sean said, looking round the wood panelled walls and thinking it was way out of reach for a police sergeant.

"To allay your suspicions I inherited a much larger property from my mother. She was his legal secretary and the house my father's bribe for her silence over my birth. Judge Osborne was a respected and wealthy man who prized his social standing both here and in London. He didn't wish it leaked he had fathered a little bastard." She led him into a spacious drawing room and slipped off her jacket, turning to him before unbuttoning her blouse. "Don't look so shocked." She frowned. "It's why you're here, admit the truth."

Sean watched in silent disbelief and admiration, undecided if the situation had run out of control or turned into something far more delicious.

"Because of the way he treated both me and my mother, I sold that house and bought this one." She threw off the blouse and unzipped her trousers, sliding them over her hips until treading them round her feet. "I saw it as my new family home, a place to raise my children once I found the right man. However," she huffed, "such a man has so far eluded me." She unhooked her bra and dropped it with other discarded clothes. Dressed only in a black lacy throng she placed both hands on her hips and raised her eyebrows in question. "So, what are you going to do about it?"

"Stunning," Sean whispered, staring in anticipation of the beautiful offering before him. He saw only two options. To dive in and accept the consequences or retreat, but to retreat meant losing everything. "We're still in police time," he said, checking his watch but thinking, every sacrifice should be made to gain inside information.

For seconds she stared back in disbelief and then smiled. "So, that makes it all the more fun. Or are you turning me down?"

"Are you joking?" He stepped forward, his arm encircling her wait whilst Victoria's words raced through his mind. "You're such a pushover for a pretty face."

"Then come with me, Sir Sean. Let us see if you're handsome physic has the ability it promises."

"You sure about this?" he asked when led into a large garden conservatory built on to the back of the house.

"Of course I'm sure, so are you. It's why you came here. I've seen it in your eyes since first we met."

A large daybed between potted ferns and palms gave an almost jungle atmosphere as he watched her lay back shedding her thong in the process. She beckoned him and he shed his own clothes with practised speed, his mind firmly entrenched in base instinct. When he lay beside and kissed her she responded with open hunger, accepting his finger over her skin and then inside of her, her breath shuddering in barely audible whispers. When he entered her he did so with gentle care before pushing down full and deep, listening to her muted gasps of pleasure. Weight on elbows, he moved with rhythmic thrusts, guided by her murmurs and her shivers until her small utterances seemed to convey sublime bliss. Against his will he could not help but compare her to Victoria. Figure-wise and love-wise he gave both ten out of ten before reducing himself to zero as she arched against him, her soft cry causing him to plummet into divine ecstasy. When finally he rolled away he clasped her hand and listened to her silence.

"Thank you," he whispered.

"No, thank you." She squeezed his fingers. "It doesn't

happen very often so when the opportunity arrives I need to feel certain, and believe me," she squeezed again, "you filled every need and joy. Why are you single, what is some woman missing? Why don't you have a wife or at least a regular girlfriend?"

Sean hesitating on mentioning Victoria. "I had a wife. We married too young and for the wrong reasons. But she did give me two wonderful daughters. We floundered on the old problem of reconciling police work with marriage. Camilla grew fat and bitter, sliding into a mindless and grabby world from which, thank Christ, I was excluded." He sighed. "Now she's history, but I still love my girls, one just thirteen, one sixteen. Each a princess. I'm taking them to Timpton village fete tomorrow."

Anjali turned her head, casting eyes on him, staying silent and thoughtful for a moment. "Then we must meet up," she said finally. "I'm helping with a bunch of guys from Universal Youth. We run some of the stalls, do dance and gym displays. We also have a cricket team playing against the village team. Top members play, Lord Rolton, Rashid Bayat, Richard Cranby, who is also a lord, even Chief Hackett."

"He's the one who suggested I go, said it was a fun family day out." He paused and decided on a chance. "He may even introduce me to senior members of DI."

"Sean, the village fete with its maypole and dancing is the heart of merry England, not some medieval sect." She let got of his hand and looked to a wall clock. "The down side of making love in police time is I still need to sign off." She rolled away and stood. "And no doubt, Sir Sean, you also have duties."

Sean lay for a moment shading his eyes from the setting sun beyond the conservatory glass. She still looked magnificent, still highly desirable and surrounded by tall palms and ferns, she appeared like a taut feline beast of the jungle.

"And what is my duty?" he asked. "Other than to remove organised criminals."

"At this moment in time, your duty is to tread carefully."

"You mean if I get too close, DI might kill me?"

She turned at the bottom of the bed, legs astride, hands on hips, definitely a jungle creature in the guise of a woman, he thought.

"When and if you get close, I think you'll find Directus Iurisdictio a bunch of waffling old men. They might even welcome you, but they're not the threat. If danger comes it will be via the Death Heads or Routt. It's common knowledge you are here to whack them, so they would not be above whacking you first."

"As you're so knowledgeable, tell me, Samantha wears a skull, is she one of them or a camp follower?"

Anjali shook her head. "Samantha is an enigma, but she's rather sweet. I see no danger there even if she is a camp follower."

"And what about Dark Angel, whose side is she on?" He watched her retrieve the thong, pulling it on to ensure the lace lay smooth and flat.

"Now that spirit has a mind of its own." She walked away to find her clothes, forcing him to snatch up his own and follow. "To my knowledge she only goes after bad boys. But if you get too close it doesn't mean she won't bit," she said over her shoulder.

"So how close am I?"

"Possibly closer than you think, watch the shadows. She'll be somewhere hiding and she'll do anything to evade capture."

"Anjali, tell me all you know." He began to dress as she did.

"I've already told you. The Death Heads are removing anyone that gets in their way. By gang retribution, Salem or Dark Angel," she shrugged. "I don't know, who or where she is can only be guesswork. Chief Hackett dismissed my theory, so does everyone else." She tucked in her blouse and pulled the zip on her trousers with a sound and movement indicting definite closure.

When the Mercedes and Corsa drove off Routt followed, aware the pickup followed also. Both lead cars went straight to the police station. Routt parked on a yellow line and made sure Salem stopped behind before climbing out, the same time a slim female figure left the pickup. As the van was stolen Routt gave it no further concern and headed for an arcade entrance and café across the street. He turned once on the opposite pavement and saw the girl ready to cross, a mobile clutched to her ear as she looked right through him. Dressed in skinny black jeans, T-shirt and leather jerkin, he figured her a member of the Death Heads. He smiled at that, he certainly planned to give her plenty of head and death would come with her tits ripped off. He felt it about time he presented the police with a new murder, they were becoming too slack in their search for him. It would also divert their attention, giving him time to concentrate on Osborne's little bitches.

* * *

Sean led the way in his Mercedes letting his last conversation with Anjali ground all thought back into reality. Because of this he noticed the black van parked on the corner but gave it no further thought until it appeared in his rear view mirror as he turned into the police station. Good guys, bad guys, he had no way of knowing. Parked behind the police fence he watched the van stop opposite on a yellow line, his skin goose-pimpled as primeval awareness sensed evil. Poor sight lines did not allow a view inside the cab but someone large rocked the vehicle's springs on exit from the passenger side. A bus blocked further observations the same time Anjali's Corsa drew up beside him.

"I think we're being followed," he said, walking with her towards the main building.

"Black builder's van," she replied knowingly. "I'll report it. Or maybe the Chief Constable is checking up on staff's extra-curricular activities."

"Could also be Routt. Remember we're both targets."

They entered the station lobby through swing doors where dayshift were busy swapping with nightshift, exchanging information, moans and side cracks.

"Any activity?" Anjali asked Berty who pulled a jacket over wide shoulders.

"All quiet, not even a domestic. A career burglar fell out of the window while trying to escape. He's been given poor recovery chances. Report of a stolen black transit van, nothing interesting."

"It's parked across the street," Sean told her. "Looks like someone doesn't hold the police in high esteem."

"Cheeky bastard." Berty picked up the phone and spoke rapidly.

Sean followed Anjali through the uniforms and up the stairs. "A burglar out the window sounds like Dark Angel," he said thinking, least now I know it's not you.

"Or some junk head so out of his box he would fall off the kerb. Don't read every criminal incident into Dark Angel. I'll check his name and record."

"Now we're off duty, care for a drink? It's past 18.30 hours." They turned into a deserted corridor.

"Nope." She shook her head. "I must file my report then I have netball practice."

"You going to report our afternoon investigations?" He patted her backside and she put out her tongue.

"I should warn you, Sir Sean, close circuit TV covers all areas and any underhand fondling of an innocent junior officer will be frowned upon."

"Then I had better leave you in peace," he paused, unable to contain his nagging worry. "That van, it could be Routt, you want I should stay?"

"Sean." She shook her head and touched his cheek. "Rest assured I am amply protected. If Routt is following me, someone will know. Go and enjoy your pint of Guinness and vindaloo. We'll see each other at the Timpton village fete tomorrow. I look forward to meeting your daughters."

He left with his unease intact, but then realised if the van driver had been Routt, then maybe his target wasn't Anjali but some big shot detective whom Hackett promised would put Routt back behind bars. "Thank you very much, Chief

Superintendent," Sean muttered going into counter
surveillance mode.

Leaving the car he walked to a pub off the high street,
constantly checking his surrounding but saw only late
shoppers and early youngsters out for their Friday night
binge. Along the busy pavements no one came near who
appeared big or bad enough to be Routt. Once he caught a
fleeting sight of a small figure that may have been Samantha,
but then be thought no, the hair looked different. Besides,
why shouldn't she be out and about with her friends?

The pub had been divided into two bars, one for the old
boys who sat in their allotted places moaning about the
economy, the young and the parasites of parliament. Sean
nodded greeting under their watchful eyes before perching
himself on a bar stool and ordering a Guinness. From his
position he had partial view into the saloon bar where a
much younger and more affluent crowd exchanged cross
chat and flirtations.

When Sean received his first pint the old boys returned
to their moaning and the landlord to his younger customers.
Only then did Sean wonder how Anjali knew he would be
drinking pints of Guinness and eating vindaloo. Maybe she
had her own spies. After his second pint he extracted a
mobile and texted a message *If you need me call.* Half way
down his next pint a single *x* came back.

Three pints later at 21.00 hours the old boys were
populating the deserts with street yobs. When they started
on church, gays and transsexuals he headed for the high
street restaurant and a chicken vindaloo. He kept sharp
watch but saw no one until settling under a picture of the Taj
Mahal, his back to the restaurant wall, his eyes on the busy
pavement beyond the window. Samantha appeared
momentarily, her cute boyish features peering in through the
glass before darting away again.

The same girl or someone like her. The hair style looked totally different from their morning encounter, more like a black shaped helmet and her face had no makeup. He shrugged, maybe someone like Sammy searching out her girlfriends or simply wondering aimlessly. Of one thing he felt certain, she had no interest in him, unless of course she spied for the Death Heads. But Anjali thought not. Trust, trust. He began to eat. Who the hell did he trust?

At 22.30 hours he purchased two bottles of wine then headed for Dolores and Berty. On leaving the off-licence he again caught sight of the same girl through the throng of youngsters milling from pub to restaurant to club. This time she walked ahead of him but glanced back once as if checking he followed.

Cutting through ancient cobbled side alleys he took a diverse route towards St Michael's Manor. No one followed. No revellers here only shadows of terraced houses and dark empty roads where the council's austerity measures had turned off most street lighting. On the third turning downhill the road straightened passing a small ornamental park where shrubs and bushes lay just beyond the light from a solitary street lamp. Two hundred metres ahead a short slim female figure walked out of the shadows, becoming clear only on entering the area of light, the same girl who had spied on him in the restaurant. No coincidence, he thought, it had to be Samantha heading for home, except out of the darkness followed a much larger figure, someone moving fast but with stealth and menace.

Sean quickened his pace but when he heard a surprised female squeal he began to run. He found no one by the open park but in darkness beyond came scuffling sounds along with half choked protests. Sean drew one of the wine bottles from its bag and holding the neck in his fist advanced into the park. Twenty paces along the path the outline of two figures struggled on the tarmac amidst muted protests and grunts. The larger pinned the smaller to the ground holding one hand over her mouth while savaging with the other beneath her clothes. To gain momentum Sean ran with the wine bottle at shoulder height before swinging it full force against the assailant's head. Showered by wine and shattered glass the thug jerked forward but instead of falling as expected he twisted up on his feet, his fists clenched, his expression a mask of animal fury. Sean knew instinctively he faced Routt, knew he now had to fight for his life. The massive fist came at full force, driven by rage rather than skill which allowed Sean to side step and parry the blow with his right arm, causing it to bounce off his head. The power of impact still staggered him backwards and over. For seconds Routt postured in triumph and Sean snatched the opportunity to regain his feet, his own fists coiled into tight balls.

He struck Routt's face so the other's blow lost impetuous but still caused Sean to feel as if struck by a cannon ball. Again he went down, rolling from the force of Routt's boot against his ribs. Momentarily defenceless he lay partially dazed, realising he faced deep trouble until a small female figure leapt high in a double dropkick which splattered Routt's nose into a flat pancake of bloody cartilage and skin. Routt screamed, staggering in a circle while Sean regained his feet. Unable to find the second wine bottle as a weapon he again struck Routt full in the face moments before the girl delivered a second dropkick. This time came the distinct crack of cheekbone leaving Routt to wail with the grief of a stricken animal. Blood running from his mouth, ears and what remained of his face, he screamed vengeance while running away in defeat. Sean staggered after him, then stopped to rest both hands on his knees, his breath hoarse, his strength gone. For seconds he saw the female figure silhouetted by the streetlight, then she stepped silently away into the night.

"Fuck." Sean stood and searched his body for damage,

sighing relief as he winced but found no broken ribs. Across the street a light snapped on in one of the houses and an elderly bitchy voice yelled in complaint.

"Stop that noise or I'll call the police. You bloody hoodies got no right in this neighbourhood. Clear off to the estate where you belong."

Sean searched the ground and found his surviving wine bottle. "Bloody old fart," he called back and left the park.

No sign of Dolores when he entered her house. The hall light shone bright but he heard no sound, the kitchen stood empty. "Sammy," he called and listened to the following silence. If the girl had been Sammy she clearly intended to stay hidden. He wanted to thank her, after all she had saved him from a brutal beating, maybe even saved his life. On the first floor landing he looked at the three bedroom doors and knocked gently on each. Again silence and when he switched off the light no glow came under the door from an internal lamp. Weary of his landlady's warning to keep out of her rooms, he headed upstairs fumbling for his mobile. The desk sergeant answered, clearly irritated his studies had been interrupted.

"Fagan here, SOCA. I just intervened during an assault on a young female. I believer her attacker was Routt."

"Did you arrest him, sir?"

"No."

"Was the young lady hurt?"

"Don't know, she ran off."

"So you're the only witness, sir. Yes?"

"Correct."

"Want to come and make a statement?"

"No. Look, I thought you guys were after Routt."

"You sure it was him?"

"I'm sure of nothing. He was big, bad and violent."

"Friday night you always get nutters looking for a punch-up. I'll inform our patrols but if you wish to take this further you have to make a statement."

Sean didn't bother to reply and entered his room. "Useless sod," he said to himself and stripped off. Looking into the mirror he found bruising to his chest and cheek. Nothing serious, he thought, fingering his face. He bet Routt don't feel so lucky. He sure picked on the wrong girl. An enigmatic spirit Anjali had called her, that's if it was Sammy. Mother involved, daughter involved. Could she be Dark Angel? He washed himself, pulled on a tracksuit and opened his wine. Listening to adagios through his iPod docking station, Sean stretched on the bed and sipped St Emilion, pondering the day's events. He figured if Routt had attacked Sammy, it was reasonable she somehow had a connection with Anjali and Charlotte. Was that through Directus Iurisdictio or the Death Heads? Or maybe one woman had Sammy as a girlfriend. Were Charlotte and Anjali bisexual, or all three of them sisters in blood? Time to move closer, he thought, Hackett might throw some light.

CHAPTER 12

Sean woke at 07.30 hours and lay contemplating the ceiling, pleased he had a day out with his daughters but guilty he had neglected them for three weeks. He knew fatherhood required more effort, particularly under the threat of their mother levelling their brains down to the benign. When time allowed, memories still filled his mind of long ago, when Saturday mornings had brought both girls leaping into the bedroom with their teddy bears and books, wanting stories, wanting cuddles, wanting to sing along to the radio between planning to help Dad in the garden, going for walks in the park or to the market. He had loved his wife then and thought maybe she had even loved him. The girls united them. Except the need for a home, the cost of a mortgage, cars, the expense of living, feeding, clothing and providing had demanded money and money demanded greater ambition with longer hours at work until the purpose of work became superseded by the work itself. Now he stared at the ceiling of a lodging house, alone. Life sure was a bitch, he thought, looking to the nearly empty wine bottle and shaking his head in self-rebuke. But at least the day's activities would enable him to both work and be with his girls simultaneously. Hackett had information to give, maybe names which might open a way into the dark corners of Directus Iurisdictio.

Showered and dressed he checked emails on his iPhone. The first came from Heidi which he read with hand against forehead. *Rashid Bayat is a major benefactor of Universal Youth, but when I approached MI5 for more info they snapped shut. That indicates Rashid is a possible high grade suspect. I then tried them on Directus Iurisdictio to have them claim they knew nothing, which means they're not divulging. Try Victoria.*

"Oh I will," Sean said, remembering his meeting with

her that evening.

A second email had the heading CAT which Sean read remembering Victoria's warning not to upset them. *Just because you don't see us doesn't mean we are not close. Beware of oysters. Enjoy your day, we'll be watching.* The signature read *Freddy Fox, Col.*

"Oysters, what bloody oysters?" he said aloud. "And where were your meatballs when I needed them last night?" He closed the phone and left the room thinking, I'm going to a village fete what could be safer?

On the ground floor Sean found Sammy busy at the stove, at least until she turned, then her nose wrinkled as if she had no recognition of him. Her hair looked different, shorter and gelled like a boys. Her skinny jeans outlined the same tight waist and rounded, slender hips, all effeminate yet her shirt showed no definition of breasts. Out of courtesy Sean glanced briefly thinking she might have worn some binding or restricting garment instead of a bra. He made to speak but the other cut in.

"Confused? That's our party piece. I'm not Sammy. Samantha, except for gender, is my identical twin. I'm her brother."

"You have the same tattoos." Sean pointed to the curling flower on the boy's arm.

"Same face, same eyes, same voice, same tattoos. We're identical weight and height, both ballet dancers, both into martial arts, both members of Universal Youth and often wear the same clothes on account she's always raiding my wardrobe. In retaliation I frequently wear her jeans. Sometimes she adopts a masculine manner, sometimes I adopt her effeminate manner. But I assure you I am not. I'm all for the opposite gender. The name's Sam." He held out his hand, slapping Sean's palm rather than gripping it. "Tell me, why aren't you fat like other policemen?"

"Because I'm not a policeman. I'm an officer of the Serious Organised Crime Agency," Sean said, still unsure if the boy spoke truthfully or Sammy played some elaborate double gender hoax.

Sam looked him over as if mulling the information, his arms hanging ape like while minutely moving head and shoulders in a display of masculine posturing. "Does that mean you're fit?" he asked.

"Not so fit as I should be."

"Well, if you need a personal trainer come see me or Sammy. It's how we make money when not dancing."

"So, I bet you could both deliver a double drop kick with ease," Sean said, watching his eyes.

"As a great fighter once said, we float like a butterfly but sting like a bee."

"I need to talk with Sammy over an incident last night."

He shook his head. "She's gone already. She's playing ballerina on one of the floats at Timpton village fete, then working the stalls. You going? I'm doing a martial arts demo, then maybe the cricket team if they'll have me."

"Sam," Delores called descending the stairs in full skirted Victorian dress. "You ready?" She stopped at the sight of Sean. "My son," she said as if by way of some explanation. "I believe you've already met my daughter, Sammy. Sam, Sammy, identical in everyway. Even I get confused on occasions. We're all hosting at the Vicar's garden party." She brushed over her dress. "This year it's champagne, oysters and canapés. Only £20 a plate. You will come?"

"Oysters," Sean repeated, remembering the warning in his email. "But of course, I'm bringing my daughters, making it a family outing."

"How old?" Sam asked.

"Thirteen and sixteen." The boy nodded and from his grin Sean knew exactly what had entered his mind. No chance, he thought.

"You drive, I can't, not in this skirt," Dolores said to her son. "You'll enjoy today." She looked to Sean. "Timpton village fete always has something interesting." She went out the front door leaving Sam to lop behind.

Sean remained standing in the kitchen thinking, mother, son, daughter, all a bit weird. Kind of too weird what with Berty and all. How can she confuse son and daughter? Unless ... He shook his head and wondered if he should check the bedrooms. Maybe this was all bluff and Sammy lay nursing a bruised lip. Instead he imagined Berty striding from the bathroom in iron corset, imagined the row if not the punch up that would follow over his invasion of her privacy. "Boy, girl, girl boy," he thought, huffing breath as he left the house.

"You sure he will come?"

Justitia heard the question over her mobile while watching Timpton village fete swell in numbers. The Grandmaster's voice sounded with its usual upper class drawl, this time followed by the crack of cricket ball on bat, some clapping, then the master's voice again. "Oh, well played, well played."

"Everything is in place," Justitia answered. "He has arranged a meeting and in the heart of middle England amidst a family outing he will suspect nothing. I expect him dead by 2 pm. We have a medical team on standby to whisk the body away. We'll put it out someone fainted so causing minimal disruption."

"I trust your judgement."

"Have no fears, Master. All will go as planned." Justitia switched off and bit her lip. This was wrong, she thought. Never had she killed outside of the criminal fraternity. This person had committed no crime. His threat lay only to DI's security. Yet for her own life she dare not disobey the sacred laws.

Sean ate breakfast in a café off the high street, retrieved his car and arrived for his daughters at 10.30 hours sharp. A gold coloured Jaguar and two golf trolleys stood on the drive of the detached house. Sean pressed the doorbell and listened to the electronic chimes ring out Rule Britannia.

Camilla answered over the intercom then pressed the remote opener. In the brand new have everything kitchen, he found his ex-wife droning over her mobile, Bradley her husband sat staring at the screen of his tablet. Neither greeted Sean until Camilla momentarily broke off her conversation.

"You finally made it then." She spoke as if in accusation before putting the phone back to her ear.

"Ran all the way just to see you," Sean said, figuring she looked even fatter than last time. And to think you were once so slim, he thought, as she stood with mouth slack, a bulbous ring of flesh hanging over the waistband of her trousers which strained to contain the wide expanse of her sagging buttocks. Bradley remained transfixed to his tablet screen.

"Trying to buy new clubs on EBay," he said in explanation. "The ones I got are no good in warm weather. You need sets for each season."

"You do?" Sean tried to inject interest into his question then turned as Sophie came running into the kitchen, arms wide and eyes bright.

"Dadda, missed you." She wrapped him in a hug and squeezed.

"Missed you too my little sweetheart." Sean kissed the top of her head and felt the burn of emotion swell from his heart.

"Just grab my things," she said and left with the speed of her arrival.

"Hi Dad." He heard Becky his eldest call from somewhere upstairs. "Down in a mo."

Sean muttered fatherly patience. Neither of the other two made eye contact. Mobile to ear, Camilla sprouted disenchantment against some fellow golf club member while Bradley sat in vacant contemplation of the electronic images, as if he suffered under the effects of subliminal psychotic induction. Sad, Sean thought and found relief only when Sophie came bouncing back into the room. Though tall and skinny, her thirteen year old body had already taken the distinct shape of developing womanhood. Sean sniffed disapproval at the sight of her minute shorts over black tights. Rebecca followed. She also wore thick black tights but under a skirt clinging in elasticated contour across stomach and rear, the hem only an inch below the extremes of decency.

"You can't possibly wear ..." Sean's protest became lost as Camilla abandoned her mobile.

"Darlings you look gorgeous," she said, hugging both girls and smothering them with kisses. "Don't stay too long, your Dad will want to go to the pub and I'll be cooking your favourite meal."

"Don't worry, Mum," Sophie answered, shoulders swinging. "Enjoy your golf."

Sean decided on silence. Neither girl would change their outfits but simply stay at home. No point in ruining the day by being grumpy. Grumpy dads, he discovered, got nowhere. Camilla returned to her rabbiting while Bradley continued staring at his screen. Dead minds, dead people, Sean thought, not caring when neither acknowledged his departure.

Becky occupied the car's front seat, Sophie the rear. Both engrossed with their electronic gadgets.

"How's school going, Sophie?" Sean asked, hoping to distract them.

"Can't wait to leave," she answered, not looking up.

"Why? St Monica's is one of the best boarding schools in the country."

"Yeah, but girls only, no boys. I'm being deprived of social contact. It's against my human rights."

"You won't say that when they start making a nuisance of themselves," Becky put in.

"If I don't meet them I'll never know."

"Listen," Sean said, taking his chance. "With the non-existent skirts and shorts you two are wearing, boys will be everywhere and I can guarantee you'll think them pests." He nodded fatherly wisdom.

"Oh, Daddy, Daddy, you're so yesterday, so out of it," Becky sighed and returned to her texting.

Sean sniffed. "Decided on your gap year yet?"

"Sort of, just don't know who to go with. Maybe Paula, maybe Melissa, maybe Brad, maybe all of us," Becky answered, not looking up.

"Brad," Sean scowled.

"Yeah, he's gay. Figured on Thailand, India, China and Aus. Back through America. We're going to join Universal Youth first. That way wherever you go you got a contact the other end. It's safer, except I also want to do Madrid, Rome and Paris. Brad agrees, we got to keep Europe together. It's our only chance."

"Gay," Sean repeated. "That's OK then."

"So is Paula." Both girls giggled. "Hey Dad, there's a brave new world out there. Stop living in the past."

"Gay," Sean muttered, thinking St Albans branch of Universal Youth was but a tiny part, these people covered the globe. By recruiting the young their power and influence could only grow. And if Street Security, the neo-Nazi gangs, recruited from Universal Youth they too would grow.

Sean parked behind Timpton church and walked towards the high street, conscious both girls attracted young male attention. Occasionally he cracked his knuckles and gave bad bear looks. Both girls appeared totally dismissive of any attention but by the time they reached a viewpoint for the big parade, Sean counted at least six youths lurking in near proximity.

Sophie hitched up onto a wall for a better view, Becky continued texting. Sean saw no sign of Hackett, no sign of any face he recognised. A band struck up some distance along the road and spectators strained forward, the same time Sean caught the faint waspish sound of a speeding model aircraft engine. Overhead the tiny circling craft slowed, hovering until it found its surveillance target, then as if the remote operator felt undecided, it suddenly darted towards the playing fields. Sean recognised it as a Tarantula Hawk micro surveillance drone, a twenty-four inch wide platform holding a CCTV camera and powered by horizontal rotating blades, the type used by SOCA and Special Ops. So what's with security videoing a village fete? Maybe it was an exercise, or maybe it was real. No one else seemed to notice.

The band arrived thumping drums amidst cheers and clapping from spectators. Then came members of the British Legion, the Scouts, Boys' Brigade, floats from local schools and Universal Youth on the platform of which Samantha gave a demonstration of ballet movements. She curtsied on passing Sean, her tutu shivering with each movement. With her body above eye level Sean paid close attention. He saw no evidence of male genitalia but certainly the definite swell of breasts. The girl appeared unquestionably female, yet in other respects she might also have been Sam. The float passed, replaced by Timpton's youth club dance troop, then the toddlers' club, each small child beaming happily and waving flags. Behind came the Women's Institute, the Girl Guides, another band and the Fire Brigade, followed by two ranks of Street Security, their SS flashes on chest and shoulders, their arms swinging as they marched with military precision.

Sean glanced to the sky, the surveillance drone had returned, circling high enough to appear like a large bird. It made no sound and drew no obvious attention. Farm tractors came next, pulling trailers which held older children dressed as yokels, behind came a trailer full of pigs, giant pigs of ancient breed. Each float received a cheer, while a teen girl dance group caused loud encouragement from the nearby group of youths. Sean watched as they followed this new attraction along the pavement, keeping parallel behind the crowd. Becky twitched her nose and Sean smirked satisfaction. Enemy diverted.

A lone community constable brought up the rear, following the parade to the sports field. Most of the crowd fell in behind, others headed for the pub. Sean considered a quick pint, least until a small boy tugged his sleeve.

"That man said to give you this." The boy held out a note.

"What man?" Sean glanced around while the boy pushed back amongst the crowd.

The note read. *Oysters and champagne bar ASAP.* H. Hackett, Sean thought, and we're going to be under surveillance. Beware of oysters. So just what are you watching for, Colonel Freddy Fox? He looked up at the drone the same time Sophie pushed off the wall. "OK, what say we watch the cricket?" He opened his arms in a display of happy expectation while fully aware of the response.

"Cricket," both girls repeated, looking at him as if he was doomed. "No Dadda," Sophie said. "You're going to buy us ice cream and then we're going to watch the dancing. I also noticed a pizza van go by."

"Ice cream." He glanced at the hovering drone which now appeared little more than a speck in the sky. "I got to talk with a friend," he said, pulling a ten pound note from his wallet. "Tell you what, meet you by the champagne bar in thirty minutes. We deserve better than a pizza."

"Champagne," Becky beamed and linked his arm.

"Young lady, that skirt is too short for you to drink champagne. I was thinking more of lunch in St Albans."

"Oh Daddy dear, you're so antiquated." She snatched the ten pounds and took Sophie's hand.

"Thirty, forty minutes," Sean called as they walked off with the crowd. The drone stayed steady, not moving until he did. That satisfied him it had no interest in the girls, but he still felt uneasy.

CHAPTER 13

Sean deliberately walked at a casual pace to give no evidence of his anxiety. This was middle England at play, he thought, nothing could happen here. Every few minutes he glanced skywards noting movement of the surveillance drone, seeing it always slightly ahead so it had vision of his face and surroundings.

The first display units held half a dozen pigs in each of two pens. All looked contented if not a little bemused by their spectators. Charlotte Osborne stood beside the first pen, dressed in jeans and sweatshirt, arms folded as she chatted to Richard Cranby, the branch president of Universal Youth. Play casual, play casual, Sean warned himself.

"Hi," Charlotte waved him over. "I believe you've met Lord Cranby," she said.

"Richard Cranby, please," he offered his hand.

"So UY is involved here too," Sean said, indicating the field of activity.

"We are ambiguous," Cranby looked to the pig pen. "What do you think of my pigs? On account of their floppy ears they're called British Lops, one of our rare breeds but getting more popular. Charlotte and I have neighbouring farms with hundreds of the beasts between us."

"A lot of pigs, must take a lot of feeding."

"Mine are free-range, they mostly run wild in fields or woods," Charlotte said. "Richard keeps his penned. We have a never ending argument as to which method produces the best pork."

"Do they find enough to eat on their own?" Sean asked, looking at the nearest pig who stared back with unblinking eyes.

"That's the problem," Cranby said. "They eat everything they find from dead dogs and rabbits to acorns, to grass. Pigs are omnivorous. If they were hungry they'd even eat us."

"Keeps out poachers and trespassers," Charlotte laughed.

"Not good for the flavour, mind."

"Or the digestion." Sean grinned without humour. "Must meet up later, I'm on my way to the Vicar's champagne bar."

"Do try the oysters." Cranby returned the mirthless grin. "And the large pork pies are mine, guaranteed free of human contamination."

"But mine taste better," Charlotte said and shifted arms beneath bosoms.

Sean waved and moved on thinking, I bet you taste just delicious.

"Cricket team comes in for lunch anytime now, we'll be over," Cranby called after him.

Sean waved again hoping Hackett realised the situation. By passing info on DI in view of Universal Youth members and possibly Directus Iurisdictio members themselves, he used the most open, yet covert way of operating, except he might also be overheard.

Hackett sat with oysters and champagne amidst the flowerbeds and lawns of the old village rectory, jazz played discreetly in the background. No one sat within ten feet making it an ideal spot for quiet gossip.

At a thatched makeshift stall, Sammy now out of her ballet costume wore a skirt which made Becky's one appear modest, while her slinky top showed a small but definite décolletage. Dolores stood at the rear, opening and placing oysters onto trays of ice.

"Champagne only." Sean grinned at Sammy. "And your ballet steps are exceeded only by your double drop kick."

"If only. For that see Sam. He's giving a display right now."

"He is?" Sean looked but the hedge blocked any view.

"Champagne as served in a rural establishment during Victorian times." She handed him a rim based pewter mug. "Ten pounds, please."

Sean fished out his wallet. "Not the same price though."

"That's because it's not real champagne, only sparkling wine. But don't tell anyone." She winked.

Sean sniffed and joined Hackett. The man sluiced down an oyster then clenched hands in an effort to hide their tremor.

"We're being watched by a UVA surveillance drone," Sean said as he sat. "Is it yours?"

"No." Hackett looked around, lingering on a woman and grandchildren sitting at the nearest table. "Wife and family," he said by way of explanation, then glanced up. "SOCA use drones."

"So do a few other agencies. On top of that Universal Youth's cricket team is coming in, does that cause a problem?"

"They're all involved, all of them." Hackett said. "But they'd never dream I'd dare tell you anything while they watched. It's why I thought this the safest place. Offices have hidden microphones and cameras, the drone can't hear us."

"So, what's the big deal?" Sean asked.

"Cobbart said we could talk freely."

"That means everything you know about Directus Iurisdictio. I need names, locations, associates."

"I can only tell you what my rank amongst them allows and that is mainly in Hertfordshire and surrounds. They're association with the Death Heads is what concerns me."

Sean sipped his fake champagne. "But the Death Heads are a criminal organisation, those who DI would destroy."

"That's not quite as you think. It's also why I am so disillusioned with DI. This branch has moved outside the remit. What they are doing is not in our charter to defend nation, justice and liberty."

"So tell me."

"Rashid Bayat and DI made an agreement. DI remove people like Grogan, Bently and their traders. In return Rashid finances DI and numerous branches of Universal Youth. But Rashid is a drug baron. His father gives critical military assistance and access to the UN throughout his tribal lands in Afghanistan. In return the UN and authorities pay him millions, plus they turn a blind eye as he ships heroin and opium to the West. Controlled by Rashid and his East European gangsters, the Death Heads have separated from Street Security. They are predominantly disenchanted Muslim who will accept the discipline and teaching of radical clerics. They recruit via council estates, football crowds and the politically lost under-classes. They remove or take over local street gangs and while they don't sell to their own community, they retain and keep a register of all other customers, who, if necessary, are then blackmailed or bribed."

"But DI are supposedly a nationalistic force for people's justice. How could they support criminals?"

"They support bankers don't they? Believe me, their sole interest is money while the higher orders cocoon themselves in self-righteous elitism." Hackett picked up an oyster from the plate before him and slurped it into his throat. "Mmm. Love them." He glanced as if worried someone may have witnessed this indulgence, then looked back to Sean. "You must realise the central purpose of DI is long term and that requires deep roots into the establishment. Rashid is a temporary means to finance an organisation whose purpose is national control. When the time comes he will be sanitised. Through Universal Youth, DI select the best future leaders and spend years grooming them to firmly believe Directus Iurisdictio is the only solution. With members help they place these recruits into politics, the civil service, security, commerce, law, the police and armed forces. Soon we will have a state heavily influenced if not governed by a secret organisation open only to the few. As I said, when DI's corporate income exceeds Rashid's contribution, they will replace him for one of their own, paying and controlling the Death Heads direct until able to disband them via the SS. Just as important, with the SS and DH they will also have their own right-wing and disciplined street armies, rather like Hitler did. Do you begin to see the wider picture?"

"I do." Sean sipped from his mug, trying to grasp all he'd been told. The conspiracy theory was more than alive, it ate at the very fabric of society. "Names, I need names," he said.

Hackett slurped down his last oyster and looked at his empty ice covered plate. "Don't get oysters very often," he said. "My one weakness, I have them here every year. But to return. There is a clear and obvious danger to their plan. What if they cannot stop the Death Heads? It is inevitable the Death Heads and SS will one day clash. That's so called Muslim radicals against neo-Nazi Christians. The result will be civil unrest on a massive scale." Both men looked round to watch the two cricket teams come in, chattering good-heartedly amongst themselves.

"Give me names," Sean said. "I can do nothing without names."

"They're here, the ones you want. Those once great who have fallen. Keep this secret, but remember my help and co-operation during any enquiry." Hackett fell silent as Cranby approached.

"There you are, Hackett," Cranby said. "I thought you were going to play for us."

"These youngsters have better eyes and speed than an old copper," he answered with a pretence of humour.

Charlotte joined them carrying a tray of twelve oysters which she swapped for Hackett's empty platter. Accompanying her, a trim bearded man of Asian appearance glanced over Sean with arrogant eyes.

"May I introduce Rashid Bayat," she said. "Without his contribution Universal Youth could not have its many clubhouses."

"My pleasure." Sean shook hands, realising that behind the man's pretention to the upper class lay the cold flesh of an alien predator.

"Welcome to our fete and please, I've brought you some

oysters. On the house, you must try. They're delicious," Charlotte said, lifting one and offering it to Sean in the palm of her hand, her smile, for his compliant trust, offering much more.

"Don't mind if I do." Hackett took the plate and ate two in quick succession. Charlotte stared at him, her mouth slightly parted.

"Don't eat oysters," Sean said, remembering the warning in his email and smelling a whiff of almonds. "They have a bad effect. So, how's business?"

"I hear you shot that gangster, Grogan, well done," Rashid said. "In my father' tribal lands we would have shot such a crook long ago. It's good to see the West is finally catching up."

"Oh, how we long for the return of public executions." Sean nodded and smiled sarcastically. "Didn't know Afghans played cricket."

"Started at prep school, continued through 'til Cambridge. Now it's only for charity."

"Rugby man myself." Sean listened to Hackett slurping down more oysters before he began to choke and wheeze.

"Touch too brutal for me." Rashid's half smile reminded Sean of a cobra surveying its victim. A sense of evil caused goose pimples on his skin.

"What do you think, Charlotte?" Sean asked.

"I love the game. And there is nothing like a hog roast after. Do try some oysters while a few remain." She pushed over the plate, too late to prevent Hackett swallowing another.

For a moment he stood empty shell in hand, his expression fixated, his face glowing red before he began to gasp for breath. The shell dropped and he clutched his chest, eyes staring, jaw moving as if attempting to speak. The next second he crashed forward tipping the table to scatter plates, ice, oyster shells and tankards over the grass.

Instinctively Sean grabbed for his drink, fumbling the attempted catch as it flipped and fell. Only then did he see the micro transmitter magnetically attached to the inner base of the mug's hollow rim. On the next table Hatchett's wife began screaming which in turn sent her grandchildren into panic, all pushing forwards amidst the startled gathering.

"Heart attack, get a doctor, an ambulance," Cranby shouted while Charlotte attempted to place Hackett's jerking body into the recovery position. Others knelt to help. Hindered by Hackett's wife who bent over her husband wailing hysterically, Charlotte tried resuscitation by pumping Hackett's chest.

A few people pushed backwards allowing more space, others lingered as unsure spectators, Rashid amongst them. Sammy knelt quickly amongst the table's spilt contents, searching round the many feet and legs. Sean knelt also but only to retrieve his mug. When finally he pulled it back the transmitter had gone, whether trodden into the ground or stolen away, he was unsure. Sammy seemed only concerned in collecting oyster shells. It confirmed Sean's suspicions. He sneaked one into his pocket then stood, empty mug in his hand. Charlotte continued pumping Hackett's chest with desperate energy and seeing her expertly dealing with the situation, others gave more room, then voiced relief when paramedics from Street Security arrived.

"Cardiac arrest," Charlotte told them, clearly relieved when one of them took over. A fourth medic brought breathing apparatus, fixing the mask before they lifted

Hackett onto a stretcher. A woman community police constable consoled Hackett's wife and grandchildren, offering to follow the ambulance with them in her car. The ambulance had appeared almost instantly as if in waiting, the logo on its sides bearing the emblem of Universal Youth. Very efficient, Sean thought. So who had listened to their conversation? Freddy Fox whoever he might be, or an unseen enemy?

"Must have a heart problem, poor sod," someone said to the dispersing crowd. Sean surreptitiously watched Sammy continue to retrieve the last shells, counting them into a bag, clearly realising one was missing. Standing she looked to the rubbish bin by the stall, then ran from the garden.

"He'll be fine," Cranby called to those still rubber necking. "Emergency over, just a simple seizure. We'll keep you informed. Right, everyone, back to the party."

"Play on, play on," someone cheered him.

Bottles of real champagne suddenly appeared on the stall and drew all attention. Sean held out his mug and had it filled by Rashid.

"Life is so uncertain," Rashid said. "One never knows when the end will come."

"No, one never does." Sean met his gaze.

"You must visit sometime." He handed Sean a card. "I too have swine. They're very useful at getting rid of the garbage."

"Cranby Hall," Sean read the address.

"Used to belong to Richard's family, built via their exploitation of India and the opium trade to China. How times change. Now I live there, poverty gives him no choice in the matter."

"So what's your line of business, Mr Bayat?"

"Family import and export. It's what we Asians are good at."

They walked slowly towards Cranby who talked with Charlotte.

"So are you going to join us?" Cranby asked.

"Join?" Sean glanced between them.

"Universal Youth," Cranby said. "You never know what it might lead to." He winked. "We have more than one Cabinet Minister in our ranks. Onwards and upwards, as they say."

"It's certainly tempting. Perhaps later we can talk, but will I need to breed pigs?" Sean asked.

"Rare breeds. Keeps old England alive and well fed."

"Lunch," a voice called and brought a general drift of both cricket teams towards the rectory.

"Must excuse us." Cranby moved off with Rashid leaving Sean alone with Charlotte.

"Do you think he'll be all right, Hackett?" Charlotte asked.

"What do you think?"

"We must talk. Call me, Anjali has my number." She half smiled and turned to leave.

"How about tonight? I'll come to your place."

"Halsham Manor Farm five miles out on the Codicote Road, but not tonight, I've something on with Anjali. Something which has to be done."

"Tomorrow?"

"Look forward to it." She tipped her head a little, eyes wide, a gesture which gave certain promise.

"Seven, I'll be there," he said and watched her departure, watched the gentle sway of her hips below a slim waist, a figure every bit as delectable as her sister's. "Life is certainly becoming interesting, he said quietly and looked upwards. The drone still hovered, a grey, almost invisible speck in the sky. As if aware of his observation, it suddenly darted away until lost in the haze.

Sean left the Vicar's garden pushing buttons on his mobile. Cobbart answered immediately.

"Do you have a spy drone over Timpton village fete, over the sports field?"

"No, but CAT might have."

"Can you find out. Someone overheard a very interesting conversation concerning Rashid Bayat, a leading drug baron who operates the Death Heads. He's part of DI's plans for national domination. You need to watch him."

"Message received and understood."

Sean switched off and went in search of his girls. So who was meant to die from cyanide poisoning in oysters, Hackett or me? Who is listening in the sky? And what are those two women going to do at Halsham Manor Farm tonight, lay themselves as bait for Routt?

CHAPTER 14

Sean left the garden and returned to the busy playing field. The pigs watched him go by, staring at him with narrow beady eyes.

"So what do you guys know that I don't?" he whispered at the nearest who shuffled back.

No sign of the drone, no sign of the girls. Maypole dancing had drawn spectators to one end of the football pitch while around the stalls people bought homemade jam, jars of honey, allotment vegetables or tried their hand at skittles. The sun shone, people smiled and children laughed. Sean let out his breath and for seconds closed his eyes. This place represented the green fields of county England and amidst its rural pastures the DI had committed murder. What he did not know was the intended victim, himself, Hackett, or maybe both. He fished for his mobile then punched in Heidi's number.

Her voice answered within seconds. "It's Saturday lunchtime, Mr Fagan, and I'm feeding my cats."

"Heidi, a favour."

"I do more favours for you, Sean Fagan, than a mistress for her lover."

"Oh Heidi, if only. You're so good to me, thank you." He listened to her huff sharp breath then continued. "Chief Superintendent Hackett of St Albans Constabulary has just suffered a heart attack. Except it had all the symptoms of potassium cyanide poisoning, even with the smell of almonds. I need you to check round local A & Es, glean any info you can."

"No problem, boss," she answered, her voice immediately in business mode.

"Cheers." Sean switched off and continued the hunt for his girls. He found them by the toffee apple stall, each with a half eaten apple on a stick. Next to it stood a recruitment stall for Universal Youth and behind the counter, Anjali and Mrs Gosling.

"Guess what, Dad, we signed up. Now we can go to the gym in Barnet for free," Becky said.

"And they got youth club every Tuesday and Thursday in the Town Hall. Plus we got a free toffee apple." Sophie came and put her arm around his waist. "Do you know Anjali?" she said as Mrs Gosling cleared off.

"We have met." Sean tried a tight smile. "So what's this cost you?"

"Nothing," Anjali said and raised her brows in expectation. "But you may volunteer a donation which will be gratefully received."

"Thanks Dad, 'cos we only got pocket money and that ain't enough." Sophie nodded agreement.

"Twenty pounds would help with administrative costs." Anjali clasped hands with a look of angelic serenity.

"I bet." Sean clenched teeth and extracted his wallet before moving close to the counter. The girls allowed him generous room, their interest now wondering to some boys who shuffled close by with a keen interest in the girls' legs.

Sean sniffed and leant towards Anjali. "Via enrolment you have their names and address," he whispered.

"We need to send membership cards. It's all on computer." She tapped her laptop. "Details are sent to HQ. Soon as they said Fagan I guessed they were your girls. Fagan is not a common name."

Trust, he thought. Could he trust her when maybe her sister had tried to kill him? Universal Youth knowing where his daughters lived did not help his unease.

"Their mother is touchy about giving their address. She won't like it. Send the cards to me, I'll pass them on."

"OK." She ran a finger over the laptop keys. "For you I'll cancel their address and put yours in, don't want anyone upset."

"I appreciate it." He touched a small finger to her hand and to show good will, "How about dinner tonight?"

"Sorry," her nose wrinkled. "Got a date with my sister out at her farm."

"What if Routt turns up?"

"Then he'll have a nasty surprise," she said, suddenly flat, her shoulders stiffening.

They're definitely hatching something, Sean thought, time to get close. "OK girls, lunchtime." Sean turned to his daughters who were now chatting up the boys. "We leave this good lady and these gentlemen and head for St Albans."

Becky handed one boy her empty toffee apple stick, Sophie copied her with another.

"Cool," the boy said, toying with his Street Security badge as they walked away.

"No meat," Becky said as they walked down St Albans High Street. "We're veggies now. Smoking, alcohol and meat are bad for you."

"I agree, but meat's OK."

"No, makes you fat." Becky patted her flat stomach.

"And you drink alcohol, bad father." Sophie pointed an accusing finger.

"Only on social and festive occasions," Sean said defensively.

"Mum said you go to the pub every night."

"Doesn't Bradley?"

"Mum won't let him."

"That's why I went to the pub. Besides, it's a great place to contemplate the philosophical meanings of life."

"You a philosopher?" Sophie looked up at him, nose wrinkled.

"Of course I am. It's the only reason I go to the pub. As Descartes said, I think therefore I am, and because I am, I drink a pint so I can think."

"Rene Descartes said that?" Becky asked, head back.

"Maybe slightly obscured from the French translation, but roughly correct." He raised a hand. "I know, let's try Moroccan food." Sean pointed to the sign as a way of escape on seeing the restaurant. "Then you can have couscous and veggie and I can have lamb."

Inside both girls approved of the Moorish decor and the food. Neither did they object to him having a glass of wine.

"So what's new on the street?" Sean asked.

"Nothing new in Barnet," Becky turned up her nose. "Ever."

"Except Universal Youth," Sophie chirped in. "I bet they're fun."

"OK." Becky leant forward in challenge. "You're a policeman, so whenever you want a policeman, why can't you find one? But you can always find Street Security. They're taking over."

"They been bothering you?"

"No, the opposite. When you can't see a copper outside of his car, Street Security are patrolling the High Street, sorting trouble. Me and two girlfriends, we had some boys following us we didn't like, and we had to cross the common to go home. So my friend, she's got this number to call on her mobile. So four Street Security turned up including a girl and they escorted us home. Like they were real cool, black T-shirts, jeans, berets. Anytime we need help they say, call 'em. We could join, but I don't want to, prefer UY."

"Just keep away." Sean looked to each. "Be careful of these guys, OK?"

"Dad, you're such a fusspot. Can I have an ice cream too, please?" Sophie asked.

"Sure, sweetheart." He looked back to Becky. "They didn't sell you drugs or anything?"

"No," she shook her head. "But one of them gave me a little book on how we should support our nation, look after the old, keep out the unwanted. I read it cover to cover. Bit rightwing but it makes sense. They have meetings at Universal Youth."

"Be very careful of those who preach extreme values, be they religious or political. There is little difference between rightwing head-bangers, Islamic head-bangers and leftwing head-bangers."

"I'm not daft, Dad. If this was the swinging sixties I'd be a flower child."

Sean had them home by six then phoned Victoria.

"Change of plan, but I need to see you."

"I trust that's a romantic overture and not some official request."

"Both, but romance first."

"That's what I love about you, Sean Fagan. Your lust precedes all."

Sean headed straight for her flat in Maida Vale thinking lust might have to wait. Directus Iurisdictio and associated dark forces were creeping and none seemed to realise. They had killed once today and he felt certain they planned to kill again. But this time he wanted solid evidence. He wanted to be there as a witness.

CHAPTER 15

"Understand little star, if you want money, if you want to be with men of power, then you have a price to pay," Salem said, forcing Sammy's face forwards over the table.

She felt her tights and knickers pulled down, felt him fumbling at his flies, then the hot, sticky head of his penis against her skin. "No, fuck off," she shouted and tried to stand, struggling against the force of his fingers over the back of her neck.

"You are now my Bacha boy, fucking you is my right. Disobey and I will beat you, maybe kill you. Give me pleasure and I make sure you become Rashid's whore." With his free hand Salem parted one side of her buttocks, searching with stubby fingers before thrusting himself into her anus, sending her solitary scream into every corner of the empty house.

Eyes tight shut and fists clenched, she suffered his pummelling with muted protest, swearing vengeance, knowing that as of now her commitment exceeded all else. Her oath of allegiance to CAT allowed no going back or escape.

He finished quickly, grunting as he shuddered his sperm inside of her. For seconds his hands rested to span her waist, then he extracted himself. "Shit," he said and moved away.

Sammy stayed face down, her eyes closed, her white knuckled fists pressed against the hard wooden table. After moments she heard him mumble then go into the bathroom, only then did she stand and straighten her underwear.

Sitting on the bed she attempted to control the rage and humiliation which trembled her body, telling herself the situation with Salem was of her own making. HQ had recruited and trained her for covert operations in which the transsexual nature of her gender might be used to advantage. Bacha Bereesh dance boys were used throughout Afghanistan. As one able to adopt both genders with licentious attraction to certain senior mid-Asian males, she had been deployed to penetrate and gather intelligence. On entering the arena she had full understanding of the possible consequences. Now it had happened she accepted it as a duty with no right to complain. But she would kill him, kill him as a duty not unto others but a duty unto herself. She listened to his return, not looking round as he poured himself a drink, clinking whisky bottle against glass.

"So, how does it feel to be my little Bacha boy, ah?" He laughed, walking round to face her. "In my culture we fuck only whores and Bachas, you are both. Now I own you, I am your master to use you as I please. If I say dance, you dance. You can make much money. Tomorrow I take you to Master, to Rashid Bayat. You dance for him and jihad Death Heads. He give big meal for Bently, celebrate shipment of heroin. But I think only pigs will eat." He knocked back his whisky.

She stared at him, not showing any expression. "I thought Muslims didn't drink."

"That's good Muslims. I, Salem, bad Muslim. It's why I do jihad, to pay for my sins."

"Will Rashid Bayat fuck me too? Will your friends fuck me?"

"Maybe. But I think Rashid prefer proper women. But you don't worry, I fuck you plenty."

She stared at him, trying to judge the gullibility of his ego, thinking this was an opportunity to consolidate her position. "You want to kill Routt? I know where he'll be tonight." She watched as his eyes flared with the intensity of hate. Teeth bared, he threw aside his glass and grabbed her T-shirt.

"Where, where this pig? You tell me, I cut off his balls."

"A trap is set at Charlotte Osborne's farm house. Half a mile passed the piggery you turn left along a drive. Because of open meadows, the only way to approach unseen is through the wood at the back. That way you get close to the house. After dark Routt will be there trying to creep unseen through the woods. He goes to rape Charlotte and her sister, then kill them in vengeance. But they know, they have a trap and they will kill him instead."

"How you know this?"

"Because I am Charlotte's close friend. I have links between Universal Youth and the SS."

"She has men there?"

"No, this is private. She don't want others involved."

He let go of her shirt and stood back. "You clever girl, you tell me truth, when I take you to Master I make sure you sit beside him. You tell me lie, then I give you to my men. When they finish, you will pray to die. OK, you here eleven tomorrow morning, now go."

Sammy left the house and headed for her car smiling over clenched teeth. When the time came she would enjoy killing Salem, or maybe Routt would kill him first; even better they might kill each other. Then the pain would be worth it. But first she must report to Charlotte and hoped telling Salem about tonight would not cause her displeasure.

* * *

171

Salem watched Sammy pass the gate then picked up his mobile. The answer came immediately.

"Slight change of plan, Master," Salem said. "I have chance to kill Routt. I take his head and say he stole drugs for Bently."

"But the shipment is safe?"

"In warehouse as ordered, taken from the transporter by my most trusted men. The rest we place in cellar of Cranby Hall. When Rashid realises part of shipment missing he will blame Bently, who will blame Routt. But I will bring them Routt's head and say he confessed to stealing for Bently. I will rise to take Bently's place. We then control Death Heads. You send assassin to kill Rashid. Him gone we have everything, heroin, gangs, all people."

"Well done, Salem, you will be richly rewarded."

"No problem, Master." Salem switched off. "Rich indeed, for I will take all."

CHAPTER 16

Heidi's call came through as Sean reached the outskirts of London.

"'Fraid Hackett's dead," she told him. "The guy suffered a second and massive heart attack. When I queried that, the hospital said he had a history of related illness. An emergency team had been present and the death certificate signed-off by a doctor."

"So, no autopsy by a forensic toxicologist? How convenient. Evidence of potassium cyanide needs a dedicated examination."

"If you've got proof act fast and get it up front, boss. The body is already being released back to the family."

"OK, cheers Heidi, I'll be in touch." Sean switched off the hands-free speaker and tapped fingers on the steering wheel. Slowing the car to stop at traffic lights he looked at those who pulled up in lanes beside him. He saw beautiful people, fat, ugly, handsome, young and old, people innocent of the secret conspiracy creeping under their lives. Or maybe some were not so innocent, maybe the spreading influence of Directus Iurisdictio might be greater than imagined. If they had penetrated the police and Government, why not the Health Service? Amongst those who were trusted they could use hospitals to commit or cover murder. Or maybe he speculated too far, maybe. He moved away from the lights, perhaps the planned operation that night would tell him.

Victoria opened the door to her flat wearing a translucent negligee, the light behind silhouetting her body to perfection. Stunning, he thought and no doubt carefully rehearsed for full impact. Sean kissed her while edging her backwards to close the door.

"You're early, I'm still changing," she said in mock surprise and then sniffed. "What's that disgusting smell?"

"Oysters." He fished in his pocket for the offending shell.

"I would have preferred flowers or perfume."

"Hackett is dead, I believe poisoned by cyanide spread on this and other shells. It's imperative your forensic boys check, like now."

"Whatever happened to romance?" She turned on her heel, still making good use of the back light while fishing a mobile from her negligee pocket. Speaking quietly she moved from hall to kitchen, returning with a small plastic container. "In there," she said, removing the lid then resealing it over the slimy article. "In ten minutes a courier will be here, but then we have the whole evening."

"Afraid not, something important has come up. I may be able to pin Dark Angel and prise an opening into Directus Iurisdictio."

"Is that so?" She moved close, her breast against his chest. "You going to tell me who?"

"I'm always open to a fair exchange," he said, his hands sliding down over the curve of her buttocks.

"Well, if you tell me something I can get to grips with, something that will lighten me up, I'm sure you'll be able slip past my defences and really open me to an exciting outcome. So, enlighten me." She gently pushed with her pelvis.

"Dark Angel, alias Justitia, may possibly be Charlotte Osborne, possibly her half sister Anjali Robson and less likely, a young and strange creature called Sammy." He kissed her, long and full, accepting the full pressure of her embrace. "OK, your turn."

"Information received from agents stationed in Afghanistan is that two thousand five hundred kilos of heroin went missing from a UN compound three months ago."

"Careless of them," Sean said, his hand parting her negligee.

"Or deliberate, in exchange for important info on the Taliban. Rumour has it the whole consignment came from the tribal lands of Rashid Bayat's father and is heading this way. Forewarned, Border Control is watching but as yet no sign. That means it's gone some place else, or passed Customs due to insider involvement. You may have noticed, not all officials are honest."

"Rashid's a drug baron, that figures. Position and money could buy him protection." Sean explored with one finger causing a delicate shiver on her skin.

"Plus he's the highest contributor to Universal Youth, an organisation supported by world governments," she said. "Playing the philanthropic gentleman he moves amongst influential circles manipulating and compromising all he can snare, particularly those of rank. Those who are fiddling their expenses and bank accounts are easily persuaded to comply."

"Including members of Directus Iurisdictio?"

For seconds she closed her eyes and nodded. "Absolutely, except this consignment stands to make him and the Death Heads a fortune, millions and millions. Directus Iurisdictio's long term plan for Street Security is for them to become an organised street army, disciplined, right-wing and under DI control. An irregular force on the streets would be very handy to prevent future riots and sort out suspect terrorists. Unfortunately as a breakaway Islamic group, the Death Heads are not playing the English game. They are imposing Sharia law amongst Muslim communities and sounding more and more radical, much to the alarm of the communities involved. The prospect of a clash between the SS gangs and the Death Heads seems inevitable."

"So do something." He rotated with two fingers and she closed her eyes again, pausing before she answered.

"We are. We're sending you in to get proof of criminal activity. If Bayat receives these drugs he'll use Death Heads nationwide to sell them. With such a fortune he'll take control. DI know he's a drug dealer, know where his donations come from. But they want his money. However, this time he has made himself a direct threat to their long term strategy. I guarantee they've voted to liquidate him. All you have to do is make sure they don't fail. Then bring us the names of any DI member involved so we can blackmail them to become informers. So thinks the Witch."

"Removing Bayat is possible, splitting DI ranks is something else. They're too secretive." He threw off his jacket.

"Directus Iurisdictio's inner chamber sanctioned the Death Heads, albeit very reluctantly, as a field trial along the path to global domination, but if they see it all going wrong, some like Hackett will talk. If any in DI know where these drugs are, they'll speak out. Use that brutal charm of yours. Let's split this whole thing open."

"Is that all?" he said, moving her backwards, positioning her legs against the couch so she gently folded down beneath him.

"As your field handler in Operation Deepcut I'm ordering you to go where others dare not." She reached down to unzip his flies, then searched inside with firm and slender fingers.

"Who am I to say no?" he whispered, allowing her to take firm hold of him, jumping when the doorbell rang clear and sharp. "Bugger."

"The courier. Wait here and don't move."

She pushed him off while swinging her long naked legs to the floor. He watched her fetch a dressing gown then enter the hall carrying the plastic box with oyster. Sean rolled on his back and huffed breath, cursing each second until he heard Victoria's voice.

"Oh hello, this is unexpected."

Instinctively he shot from the couch and grabbed his jacket, still struggling with the sleeves when Alice Sibree, head of MI5 entered the room. Victoria came behind followed by what appeared to be a huge android in motorcycle helmet and leathers. He held a smaller helmet as if it represented a royal crown.

The Witch looked Sean over and grimaced. "Yes, quite unexpected I see." Dressed in grey trouser suit, her hair razored yet tussled, she assumed instant command, taking the plastic box from Victoria and handing it to the android. "Give it priority A, I'll make my own way back," she said and turned to Sean as the courier left. "I hear you lost one of our informants."

"I lost nobody. But if that oyster shell contains cyanide then I think someone tried to murder me, only Hackett's greed got him murdered instead."

"In my opinion, Mr Fagan, your importance doesn't qualify you for all the risk associated with murder. However, Hackett had a place with St Albans Directus Iurisdictio and he agreed to give us names. I arranged with Cobbart you should be the go-between. You failed."

Sean glanced to Victoria who stood to the side, her eyes wide and lips compressed.

"Well thanks very much for informing me, there is nothing like co-operation between agencies," Sean said.

The Witch sniffed. "Mr Fagan, at this moment there appear many things of which you are unaware. However you are the only person currently in that field with a known reputation for killing criminals. I'm told you have also made contacts. You will use both advantages to join Directus Iurisdictio immediately." She straightened her shoulders and clasped hands together.

"Madam, John Cobbart is my boss, not you."

"Wrong, Mr Fagan. In this matter I am Cobbart's boss and therefore your boss. If you join DI they will no longer be suspicious of you. We need information on Bayat and this drug shipment."

"And what if DI ask me to kill criminals?"

"Then use your discretion, Mr Fagan. We believe DI has seriously infiltrated the House of Lords, the banking system, the civil service and might even have members in the Cabinet. Due to your status as a senior SOCA officer, your future victims will probably be amongst such honourable people whose greed has disgraced their company. You will inform us so we can take necessary action."

"And shoot me when done," he added with glib sarcasm.

"Always a possibility."

Sean stared at her, realising now why they called her the

Witch. "So I join DI, bust this drug baron Bayat, shoot a few lords in the Upper House and report DI members' names. All unofficial and without any backup."

"Not quite. The Combined Agency Task Force, CAT, also have operatives in St Albans and they will be watching. We track your mobile constantly, we know of the warning messages you have received but as yet cannot identify the caller beyond it being female. We also have another highly placed informant who will let us know of your situation and possible victims."

"And just who is that?" Sean asked, placing clenched fists on his hips.

"As you were so careless with the last informant, I cannot possibly tell you."

"So, no trust."

"Duty does not require trust, Mr Fagan, only obedience."

"Listen, madam," he said through tight teeth. "Has it ever occurred to you that to carry out my duty I might need information from this person which I cannot get from anybody else?"

"In that case, I'm sure he'll inform you." She glanced him over. "By the way, Mr Fagan, your flies are undone."

"Bollocks." Sean zipped up as he watched her leave, Victoria faffing around her. She came back hand over mouth.

"Sorry about that," she said and burst into giggles.

"I don't think it's funny."

"Oh don't be so huffy, darling." She came and put arms around him. "I'm still your operational handler and I need to debrief you, so come and make love to me."

He carried her to the bedroom and removed his clothes while watching her throw aside her dressing gown and negligee. He never tired of seeing her naked, her skin toned and smooth without bulge or unsightly fold. When he entered her he did so gently, feeling her swallow him with a silent hunger. In all too short a time he raced towards heaven, arrived, then rested down feeling he had been cast aside.

"Next time I promise we will be undisturbed," she said.

He kissed her then drew away. "If I live."

"So let's increase your chances. A small gift, with love from me to you." Victoria slid off the bed and parted clothes in one of her many wardrobes before pulling out a black attaché case. Whilst Sean dressed she placed the case on a side table, waiting for his attention before opening the lid.

"For me?" he said, lifting the Glock 9mm automatic pistol from inside.

"Plus three magazines and four hundred rounds. It's unregistered, so don't get caught with it." She replaced the automatic inside and handed him the case. "Stay safe, my love," she said and kissed him.

"I'll do my best."

Minutes later he headed for the motorway. At best he had an hour before full darkness, barely time to reach the location and find a hide.

CHAPTER 17

"You go wait, but get back quick if I call," Salem said to the minibus driver before signalling his men to follow. Dressed in camouflage fatigues with jihad head bands in place, the men clustered round their leader, swaggering with the aggression of street thugs as he handed them sealed plastic bags.

"Inside is chloroform rag. Don't take out 'til you have Routt. I want him alive, I want cut off his head and balls. You don't kill. Use clubs not knives, then rag with chloroform so he lie still. All mobiles switched off except to vibrate. You see him, you signal. Then we all get him. OK, let's go."

Each helped the others over the boundary fence then followed their leader in tight Indian file, skirting open fields scattered with pigs and metal sties. Within ten minutes they had entered woods bordering the rear garden of Halsham Farm. On Salem's signal all spread along the tree line and crouched behind low fencing designed to keep stray pigs from entering the formal farmhouse garden.

Salem pushed between bushes and searched over the lawn which gave way to a paved area stretching the length of the house. Outbuildings and walls enclosed both sides so anyone who approached the rear garden had to pass this way. From his position Salem saw straight through the kitchen window, the last evening light giving a clear vision of the interior. He leered when he saw the Osborne woman appear and sit at a table. She looked more naked than dressed. Maybe this evening might be blessed with other entertainment than simply beheading Routt.

For half an hour he sat watching the outbuildings and garden become walls of darkness under the encroaching night. Slowly the woman became lost in black shadow, bird song ceased and somewhere an owl hooted followed by the grunt of distant pigs. Where was Routt, he thought, that little bitch better not have lied.

In a quick reconnaissance Sean drove past the wrought-iron gate of Halsham Farm, then doubled back before parking in a lay-by near Ayot St Lawrence. He figured the return walk about twenty minutes, ten to fifteen if he tried to cut across country. Half a mile down the lane he vaulted the fence and made his way round fields to a wood at the rear of the farmhouse gardens. Pigs grunted in the rapidly failing light and the forest looked black. He had no idea of tree density but figured such a property would have horses, so somewhere through the black band of vegetation lay a bridle path. It took five minutes to find and another ten to manoeuvre through pitch darkness. During the time he considered his plan of action. He figured Routt would approach from the rear, through this very wood, then try to break in or maybe entice the girls outside. If wise, both girls would be armed, but then so might Routt. Best, he thought, to find a position which gave a clear view and line of fire. Wind rustled the trees covering the sound of his approach but to be safe he cut through bushes and came out of the tree line left of the farmhouse. Hugging the night shadows of a hedge he traversed round to a stock-fence protecting the gardens, then lay back on the ground, lifting the wire mesh to wriggle under, continuing on elbows until below a garden trellis. Every few metres he stopped and listened but saw no sign of light or life. Dogs, he thought, a farm has dogs. Why aren't they barking? She's sent them away. Doesn't want Routt scared off. If Anjali and Charlotte were inside they were keeping a low profile. Or maybe they had something brewing. In the silent night he edged forward finally stopping ten metres from the house under concealment of ornamental bushes. For minutes he lay watching and listening until the squeal of a cat centred his attention, that and a shadow black on grey which flitted before the house. Unzipping an inside pocket he slipped out the Glock automatic, aimed and waited for light.

Within the solid walls of Halsham farmhouse Charlotte gripped the shotgun while watching darkness close in on her, cloaking her in the first unease of loneliness and isolation. How she wished for Anjali's comforting strength. The abrupt ring of the telephone on the kitchen dresser sent her reaching for the receiver and hope of a friendly voice. No one spoke. She heard only a hollowness intermingled with the expulsion of coarse breath. A shiver gripped her and translated to a quiver in her voice.

"Who's there?" she asked, and listened to the line click dead. Isolation again closed like an oppressive shroud, pushing all remnants of warmth from the room. Ghosts of time past filled corners and shadows, her mother's cowardliness, her father's hands and his abuse. Routt was close, she knew it. The call had been to check if she was there. Maybe he had looked through the windows. Dusk became darkness. She wanted to switch on lights but that would mean Routt would see her through the curtainless window, alone and near naked. But then that was her plan, to entice him into the open by making herself bait for his trap. She shivered and when the phone rang again leapt from her chair, shotgun ready. Holding the receiver she listened but did not speak.

"Is that you Charlotte?" Anjali's voice came harsh and panting as if she was running. "I got caught up giving statements over Hackett's death."

"I'm OK. Just scared. Someone phoned. He's here, I know it."

"OK, I'm on the drive," Anjali said and switched off.

Charlotte sat in the stillness, the shotgun gripped to her chest as the minutes ticked by in stony silence. The squeal of a cat brought her own scream of terror, which twitched her skin and froze her to immobility. The dogs had been placed in kennels but the cats had been deemed safe. "Please, don't hurt them," she whispered.

Clouds shifted round the moon and brought brief silver light but still she had no ability to breath or move. A click sounded against the window. It would be easy to break the ancient glass, to smash the glazing bars from their frames, to climb into the room. She sensed his presence clawing the air and under her clothes, creeping across her skin, probing her, desecrating her body as her father's hands had desecrated her childhood so many years ago. Tears welled in her eyes and rage trembled the shotgun as she slipped off the safety and aimed at the window.

"Die you bastard," she whispered and took first pressure on the trigger.

"Charlotte, are you in there?" Anjali's voice sounded from outside.

In a second Charlotte was at the back door, throwing open the locks before wrapping arms around her sister.

"Quick, he might be out here." She pulled her inside and refastened the bolt. "Where's your car? I never heard it."

"I left it outside the gates," Anjali said. "I came on foot so he wouldn't realise there are two of us. The cats are terrified. Why are you in the dark?"

"Hiding, I suppose. I didn't want him to see me. Not yet, I feel so vulnerable in this." She used fingertips to pluck

184

her nightdress. "He phoned, he knows I'm here."

"Charlotte, that's the whole plan. We're here to bait the trap but waiting for him to break in doesn't give us the best chance."

"I've thought of that," Charlotte said. "So I show myself by the window or open door, which will entice him from cover. Then we shoot him as he approaches the house."

"Sounds scary."

"All of it's scary. But the more vulnerable we look the more he'll take chances. Come into the hall and I can put on the lights without him seeing." She grasped Anjali's hand and led her from the kitchen, closing the internal door before switching the lights. The brightness made her blink. Unlike herself, Anjali was dressed in jeans and shirt, her hair tied back, her feet clad in trainers.

"We only have one chance," Anjali said. "This man is crafty, agile and brutal. If he manages to get hands on either of us, we're done for."

"Then listen to my idea," Charlotte said. "He wants more than death he also wants sex, so we let him see it. Moving before the window with strong lights behind it will make my nightdress translucent. There are also security floods under the eves. As he comes forward he'll see only the near naked silhouette of a woman who, because of internal light, will be unable to see him. He'll realise that and hopefully be bold. You hide behind closed curtains in the sitting room with the window open and the shotgun tracking him down over the paved area. When he's twenty feet away the floods will come on and you fire. Shooting him outside will leave no pellet marks on the wall. It will also be easier to clean up and drag him to the pig pen. I've not fed them, so in a day most of him will be gone. No one will know he was here. He will vanish as all victims of Dark Angel have vanished."

"A fitting end. OK," Anjali grimaced. "So let's hope it works."

Charlotte lifted a shotgun from the hall table and handed it to Anjali. "It will work and for extra safety I also have a pump action gun under the window."

"I think a smaller weapon for close quarters might also help. Do you have anything at all, other than pitchforks and kitchen knives?"

"Father's automatic, but I'm afraid it's very old, so is the ammunition."

"How old?"

"Fifty years or so." Charlotte shook her head. "But it's always been cleaned, it should work."

"I'm unsure the ammunition will. Where is it?"

"Under the pillows in my bedroom."

Anjali checked her watch. "OK, decision time."

"I'm bait," Charlotte put in quickly. "No arguments, it's my plan, I should take the risk."

"I'm better trained in self-defence. Plus you've had more practice with a shotgun. It's logical I should pull him in. I'll also have the pistol."

Charlotte huffed breath. "It's pointless arguing. OK, we share. But I go first."

"No, me first. I'll feel safer. You kill the brute. So what do I wear?"

"Search the cupboards in my bedroom," Charlotte said. Shoulders slumped she watched Anjali ascend the stairs, switching on lights as she went, clearly wanting Routt to see her through the windows and set his blood on heat.

Left alone she gave final adjustment to the many lamps she had set around the hall and in the living room. When turned on they would give a strong back light to any figure passing in front. Anyone outside would see a clear silhouette through any loose clothes. She waited five minutes before Anjali returned, descending the stairs in a slow, graceful walk, her figure draped in a silk evening dress, two thin straps holding the front, the back scooped to below her waist. In her small hand the Browning 9mm automatic looked huge, like an alien mechanism attached to some exquisite goddess.

"You look gorgeous," Charlotte said.

"Let's hope Routt thinks so, least enough for him to come charging in. Just don't leave it too late before you fire. I'll be wetting myself." Anjali stepped before the lights and unlocked the back door, holding it closed, the pistol behind her back.

Charlotte suddenly felt frightened for her, more frightened than she had been even with their father. "You sure, Anjali?" she asked.

"For you, for us, for justice."

Both jumped when the front door bell rang. "For Christ's sake, who, not him?" Anjali refastened the bolt and together they moved to the entrance hall. Charlotte swallowed, squared her shoulders then switched on the door video camera. "Sammy, what the hell are you doing here?"

"I came to warn you," Sammy's voice sounded over the intercom. "Salem's outside looking for Routt."

Anjali opened the front door allowing Charlotte to yank the girl inside before locking it again. "How do you know?"

"I heard it via the Death Heads. Salem has been organising his own tight individual group. They're secretive, don't mix and will do anything he asks. Salem wants Routt and Routt wants you two. Salem will kill him for you."

"You think we'd rely on that thug?" Charlotte narrowed her eyes. "You didn't tell him what we planned, did you?"

You told me to gather all the info I could, I needed his confidence. I thought he might be useful," she said, looking to Anjali for support.

"Stupid girl." Charlotte twisted her round, slapping hard at the rear of Sammy's jeans. "When I have the chance you're going to get such a spanking."

"But I only wanted to help," Sammy sniffed and looked down.

"She has a point," Anjali cut in. "If things go wrong and the police investigate, Salem's intrusion means all blame can be placed on him."

"The last thing we want is police," Charlotte huffed breath and looked up at the ceiling.

"But if it came to it, see it from their view. Three helpless females trying to protect themselves from murderers and rapists," Sammy said with wide innocent pretence. "Such horrid men, all of them, but if you like I'll kill Routt myself."

Charlotte smiled with love, then drew her close. "It's our intention to bait Routt with our bodies and draw him into the security lights on the paved area. Once he triggers the movement detectors the floods will leave him a standing target in open space. When he's dead we'll feed him to the pigs. It's a plan but it's dangerous, messy and I don't think you should be involved."

"I'm already involved." Sammy stood back to look between them. "I want to help and I'm here to help, I'll do anything, anything, you know that." She returned to hugging Charlotte.

"A third gun outside increases the odds in our favour," Anjali said.

This time Charlotte moved away to stroke Sammy's cheek, staring at the girl in decision before handing her the shotgun. "OK. I know you're a good shot because I taught you. Just watch your field of fire."

Sammy nodded eagerness, then allowed herself led to the back door where Charlotte gave her spare cartridges. For a moment Charlotte looked to her sister and then drew a hand down Sammy's body, this time only to gently pat on the girl's backside. "Surprised?" she said to Anjali.

No." Anjali smiled. "I've always sort of known. After our father's abuse I almost went that way myself but finally chose another path. Few men have the perversity to do as our father did. Most men are good, and rejecting them somehow didn't fit."

"Well it did for me. And Sammy is a very special with more attributes than are apparent." She kissed Sammy's nose. "OK, to work. I'll switch off all lights so you can slip out through the back scullery window. To the left of the paved area bordering the lawn are rhododendron bushes, hide there. If you see Routt don't shoot unless you have a clear and open target. And for Christ's sake don't fire at any window or you might hit one of us. If Salem grabs the body, let him."

"Yo, I hear," Sammy said and brandished the shotgun in determination.

"If by chance he sees you and makes a grab, scream and I'll be there. OK, follow me." Charlotte led her through the darkened kitchen and entered the back scullery. Silently she opened the window and placed a chair beneath. "You sure?" she asked, holding the grey outline of her lover at arm's length.

"For you, for England and St George." Sammy hugged her.

"Take care my little one," Charlotte said as Sammy stepped onto the chair and slipped her legs over the sill. Seconds later she vanished into darkness.

Charlotte stayed listening for any sound until satisfied Sammy had reached her hide undetected, then closed the window and returned to the hall. "So then there were three," she said, collecting a pump action shotgun from the table.

"And God knows how many more out there," Anjali said, plucking the gossamer material of her dress. "OK, let's do this, let's get the animal dead."

Charlotte switched power back to the movement detectors on the patio floodlights then kissed her sister's cheek. "I have no sense of guilt, do you?" she asked.

"No my sister, just cold anger at our betrayal. And now to battle."

Charlotte entered the unlit family room, opened the window and parted the curtains before easing the shotgun muzzle beyond the frame, allowing herself an arc of fire covering any front approach to the door. Kneeling beside the wall, she pulled the wooden stock to her shoulder.

"Ready and waiting," she said to Anjali.

The paved area outside immediately flooded with a long corridor of light as Anjali opened the rear farmhouse door, allowing the concentrated blaze behind to cast an elongated shadow of her figure.

"Who's there?" Anjali called. "Whoever is out there, show yourself."

Nothing moved, not a moth or a bat. Even the cats stayed hidden. They waited, waited for minutes.

"Show yourself or I'll call the police," Anjali shouted.

Through the open window of the darkened room Charlotte watched her sister's shadow move on the ground, first in profile, then frontal, the lesser shadow of her dress taut over spread legs. Then the light faded to a crack as she partially closed the door.

"How long do we keep this up?" Anjali said in a whisper.

"I know he's there. One more time and we'll rethink," Charlotte whispered, watching as Anjali again filled the yard with light.

The cat came from nowhere, seemingly out of the sky as it flew in a wide arc, twisting its body, trying to control its landing. Charlotte heard the squeal of pain as it hit the wall and held the shotgun ready, her attention momentarily drawn to the cat. The next instant a hand grabbed the muzzle and half yanked the gun from her grip. The jerk caused her to fire, the shot going upward, the sound crashing in on her ears. A second shot came as her fingers were jerked against the double trigger. She could hear the cat screaming; hear her own scream as a third and forth report flared in the darkness. Immediately all pressure came off the gun. Anjali was shouting as Charlotte fell backwards against the sudden release. The enclosed discharge of gunfire rang in her ears as she rolled, fumbling to reload the smoking breech. By the time she had regained her feet Anjali was in the room, her dress ripped from bodice to navel, her face and naked breasts flecked in blood.

"My God, what has he done?" Charlotte wiped her cheek.

"It's OK, it's his blood. One of us hit him, enough to make him let go. He came along the side of the house, grabbed your barrel then grabbed me. Lust was his undoing. He should have concentrated on the shotgun."

"Shit, what do we do now?" Charlotte said, looking to the window and locking it as shouts sounded from the night.

"Go after him. If he's wounded he might be down in the yard. We can't risk leaving him near the house, he'll be found, which means the police will come."

"What if he got away?"

"Then he'll die of his wounds or be back."

"Pray he dies."

"We can't rely on prayer. But if Salem is there he could be the answer. Maybe that's him fighting with Routt now."

Anjali unhooked a raincoat from the hall stand and shrugged into it before opening the door. "Least we know the automatic works," she said, holding it in readiness to step outside as Charlotte also took a coat.

"I'm not sure about this," Charlotte said, triggering the outside lights as she followed Anjali and relocked the backdoor. For a moment both stood as if each waited on the other's bravery. Shouts from the wood indicated a number of men.

"Not English," Charlotte said.

"Urdu, must be Salem and his gang."

"You OK?" Sammy said, running into the light, shotgun in hand. "I think I hit him."

"A few pellets maybe, he's still up and dangerous."

Charlotte stared across the emptiness of the walled garden standing on two sides of them. She knew of only one way Routt could have run, the same way they must go to find him, towards Salem and his men. Anjali started forwards causing Charlotte to follow, her finger against the shotgun's trigger, but when the courtyard lights gave way to darkness, even Anjali hesitated.

"Will Salem try to rape us?" she asked Sammy.

"Not until they have Routt. Salem's hatred is greater than his lust."

"This is crazy, leave him. Let's go back," Charlotte said.

"And go through it again? If Salem kills Routt, fine, but we have to be sure."

"We'll never find him," Charlotte said. "He might have made it to his car or be lying in the woods. Leave him to the pigs, they'll eat him dead or alive and if they don't, then let Salem kill him."

"Sister, we have to find out. I'm not going to live with the dread of him returning. I need to know, you two wait here, I'll see what's going on."

"Don't." Charlotte put out her hand. "He might be

there. Salem and his gang might try to rape you."

"I'll shoot their bollocks off first."

"I'll go with you," Sammy said. "I know Salem."

Charlotte's protesting hand waved helplessly as she watched Anjali and Sammy's shadows merge into darkness and disappear.

"Don't leave me," Charlotte whispered as a shiver clutched over her skin. "Don't leave me behind." She took a step to follow, then another and another.

When light flooded from the house Sean crouched immobile, hoping to blend with the undergrowth. To his right came a rustle of foliage and branches bending against someone's weight, then silence. Sean held his breath, either Routt lay very close or they were not alone.

The sound of Anjali's voice calling clear and fragile over the night air came amidst a tremor of fear. "Show yourself or I call the police,"

Sean stayed down, watching, waiting for any movements. When the light went out he carefully shifted position, manoeuvring himself for a better view, then went to ground again as light shone from the farmhouse doorway a second time. Anjali's silhouetted figure stood clearly visible, taunting Routt forward with a body that appeared almost naked. These women weren't cowering, they were challenging Routt to do his worst. The rustle of undergrowth again sounded from his right followed by a second movement that bunched with another.

The squeal of a cat, the dual bang of a double-barrelled shotgun fired in rapid succession, followed by the snap of an automatic pistol and the flare of a second shotgun cracked the night air with vibrant explosion, but not enough to hide the terror in Anjali's scream.

Sean was on his feet instinctively, sprinting to her aid without thought or consideration. The same instant figures came out of darkness on every side. He juddered under the impact of a fist against cheek, then a blow dropped him to the ground before he smelt the reek of chloroform.

In some numb and binding place, he grew conscious of being dragged by his feet. All around men were mocking, kicking him, one of them shouting. "I cut his head off, cut his balls off, feed him to pigs." Someone put a knee on his chest and started ripping at his collar. He had the sense of a blade floating over him while ghosts hovered either side. Then suddenly the shouting increased and the shadows moved back.

"Hey, you want fucking?" a male voice said.

A solitary female figure came into view as if fallen from a star speckled heaven. Somewhere an angel spoke. "Touch me and I kill you. My God, that's not Routt, it's Fagan. Is he dead?"

"Sure, they split his head, but I still feed him to pigs, then I fuck you."

"You know who I am, Salem? I am Justitia. Touch me and you are dead. All of you dead."

Sean heard their breath, heard them move further back. "I'm not dead," he whispered without sound

"What a waste," the angel said. "Bury him, here, now. Then go find Routt."

Feet moved, people walking away, the ghosts above him

vanished and the angel flew away. For a time Sean saw only stars, then heard the clunk of spades. He lay listening, trying to move, then sensed himself rolled over into a hole. He heard voices, then the thud of earth landing on his chest.

CHAPTER 18

Charlotte hated the dark, hated her fear and returned quickly to the light. There she waited with shotgun ready, aiming it at shadows until one emerged as a figure.

"It's me," Anjali called, as she came forward. "And for Christ's sake, don't point that thing unless certain of your target."

"Sorry, sorry." Charlotte touched her, flustered by her sense of relief. "I thought I saw something, someone."

"Sammy, have you seen Sammy? I lost her in the dark. We searched around, saw nothing. We didn't speak to Salem, just crept close for a view. They had someone on the ground but we couldn't see, except it wasn't Routt. A poacher, one of their own, I don't know. The body didn't have Routt's bulk. Then I lost Sammy."

"Maybe she's hiding, waiting for us. Come on, let's go back inside. Please." She took Anjali's hand and hurried her towards the house where she quickly unlocked the front door.

Still outside, Anjali removed the raincoat and then the remains of her dress. Naked except for a string she folded the dress carefully within the coat. "No time for modesty. We have much to do. At first light we clean any blood from the flagstones. Right now we dispose of everything possibly contaminated. Fetch a bin-liner, all outer clothes go inside to burn or bury. We must cleanse our bodies and ensure he left no mark or forensic evidence," she said, and led into the house. "Everything must point to Salem, not to us."

"Thank goodness for police expertise." Charlotte closed the door behind them, relieved to have the safety of a lock between themselves and the outside. "What about Sammy?

I can't leave her out there."

"With Salem and his men searching the area, Routt would have run. Sammy knows Salem so maybe she's keeping low 'til he's gone. My guess is, ten minutes and she'll be back," Anjali said. "OK, I'm going to take a shower. I suggest you do the same and find new clothes."

"There're towels in my bathroom," Charlotte said. "Use what you need."

"Thanks." Anjali walked up the stairs while Charlotte fastened the door bolts.

Alone she went to the kitchen, unrolled a bin liner and placed the torn dress and coat inside. Still with shotgun, Charlotte carried the bin liner upstairs and began to remove her coat and nightdress. A minute later she heard the shower stop. Anjali emerged with wet hair bundled into a towel; a second towel loosely draped her body.

"At last we act as sisters," Charlotte said. "If only we had grown up together, how different life may have been."

"If only. But our father separated us, separated our mothers. He wasn't interested in family, only lust."

Anjali dropped the towel. "Look me over for any scratches. We must ensure there is no DNA content under Routt's nails via marks on my body that will need explaining. When you have a dark secret it is best to be over cautious."

"It's not a dark secret," Charlotte said. "It's simply our secret. Routt hunts us as a predator. Do we allow ourselves to be victims a second time? Those who should protect us do not. Instead they protect the life of Routt. It is our right to take action," she said, examining Anjali, turning her, searching over her skin. "Or do we meekly allow ourselves slaughtered?"

"Then why do I feel guilt?" Anjali said. "I don't want guilt, I want justice."

"Listen sister, our father as a judge stood as a figurehead of law, the pinnacle of justice. Yet he used his position to hide his sexual abuse of us, his own daughters. No one would believe us. My mother said nothing, just beat me and called me a dirty lying little whore. And when the truth was obvious she ran away, committed suicide. She deserted me. No one protected us."

"My mother did. She drove their car into a wall and killed them both."

"That doesn't make you guilty, Anjali. It makes you a victim. Your mother sacrificed herself to stop his abuse of us both. She showed the Dark Angel an example of love and duty. And it is why I never hesitate in carrying out my own duty. We are not guilty, the law is guilty in its failure to protect the innocent. So long as the rights of the criminal prevail over the rights of others we have no choice but to stand up for ourselves." Charlotte handed Anjali a silk dressing gown from one of her cupboards. "You're fine, not a mark. The hairdryer is on the dresser. I'll shower then make coffee, perhaps something to eat, and a brandy. Not sure about you but I need a drink."

When Charlotte returned from the shower she had swaddled herself in a towelling robe. Anjali sat at the dressing table drying her hair. For a minute Charlotte stood behind, combing her own hair, sharing the mirror. When finished she placed both hands on Anjali's shoulders and began to massage. Anjali sighed and lowered the dryer. For a moment her eyes closed and Charlotte felt the unity of their spirit. She didn't want any darkness between them, just the open love of siblings, each being the sole family of the other. When she again looked to the mirror she found Anjali staring back.

"Is justice the acquittal of guilt, or the passing of guilt to a high authority?" she asked.

"Forget justice, there is no such thing, only retribution because most criminals don't have guilt. Time for coffee, I think." Charlotte released her grip and stepped away. She pulled on bra and knickers then fetched jeans and sweater from a drawer as Anjali retrieved her own clothes.

"Shall I bring the automatic?" Anjali asked when dressed.

"Routt's gone. Replace it under the pillow, but bring the shotgun, just in case."

The shrill ring of the doorbell made them both jump and for seconds each stared at the other's fear.

"Sammy." Charlotte broke the silence and rushed for the stairs.

"Or Routt," Anjali warned as she came behind. "Don't open 'til you're sure."

Charlotte switched on the security camera to see the black and white image of Sammy hugging her shotgun, shivering as she stared between door and darkness. In a second Charlotte had the door open and the girl inside. "Thank God." She hugged her.

"I lost you, then Salem's men tried to grab me so I ran. Been hiding in the woods," Sammy said.

"Don't worry pet you're safe now. No one is going to hurt you. Come on, time for tea or something." Charlotte led the way to the kitchen and busied herself putting out cups, bread, cheese and ham, thinking what she had done and what she still had yet to do. Sammy sat at the table, her face buried in her arms while Anjali stroked the girl's hair.

Maybe, Charlotte thought, Routt lay in the woods, his body already explored by maggots and insects, his flesh hacked open by Salem and his men while hungry pigs closed for the feast. She hoped so. She had wanted his death, wanted freedom from the fear his predatory stalking wrapped around her life. She prayed for it, prayed to be rid of him as she had prayed to be rid of her father when forced to taste his sperm. But God had never answered. She wondered about God sometimes, he seemed to have no mercy for children.

She heard the kettle click and returned from her thoughts to fetch the coffee. The tin was empty. "Could you get another from the pantry?" she asked Anjali. "Over there, behind you."

"I can't believe this has happened." Anjali said, seemingly lost in her own thoughts as she opened the pantry door and leaped back in shock. "For Christ's sake, there's a window open in here. There's blood on the shelf."

"He couldn't get through that." Charlotte came round the table. "It's too small."

"It's been smashed. Who else would crawl through? A raving psychopath fired by blood lust is like a rat, it will squeeze in anywhere."

Charlotte stood staring at the tiny square window that channelled the evening breeze against her face. "It can't be, it can't possibly be," she said, hoping to convince herself.

"Maybe, or maybe we made a mistake. When we were outside maybe he squirmed through and hid himself. He wouldn't trigger the floodlights this side of the house. Unless we search the place from top to bottom we'll never know."

"He's not locked in here with us, he's not." Charlotte

hugged herself, looking to Sammy who had raised her head, biting on her lower lip.

Anjali closed the pantry then dragged the table to wedge it against the door. "Bring your shotgun. We have no choice about this," she said, rummaging through the kitchen drawers before extracting a twelve-inch carving knife. "We do the ground floor first then work our way upwards. We leave all lights on, all rooms open. Sammy, you can stay or come with us."

"I'm not staying here by myself." Sammy came to her feet holding her shotgun. Anjali unlatched the kitchen door, her knife held ready for slashing.

Charlotte stayed close, searching for traces of blood as she switched on lights. Every room was clean and orderly. She knew it possible the blood had stopped flowing, that he had wrapped his wound with a cloth or towel. Which also meant the wound was not serious, at least not enough to maim him. Now he was just a wild and agitated animal. Charlotte followed into the dining room, through the living room and into the study. She left all lights on, all doors open and checked all large cupboards, two of them concentrating on each room, Sammy watching the hall to ensure Routt did not sneak past behind.

"Maybe he never got in," Charlotte said.

"Maybe. What's left?"

"Five bedrooms, en suite, one family bathroom and the attic."

They went slowly up the stairs, Charlotte carefully stepping over two creaking boards, indicating the others do likewise. In the spare bedrooms she checked the cupboards while Anjali looked under beds and into the bathroom, Sammy staying in the doorway watching the stairs and hall.

Charlotte's breath relaxed when faced with empty space instead of a psychopath. Each room, every cupboard meant one safer place, but one less place before the one in which he might be hidden.

"Should we do my bedroom next?" Charlotte asked, looking to the attic stairs, conscious of a growing reluctance. Sammy came to her side.

Anjali shook her head. "He's not in your bedroom. I went straight to your room when we first came back, there's nowhere to hide. I stood naked, we both did. This animal is lust driven. He would have attacked while we were vulnerable. You took a robe from your cupboard."

"I have four cupboards."

"All jammed with rails and clothes, Charlotte. The attic is the only place left. I'll go if you wish, you watch the stairs."

"I'm not scared," Charlotte said, tossing her head and walking to the bottom step. She stopped. "You will stay here, won't you?" She looked between them. "Watch out for me. There's no light inside, only on the landing but the room is tiny. If he's there I'll see him. I can't miss if I shoot from the door."

"I'll come with you. Sammy, you watch the landing." Anjali touched her shoulder.

Charlotte mounted the stairs, her trainers making no sound on the wooden treads. She put a hand to the door and was conscious of her adrenaline racing, her body pulsing. She threw the door rather than opened it, crashing it back against the brickwork, shotgun to shoulder as she stepped inside. A frame of light fell on the far wall illuminating the mattress under which she had hidden from her father. She kicked it. The room was empty. "He's not here. I told you he never got in."

"We had to make certain," Anjali said with clear relief in her voice. "But we still check your bedroom."

Charlotte returned down the stairs, her mind reliving what had been there for many years. When her father had stood in his silk dressing gown, demanding, coercing, promising, threatening. How many times over all those years had she given in, so even now the taste of him never left her? From five until she tried to kill him when fifteen. Now he had left Routt to continue their suffering. But as Anjali's mother had killed her father, so Charlotte swore her vengeance on Routt, and all men who caused women to suffer.

"He's not there." Charlotte said, passing Sammy to stop before the bedroom.

"Let me go first." Anjali opened the door. "Empty, of course." She moved inside to place her knife on the dressing table.

The room remained as left, clothes and towels littering the floor, the curtains open leaving no place to hide. The bathroom door stood wide, the lights shining on a bright, tiled interior, the fragrance of perfumed soap still lingering.

"Maybe he struggled to squeeze through the window, found it impossible and gave up," Charlotte said, putting her arm round Sammy's waist.

"So, night's work is done," Anjali said. "But lots of work tomorrow. We must ensure this place is clean of all incriminating evidence. With luck, Salem has chopped the monster up and fed him to the pigs. Sammy, can you find out for us?"

"Sure, no problem," Sammy said. "Salem will boast

about it. It makes him feel big."

"Well thanks for you both being here," Charlotte said. "I would have gone crazy without you." She squeezed Sammy. "Look at you girl, you're filthy. Let me get you a clean top at least. Then I think a drink is definitely called for."

"I must admit I was a bit scared," Sammy said and gave each a smile.

"You and me both." Charlotte went to the nearest cupboard. "No bogeymen here," she said, looking inside before glancing back. "Blue sweat shirt I think." She moved along the row. "One, two three, four, who's that hiding behind the door?"

Routt came out at her with the screech of a wounded beast, his bruised and battered face pushing between racks of clothes. The pain of his fist punching into her stomach doubled her up as he kicked her aside and leapt on Anjali. Face to floor Charlotte heard only screams intermingled with Routt's wail of lust. Trying to draw breath she turned on her back to see Anjali's legs flailing from the bed where she was pinned by Routt's bulk. Regaining her feet, Charlotte hit helplessly at his back while he ripped at Anjali's jeans, her sweater and bra were already pushed under her chin. Anjali was fumbling, one hand under the pillow, the other lashing nails into Routt's face as she tried to defend herself.

Sammy stood by the bathroom, waving the shotgun in panic, unable to shoot for fear of hitting Anjali. Next moment Anjali had the automatic in her hand. Instantly she pressed it to her attacker's head, turning her face from the expected spray of bone, blood and brain before pulling the trigger. The click of firing pin against dud cartridge momentarily carried over the noise. Routt struck out in rage, forcing her gun hand aside the same time Charlotte grabbed the discarded carving knife, screaming hate as she plunged the blade between Routt's shoulders. Shock caused him to sit upwards the same time Sammy swung the shotgun by the barrel, hitting the butt edge squarely against the side of Routt's head. Mouth open in silent disbelief he toppled onto the floor and lay still. Instantly Sammy struck again, jerking the head with a distinct thud of breaking skull. Each looked to the other then back to Routt.

"Is he dead?" Anjali asked, pulling bra and sweater down before zipping up her jeans.

"Let's take no chances. Sammy, get Salem here, hurry," Charlotte said and watched her take out her mobile before running from the room. "No other choice." She picked up the discarded shotgun and pointed it at Routt. "Let's get rid of this pig once and for all."

"Whatever you say, sister." Anjali swung her legs from the bed and buried her face in hands before filling the room with sobs.

After ten minutes Charlotte heard the sound of men. Noisy and aggressive they rushed up the stairs. Ahead of them Sammy flew past the open door before a block of military clad bodies thrust into the room. Faced by two armed women those in front bundled to a halt, pushed and shoved by those behind. For seconds all stood silent.

"Touch us and you're dead," Charlotte told them, levelling the shotgun at the testosterone driven invaders walled on the other side of Routt.

Salem wiped spittle from his chin and kicked Routt's prostrate body. "You kill him already. You steal his death from me. You pay."

"He's unconscious, not dead. Take him before he wakes because when he does he'll go crazy. Then Salem, you'll have a real fight."

"He's nothing, I cut off his head, eat his balls."

"Do as you wish, but do it someplace else. If you kill him here you will answer to a higher authority."

For seconds Salem looked uncertain then jerked a clenched fist and forearm in a gesture of masculine obscenity. "When I finish I feed him to pigs. Bring him," he ordered his men, standing aside whilst six of them lifted Routt's inert bulk, staggering as they carried him from the room. Forearm still raised, Salem turned back to the women prodding his extended gut against the end of Charlotte's shot gun. "Hey, you want I come back and fuck you?"

"We're a little busy right now. Another time perhaps," Anjali said, using her thumb to ratchet back the firing hammer on the automatic.

"Don't worry lady, one day I find you. Then I fuck you good." He sneered and left.

"Charmed, I'm sure." Anjali lowered her weapon.

"Is that it, is it over?" Charlotte asked, hearing Salem shout at his men as they carried Routt from the house.

"End of act one maybe, but tomorrow is another day." She looked down to Routt's blood smeared over the wooden floor. Sammy slid round the door post and leant back against wall, eyes closed as she exhaled breath.

"They've gone. Salem has his prize, he won't return. Look, I think maybe they also killed someone else in mistake for Routt."

"Oh God." Anjali closed her eyes.

"Who?" Charlotte asked.

"Don't know, but I saw them bury something in the woods."

"Sod it." Anjali sat heavily on the bed. "This is totally out of hand."

"So let's have a plan." Charlotte placed the shotgun against the wall. "Do we call Fagan, the police, or carry on?"

"No police, no outsiders. We spend the night clearing this room and the house of any mess," Anjali said. "No one but Salem and his men know Routt came here and as they plan to butcher him it's unlikely they'll talk. If the police do get involved we say we were scared defenceless women protecting ourselves. Salem threatened he would have his men gang rape us if we informed." She clasped hands in a pious gesture. "Play the helpless women and we are above innocence. But with good fortune no one will even come looking. Routt is missing, and it's probable he'll stay missing."

"And probably to everyone's relief." Charlotte looked between them. "But now we have Salem's threat."

"Don't worry, he's all mouth and trousers," Sammy said.

"So, are you with us?" Charlotte asked, opening her arms.

"Yo, lover." Sammy crossed the room to embrace her. "Forever and ever."

Charlotte stroked her hair. "But not tonight, my little one. You've done enough. Go home to your mother. I don't want her worrying. Act like you've had a normal Saturday night. We'll meet tomorrow."

"But I want to help."

"You have. Now, be a good girl and go." She patted Sammy's rump. "Send a text when you're safe in bed. Then I'll feel happier." She kissed her, slow and sweetly. "Now more than ever we are as one. Go."

Sammy looked between them and walked reluctantly from the room to run downstairs and out the front door.

"OK Charlotte, that leaves us two sisters with a busy night clearing this place. First light we check outside, find where this grave is, and let's hope they accidentally killed one of their own."

"Who else?"

"Yeah, who else?"

CHAPTER 19

"You are born, you suffer, you die," Sean repeated the Buddhist saying over and over in psychological hope of easing the pain. He had been hauled from the earth, lifted, carried, then dumped on the ground, sometimes in semi-consciousness, sometimes in dream. Either way, the pain stayed. When the stars faded and dawn crept to the horizon he found himself lying in a field. A horse stared down at him as if perplexed by the oddity of human behaviour. Somewhere close he heard the excited grunt of pigs.

With effort, Sean rolled on his stomach and forced himself upwards until kneeling, then once more to his feet. The horse shied back, flicked its tail but continued to stare. Without the horse's sentinel stand the pigs closed in a little. Sean checked himself for injury. His ribs hurt and his head throbbed under a congealed mat of hair and blood. He winced when fingers found the raw edge of a wound and again when he touched his cheek. There was dirt in his pocket, in his hair, in his mouth and in his ears. A rolled sheet of notepaper was stuffed between the buttons of his shirt, a scrawl of writing across the middle. *Lucky you have a guardian angel. Will be in contact for meeting 10.00 hours. Col F.*

Sean muttered and staggered a little. "Meeting, angel, shit." He turned to see six giant sows clustered in a group, all eyeing him with evil intent. Slowly he began to back off while feeling for the Glock automatic, cursing when he found it missing. "Fuck." Hoping not to agitate them further, he continued his retreat, judging the fence about twenty metres distance. To his right he saw the tower of Ayot St Lawrence parish church rising above the trees. Whoever had dumped him knew his Mercedes lay close, which allowed him to extract without further assistance, but did they know about hungry, free range pigs?

Chorusing grunts and squeals the swine moved forward

while the horse, as if in anticipation of something horrid, trotted off. Sean didn't wait, he turned and ran for the fence the same time the pigs rushed him en masse. His speed doubled under the savage squeals of the animals snapping at his legs. Panic gave strength and in full stride he used a fencepost to vault bodily through the air and over the wire, he screamed from the pain in his ribs on hitting the ground, then rolled down an embankment to a tarmac lane. Above him the pigs squabbled in angry frustration over loss of their breakfast.

"You'll all be bacon," Sean shouted, rising to his feet leaving them swaying the fence as he ran for the Mercedes. Resting head against roof he closed his eyes, regaining his breath before looking up. From the village high street a local man stared at him with the expression of one who has unexpectedly stumbled upon the devil. Mouth wide open the fellow turned and fled.

"I look that bad?" Sean said to himself before climbing in and starting the car.

Outside his St Albans digs he found Dolores' parking space vacant so backed his own vehicle straight in. Save for a lone cat the street was deserted and moments later he stood in a silent and seemingly empty house. Careful to make no sound he mounted the stairs and entered his bedroom in the attic.

The reflection in his mirror caused him to grimace. He had seen less frightening images in horror movies but five minutes under the shower and a change of clothes returned some form of human resemblance. Tentatively he dried the wound in his scalp and a cut to his cheek. Sometime they would need stitching, but not now, now he had more important things. What troubled him most was the voice of an angel, one who had declared herself Justitia and had ordered him buried alive. And what of his other so called guardian angel? An angel who must have summoned help. He knew of only two angels at Halsham Farm last night. But which was the good and which the dark angel? He had a vague recollection of making a pocket under the earth by forcing his arm over his face, then cold air on his lips as small fingers scraped soil from his mouth. No spirit, but an embodied angel who had saved his life, who may even have helped dig him out. So who had carried him?

At 08:45 he checked his mobile. One message from Victoria. *Oyster shell tests positive. LOL. V.*

That left an open question over the intended victim. Hackett, me or both of us? he thought. And who on the champagne and oyster bar poisoned them, who served them? Colonel F might have answers. Sean checked his watch. He would need to move fast for a meeting at 10. Meanwhile coffee and toast sounded good. He pulled on a heavy leather jacket and headed downstairs.

On the lower landing he listened at Dolores' bedroom then passed in silence to Sammy's, leaping back when the door suddenly opened. Sammy's squeal of fright drowned his own exclamation, her eyes wide in surprise.

"When did you get back? I thought the house empty."

"Same here," Sean said, stepping aside so she might leave the room. "Where's your mother?"

"Saturday night she kips at Berty's, you know, girls' stuff without prying kids." She closed the door and headed downstairs. Sean followed.

"And where's your brother?"

"In bed, pissed and brainless. Stupid boys are like that."

"You look like you had a hard night yourself."

212

"You look fucking shit," she said and entered the kitchen.

"You know Halsham Farm?" he asked, searching for a breadbin.

"There," she pointed. "Toaster in the corner, I'll make coffee." She filled the kettle. "I know Charlotte Osborne, been invited there a few times with Universal Youth, Lord Cranby too. All very posh. Why do you ask?"

"Why did you pick up poisoned oyster shells yesterday?"

"Poisoned." She stared, nose wrinkled. "Those oysters were fresh from market. Loads of people ate them."

"And the shells?"

"They were a mess. I put them in the bin." She turned her back and spooned coffee.

Sean slotted sliced bread into the toaster and pushed down the spring. "You know of Directus Iurisdictio?"

"Sounds like weirdo stuff, all bowler hats and secret. Don't go for that, prefer Universal Youth myself. They have better gigs, more fun. A girl has to put her faith somewhere. Not in religions which bless those who kill any from other religions, but in an organisation which looks to the goodwill of humanity and mother earth. Let's get rid of the bad guys, let's help others, let's reason and live as one community. That's why I help both the DH and the SS, I liaise between them."

"A foot in each camp?" Sean raised his eyebrows.

"Sort of. But now they both got too many head-bangers, kind of gets scary at times. This came for you." She picked an envelope from amongst others and tossed it on the table. "Found it on the doormat."

The brown envelope bore his name but no stamp or address, indicating hand delivery. He ripped with the edge of his thumb and drew out the note. *St Albans Roman theatre. 10.00 hours. Prepare for immediate action. Col. F.*

"Any idea who left this?" he asked.

"Haven't a clue," she shrugged.

The toast sprung up and Sean dropped hot slices onto a plate. "How far to the Roman theatre?" he asked.

"End of road, turn left. Gates are on the right. Five minutes max."

Sean checked his watch and buttered the toast, crunching on the first piece before spreading marmalade on the second. If action starts today, what the hell was last night, he thought.

"Coffee." She pushed over a mug.

"How old are you Sammy?"

"Twenty-two, but I can still get kid's rate on the bus."

"Truth is you do look kind of young."

She laughed. "Comes from clean, active living. I was in the army four years."

"You left, you didn't like it?"

"They didn't like me." She picked up her coffee and left.

Sean finished his toast, slotted the note in his pocket and headed for his appointment. There was more to that girl, he thought, far more than appeared on the surface.

Sean opened the door to find Meatball and Rottweiler sitting in his Mercedes, one in the passenger seat, one in the rear.

"So I get an escort to your boss," Sean said through an open window.

"Just ensuring you arrive safely," Rottweiler said and grinned a half smile.

"You mind sitting in front," Sean said to Meatball in the rear. "I get nervous about backseat drivers."

Meatball shrugged but did as asked. Sean opened the rear door and slid in behind so able to watch both. If these guys were CAT he was probably safe. If they were Directus Iurisdictio then his future held uncertainty. How many in the front seat of a car had been wired by the guy behind? A choking, painful death.

"Keys," Meatball said and held up his hand.

"You mean you don't have your own? So unprofessional." He handed over the keys. When the car started Sean glanced to the house. Sammy stood at the window with arms folded watching as if all seemed normal. Sean figured a long and earnest talk with her seemed definitely overdue. Five minutes later the car stopped outside the enclosed surrounds of St Albans' Roman theatre. All appeared closed to the public except for one side gate slightly ajar. Both men in front left the car allowing Sean to retrieve the ignition key. They watched as he passed and closed the gate behind him. He saw no sign of life, no wardens, no visitors. From experience he realised it an ideal venue for murder. Occasionally he heard sounds of traffic from the main road, otherwise only the crunch of gravel underfoot as he traversed the internal track. Gradually steep terraced seating which formed the main amphitheatre came into view. A lone figure sat halfway down. Sean descended twenty metres away, then walked around the curved seats at the same level. Sean recognised the figure, the one who had watched him on the pavement. A wax jacket hung on the man's broad shoulders and a flat cap covered his large domed head. From profile his face appeared granite cut, his features weather beaten and lined. Hands clasped he rested elbows on his cord covered knees, continuing to stare at the far distance when Sean sat beside him.

"Colonel Fox, I presume," Sean said.

"Welcome Mr Fagan. I was just wondering how many people died on the floor of this theatre, gladiators, slaves, Christians."

"So long as they were the last, Colonel."

"You are perfectly safe Mr Fagan, I guarantee it. Allow me to elaborate. I'm Head of Unit C, Mainland Security, The Combined Agency Task Force or CAT for short. We're made up of ex special forces and police units. Sometimes also called The Invisible Ones on account we don't exist."

"Well I exist, Colonel and I want to know what the hell's going on. Yesterday I was nearly poisoned, smacked on the head and buried alive."

Fox snorted a false laugh. "That makes you a survivor Mr Fagan. Just the sort we need in our intriguing little games."

"Well get this straight, Colonel, I am not one of you and I don't play games."

"It's all a game Mr Fagan. A violent, greedy and politically devious game devised by the worst of humanity, our politicians and administrators. Basically it allows one tribe to inflict its power on another. We're simply game pieces, toys used by those who believe themselves supreme. But alas for them, they die just the same as we do. You are surrounded by dark forces Mr Fagan. Be scared."

"Of you and your two thugs? Never."

"My two thugs dug you out the ground last night and carried you to safety. They unquestionably saved your life."

Sean huffed breath over mistrust and clenched his teeth. "Then I apologise. According to your note I was saved by my guardian angel."

"The Angel is what we call our surveillance drone, or platform. In the same manner as a helicopter it normally hovers between five hundred and five thousand feet. Equipped with day and night vision cameras we can spy virtually on any outside area we choose. In the manner of a guardian angel it watched out for you and your family during yesterday's fete. It watched you cross the fence into Halsham Farm, watched Salem and his Death Heads lie in ambush."

"So who is the female? I heard her, saw her outline."

"The film is still being analysed," he said dismissively. "Meanwhile let us walk. I need to clarify your position." He stood, talking over his shoulder whilst moving down the auditorium steps. "Due to austerity and lack of recognition, CAT receives little funding. We are therefore small in numbers and always seeking outside help. In consequence of your unfortunate circumstances, you are in a position to offer such help."

"What unfortunate circumstances?" Sean stopped on reaching the theatre floor.

"You mean no superior has informed you?" Fox raised eyebrows and shook his head. "Then let me explain. An internal enquiry has judged your shooting of Grogan unjustified. Until the matter is resolved you are stood down. Fortunately for you, CAT has acquired Grogan's mobile which will prove your innocence. However, this requires both arduous and delicate admin details which cannot be rushed. It is suggested that a favourable outcome might be more rapid should we combine operations."

"You blackmailing me via some kangaroo court?"

"No, old chap, I merely pass on decisions made by various ministerial departments. Talk to Cobbart if you wish."

"Bollocks."

"I'd feel the same." Fox raised his hands as if addressing the surrounding seats. "Meanwhile we have a job to do, somewhat more complex than your original brief, but just as dangerous."

Sean pulled out his mobile and rang Cobbart. No answer. That confirmed it, Cobbart knew and was hiding. Victoria's number produced the same results but a text came back moments later. *In meeting. Hear you're with CAT. Be careful. L xx V.*

"Bunch of sods."

"All of them." Fox began to walk again. "Least in CAT we have no rules or regulations. When there's a bad guy we don't bother with paperwork, we simply remove him. If it makes you feel easier I have placed operatives to protect your girls at home and in St Monica's."

"Don't fuck with me Fox." Sean grabbed the man's jacket and pulled him face to face. "Are they safe?"

"Totally safe. Now calm, please." He eased away. "But

if you're really interested in their future then help me remove a threat to all children in this nation, a threat to their parents, to their grandparents. You have the trust of certain individuals where I have not. Your country needs you, Mr Fagan."

Sean let go of his jacket. "OK, OK, for my kids I'll listen. But I warn you, if they get hurt, I'll kill all involved, you included."

"So far as those who threaten your children or others, you will have ample opportunity to terminate all concerned. As for myself, I am not your enemy, Mr Fagan. Allow me to explain the structure of CAT. Formed during the IRA troubles we removed the unwanted by less orthodox means than the laws allowed. In consequence we are not supported, sanctioned or recognised by any Government ministry or agency. However, clandestine and informal co-operation between SOCA, MI5 and 6 is frequently called upon. Basically we make Britain a safer place, our current priority being terrorism and insurrection. I understand Directus Iurisdictio, the National Street Security gangs and the Death Heads are your operation's targets. SS for Street Security is not by chance. They and the DI are basically national socialists. But the Death Head gangs are a different and more a serious threat. DI think they are a branch of the SS, but they are not. Founded by Rashid Bayat it is their intention to blow this country apart. Directus Iurisdictio might do valuable community work in killing off habitual criminals, but the Death Heads want to kill us all."

"This doesn't gel," Sean said as they passed out the back of the auditorium. "Rashid has poured millions into Universal Youth. He aspires to be part of the British Establishment, public school, Cambridge, cricket."

Fox gave another dismissive laugh. "Beware of the unseen enemy within our midst, Mr Fagan. Some facts.

219

Rashid's father is a leading warlord. In return for his help NATO have been less than vigilant concerning his drug smuggling. Now NATO is pulling out they need him to cover their backs so as to extract with minimum loss and maximum dignity before the Taliban move back. In payment for this they have allowed two thousand five hundred kilos to slip past our Border Control. Street value is two hundred million pounds. In normal times this would have been sold via Bently and Grogan. However, as the Taliban regain control, Rashid and father will swap allegiance. The drug shipment will fund the Death Heads and their jihadist activities, so giving father and son credence after years supporting NATO. It's my job, with your assistance, to prevent that."

"I don't believe our Government is that devious. They would never allow such a thing."

"Our Government didn't. But certain ministers did believing once the deal was done and NATO out they could destroy the drugs and imprison Rashid. Such is the nature and naivety of modern politics. The fact is the drugs are here, ready for distribution and sale. The street price will raise enough for the Death Heads to rid themselves of any connection to Directus Iurisdictio. Subsequently Rashid will fund and control a nationwide gang of East European Mafia with Islamic pretentions."

"OK, fine. So CAT need to act fast. What's that got to do with me?"

"Info from an operative I have imbedded in the DH informs us Bently has a meeting with Rashid today. I believe it will be his last on earth," Fox said and extracted a small digital camera from his pocket. "The latest technology. I wish you to record Bently's demise."

"Get serious Colonel." Sean stopped and shook his

head. "Maybe you could also get me an invite so I can film at close range."

"I can do better." Fox stared at him, gave a half smile and continued to stroll. "The house is hundreds of years old and riddled with secret passages connecting principal bedrooms. There are spy holes, priest holes, means by which dukes, princes and kings would meet with lovers and murder their rivals. I have a colleague who will show you how to access this network."

"Let him show one of your CAT operatives."

"Unfortunately my two available assistants had a mishap with the police during our last mission. In consequence both are wanted for GBH and would not be considered reliable witnesses in a court of law. Also you are the only person trusted by my colleague, who I might add, is also a senior member of British Intelligence."

"I'm not good at small passages."

"Don't underestimate your ability. You are highly regarded. This is your way out of difficult circumstances, Mr Fagan. Refusal will be considered desertion of your country and at the next Grogan enquiry your future may not go well."

"Fucking blackmailing bastards." Sean snatched the camera and continued along the path.

"I take that as affirmative." Fox pulled a mobile from his pocket and began to speak. "OK, he's in," he heard Fox say. "Bring your vehicle to the entrance." He put the mobile away and extracted a Glock 9mm automatic from the wax jacket. "Yours I believe, Mr. Fagan. Victoria would be most upset if you lost it. Do take more care."

Sean accepted the weapon, checked the breach and

placed it to an inside pocket which he zipped. "You think I'll need it?"

"I sincerely hope not. You're already dead, so don't let them kill you a second time." They stopped by the gate. "See the Land Rover across the road, just get in. The gentleman will explain everything. Oh, and do take care."

Sean watched Fox walk away, his hands and arms hanging in the manner of one who believes his job well done. Sean cursed the day and started towards the Land Rover. Approaching from behind the headrests blocked any vision of the interior, only when he opened the passenger door did he see the driver.

"Good day, Fagan, glad you decided to join us. Please hurry, we have little time."

"So, Lord Cranby, what's your part in all this?" Sean asked and climbed in.

"As a member of British Intelligence my part is highly confidential. However, I do have a personal interest. Precocious little upstart that he is, when Rashid Bayat began supporting Universal Youth, to help establish himself amongst the elite and powerful he demanded use of my house as his base. Refusal would have meant withdrawal of his patronage. For nation I reluctantly agreed. That house has been occupied by my ancestors for over two hundred years. If Plan A succeeds I hope I will soon resume residence."

"Well if I'm Plan A don't count on it."

"I hear otherwise. Cobbart assures me you are one of the best and totally trustworthy. I deal only with the best. I want you to bring back evidence of Bently's murder so I can place it in the right hands. With luck we can wind this operation up within days."

Sean stayed silent brooding on the best way forward as they sped from St Albans into country lanes, going deep amidst rural countryside. "Are you part of Directus Iurisdictio?" he asked finally.

"As I said, I'm part of British Intelligence and that will have to suffice. Returning to your brief. Though Rashid has taken the house and gardens I still occupy the surrounding farmland and buildings." Cranby suddenly snorted laughter. "In an affront to Rashid's jihadists, it is the reason I keep pigs there."

"How do you know Bently will visit? This could be a complete waste of time," Sean said as they slowed and drew off road to a track.

"I think not." Cranby opened his door and stepped out. "You have the camcorder?"

"Here." Sean patted a pocket and climbed out to follow him.

"Fox informed me of the drug shipment," Cranby said, walking a path between trees. "Somewhere in that house are two and a half thousand kilos of heroin. Or should be, except Bently as Rashid's distributor has been stealing it. An unknown source has informed Rashid of this, so now he'll want blood, probably in a very unsavoury manner. It's your job to record it."

"Thanks a million."

"I'm about to show you a secret passage to the cellars. The house and grounds are two hundred metres west on the opposite side of the wood," Cranby said entering a clearing. He pointed to the roof and chimneys just visible over the trees, then a small derelict medieval tower. "Built before Tudor times, used to be an old watchtower and guardhouse." He patted the wall. "I often played here when a boy, fighting off the non-believers who invaded our land. Though the house has been extended and rebuilt a number of times, a tunnel from this tower to the lower cellars still exists. In times of old it allowed the coming and going of priests, lovers and political undesirables, generally people the residence did not wish the servants to see." He stopped by the door.

"How do you know Bently's been stealing?" Sean asked, looking to the surrounding trees. All hung heavy with the damp silence of mouldering vegetation.

"This is part of my land. In the last few days I've seen men coming out of here carrying heavy rucksacks. It's too damp for storage so it must have come from the house."

Sean nodded and turned his attention to the ground while Cranby pushed open the door, lifting the edge as it dragged on the stone floor to clear a small swath of moss. A wooden ladder rested on the curved wall, a millstone beside it, its weight bearing down on a flagstone.

"I need your help here," Cranby said, grasping hold of the stone. Together they rolled it aside, then digging fingers round the edge, dragged the flagstone on top of its neighbours. Cranby produced a torch and shone it into the hole below. "They brought the drugs out this way."

"You saw them?" Sean knelt down to look inside. A tunnel high enough and wide enough for two men standing side by side led into pitch darkness.

"Four or five men over a couple of days could easily shift five hundred kilos."

"That's a lot of money. You sure it's Bently?"

"I saw him. He was here with Routt. Routt organised the men. In result Bently will pay the price, today."

"You seem very certain. Were you the unknown source from whom Rashid learnt of this?"

Cranby shrugged. "I'm a manipulator not an informer, Mr Fagan. It was probably Routt looking to replace Salem as head enforcer. Both will unquestionably face a grim execution."

"If they shoot Bently we'll need to recover the body as proof," Sean said.

Cranby snorted. "Body, these men are from third world countries following a lifestyle started in the 7th century. They'll want a show. There will be no body. Ten of my pigs have gone missing and I have reports from my field hands that Rashid's men have built animal pens against and through the French doors into the main banqueting hall. Hungry pigs will eat anything, Fagan, you and me included. So don't get caught and don't worry about a body because there won't be one. Hence the camera."

Sean blew out breath and rested his elbow on one knee while looking down into the hole. "Maybe we should just call the police on this one."

"At the moment no crime has been committed and whatever drugs are in the house can be removed or well hidden even from sniffer dogs. The situation does not allow time for the bureaucracy entailed with a police raid. And where this tunnel can take drugs out, it can also take them in. Rashid can plead he never went to the cellar, never knew any drugs were there."

"So you sacrifice Bently."

"He deserves it. Now listen in. This tunnel leads to a

lower ante cellar never used in my time. The entrance is covered by a millstone much lighter but similar to the one here. You'll need to push it aside, unless recent use has left it open. To the left are steps leading to a door and access to the main cellar. That door is always locked." From the pocket of his coat he produced a large iron key. "Original from the 17th century. Please don't lose it."

Sean accepted the key and placed it into a buttoned pocket. "What if there are people in the cellar?"

"No worry. You don't go that way. Directly opposite the end of this tunnel is a low wooden door disguised as panelling. Pull the oak peg at the panel edge and you can swing the whole thing inwards. From inside you have one of numerous entrances to a whole honeycomb of secret passages weaving all over the house, both upstairs and down. Ahead of you will be stone steps. Go straight up avoiding any side passages. Eventually you'll reach a small chamber. Holes have been cut in the carved wooden columns which support the ceiling. Through them is a clear view of the banqueting hall. In the old days it was used for watching and listening to any persons holding the wrong political allegiances. I used it to record my first wife's adulterous liaison. You see and hear everything." He handed Sean the torch then lifted the ladder to slide it down into the hole. "You can't get back up without this." He patted the top rung where it rested inside the hole. "So when you return remember to replace it against the wall. OK, off you go."

Sean played the torch beam down to the flat mud surface three metres below, thinking it an abyss into the dark hole of nightmares; nightmares over which his future and possibly the safety of his daughters were dangled by unknown persons. To go forward might or might not succeed. But to refuse left too much in jeopardy.

"A man could easily get trapped down there," he said.

"Don't worry I'll pull the stone back over to hide the ladder. When you return you lift the slab from underneath, I've done so myself.

"That's reassuring, but what if someone else comes along?" Sean checked his watch at 1300 hours. "You going to stay?" he asked.

"I'm going to report to Fox. Get things going from this end. Fagan, sovereign and nation demand your courage. Don't worry, in ninety minutes you should return with evidence. Then we can bring in police, MI5 and all the other agencies wishing to be involved. The threat from Death Heads and terrorism will be eliminated."

"Yeah," Sean said and climbed downwards until standing on the mud floor. Looking up he saw Cranby framed by the dim light, a sickly smile on his face.

"Good luck old chap," he said and slid the slab back. Sean turned into the tunnel and stared at a wall of pitch black, his tongue sliding over dry lips as he tasted the damp stale air. This place was not good.

CHAPTER 20

Only one way forward, he thought and shone the torch beam so it spread a small cone of light over the flat mud floor. Occasionally, if indentations appeared on the surface he knelt to examine them, each time his suspicions growing. After five minutes probing and walking into the void of darkness he bumped against the wall where the tunnel suddenly changed direction in a ninety degree bend. Sean stopped and steadied his breathing, for the first time feeling a twitch of panic as he wondered what the hell he was doing. Cranby had mentioned no turn in the passage and from what had been discovered since entering, Sean's faltering trust in the man had begun to fade. Within minutes of starting again, the invisible clutch of a spider's web shrouded his face, causing a startled yelp and frantic clawing to free his eyes and mouth from clinging layers. The anonymous scurrying of claws over the floor brought a second shout as he realised rats were also around. Arms outstretched he hurried forward, occasionally kicking a furry body until after endless minutes his head brushed the roof. Torchlight revealed the tunnel narrowed to a dead end which forced him onto hands and knees as he edged forward. A millstone as described by Cranby blocked further progress and he searched with fingertips until finding an edge and gap beyond. Torch on the ground he twisted bodily, exerting maximum leverage to roll the stone enough to squeeze past. On the other side he paused to catch his breath then propped on elbows, he shone the torch to explore. Ancient bricks formed the walls of what appeared to be a small subterranean wine store. Empty racks covered two walls, the one directly ahead partially panelled, the wood warped and cracked. To his left steps rose to an entrance door.

Least this bit is true to description, he thought and stood. For moments he considered the hidden passage opposite before curiosity made him climb the steps. Cranby had given him the key for a reason. He judged the latched door solid oak, a door clearly made to last. Light shone through a keyhole and he knelt to spy, finding a single floodlight illuminated the larger cellar beyond. Steps one side led upwards through an arch which he guessed gave access to the house. Several doorways occupied the back wall but what stood in the central area grabbed instant attention. For two minutes he waited and listened, hearing only his own breath, before finally certain no one moved in the cellar beyond. The cast iron key fitted perfectly, but the strength needed to turn it made him realise the mechanism had not moved for some time. It compounded his suspicion and made him more cautious. Latch raised he leant against the door hearing the creak of hinges as it slowly swung open. Again he stopped and listened. Silence. Praying no one had fitted an electronic movement detector he crossed the floor.

Three stacks of clear shrink-wrap plastic sacks stood in neat blocks, one stack only half the size of the others two. Sean concentrated on the two larger. Pressing fingers against the wrappers he caused small indentations in the white powder inside while counting width, height and length of each sack. He calculated two thousand packets between them, at a kilo per package that accounted for two thousand kilos of the imported heroin. So what of the five hundred kilos stolen through the tunnel? The third smaller stack seemed absolute proof that Cranby had lied.

Sean shone his torch to give extra light against the plastic, blowing out breath on finding the content coloured red and with the consistency of plasticine. Clearly more than heroin had been smuggled, he thought, while digging with a finger. He split a wrapper and scooped out a sample to place is within the folds of his handkerchief. So in one fact Cranby had been right. Five hundred kilos of heroin had gone missing but in its place there now stood five hundred kilos of Semtex; enough to wage a serious war. Sean quickly re-entered the wine cellar, closing and locking the door behind him. Cranby may have been right about the theft but that still left something wrong with his story, something seriously misleading.

Guided by torchlight Sean felt round the panelling beside the wine rack, found the locking peg and pulled it free. On pressure from his hand the panel leant forward then fell inwards. Beyond, a narrow stone staircase spiralled upwards allowing only the thinnest to ascend. Unable to use the torch and with his shoulders brushing surrounding walls, Sean eased himself into the crevice, careful not to bang his head on the twisting stairs directly above. He counted eighty steps before his emerged into a tiny chamber, the interior lit via holes drilled though the wall.

Perched sideways on a stone ledge he breathed relief on encountering natural light, grateful for rediscovery of the real world outside. For moments he leant head against the solid wall, then positioned himself to spy on what lay below. Three separate holes gave circular views of the grand banqueting hall, the ceiling supported by massive carved beams, one of which incorporated his chamber. Four high French windows were set in the opposite wall allowing space between to display portraits of past residents. At the top end of the hall, tapestries adorned screens behind the main table which was elevated to give view over smaller tables placed each side and ending before a huge open fireplace at the far end. Sean figured the room would seat at least a hundred though at this moment he saw no sign of food or activity. For certain Cranby had been right about one thing. Near the main table some kind of animal pen had been built against one set of French doors, the rear wall formed by the doors themselves so they might open inwards. On one side a table held a long object covered by cloth from which led an electric cable plugged into a socket. Hanging over the pen stood a wooden gallows with rope and pulley giving it the appearance of some sort of medieval torture instrument. It did little to settle his apprehension. He checked his watch at

14:38 hours thinking, so what and when, if anything, would happen?

The heavy night and morning suddenly rushed in on him and he closed his eyes. Don't nod off, he thought, but rested for an uncertain time until startled back to life on hearing a faint female scream. Eye back to peephole he found the banqueting hall remained empty but on the terrace outside a large brute of a man held a girl face down over the balustrade wall. Her skirt around her waist he pummelled himself against her naked backside, oblivious to any who might be watching, his voice rising until he shouted in triumphant lust over ejaculation.

"Batcha boy, batcha boy. You good fuck." Finished, he extracted himself, fiddled with his trousers then zipped up and walked away. The girl stood, pulled up her knickers and followed. Only then did Sean see her face.

"Sammy," he whispered. "What the hell are you doing?" Head against the wall he closed his eyes. He had judged Sammy a feisty, hard nut young female who would never willingly allow herself screwed by some gross individual who treated her like a blow-up doll. That girl would only suffer such violation for a reason. So what was her game?

The Roller always gave Calvin Bently a sense of smug superiority. The car, like the mock Tudor house on West Common, Harpenden, with its white leather sofas and glass cocktail cabinet made him feel a high achiever. A few terms in prison had punctured his freedom while dealing crack cocaine on a Watford council estate but in balance a few gang murders had gone undetected. And prison always provided plenty of opportunity to recruit. Except in this period of austerity nearly all his recruits had vanished. Business had suffered. He couldn't understand why. With the police shooting Grogan things should have picked up. The SS gangs didn't help, neither had Salem who was meant to see off the opposition and get more Death Heads selling. Useless sod, Bently sniffed. But then Salem was a foreigner, Chechen or something. He knew now he should never have employed a foreigner, couldn't trust 'em. Thank fuck they'd let Routt out, he'd soon sort the prat. Business had to pick up. He had a new supplier, Rashid, one of them Afghan wallahs. He didn't trust him, but Rashid had the goods, so what choice but to help him smuggle them from Amsterdam. Salem had taken all the risk and now they were here. Time for payback. Deep in thought he drove without consideration to the car's pedigree or elegance, swinging it passed other traffic in eagerness to collect his money. How many kilos? Two? He'd ask for five. Greed with an overhanging threat of violence always paid off. Which was why he had wanted Routt along to provide the threat. Routt frightened people but Routt hadn't shown up as requested. Bently had tried his mobile; no answer. He guessed the man was too busy killing someone. One of them SS hoodies he hoped. That left him to rely on charm and diplomacy. Bloody foreigners.

Stopping before the entrance to Cranby Hall, Bently waited for the security cameras to scan his car, then watched the high wrought iron gates swing open. Once through they closed silently behind him. This was it, he thought, me where I belong, amongst the top geezers in the business. If all went to plan this meeting would make him the leading wholesaler in Britain. No more dealing on estates or in dodgy clubs but selling a kilo a time to organised crime. With this kind of source producer he would deal only with top distributors, respectable criminals who had business lunches and wore suits. He figured himself an executive now, one doing international deals. Yeah, five kilos, he definitely wanted five kilos.

Before the Gothic heights of Cranby Hall a uniformed

servant with a beard opened the car door. Bently flicked gold and diamond cufflinks to show below the sleeves of his shiny mohair suit, the once fashionable skinny jacket and trousers too tight for his middle-aged and over-weight body.

"Bently, my dear chap." Rashid came down the grand swathe of steps, his hand outstretched. "So good of you to come. I have arranged a very entertaining afternoon."

"Got some crumpet lined up then?" Bently shook hands and followed his host back up the steps.

"Champagne?" Rashid queried as they passed through the outer hall with sweeping staircase and portrait hung walls.

"Don't mind if I do, mate. Nothing like champers to help business along." He glanced to the servants standing by, all with beards. Why they all got beards? he thought.

"The final shipment arranged via your network has arrived," Rashid said. "So payment in kind, I think."

"Well, I had to split the load up. Split loads means less risk of losing the lot if you get caught. Had me best man on it. One of your mob."

"How interesting." Rashid led into the banqueting hall and Bently felt his mouth open as he viewed the splendour. "I can see you're making a profit," he said. "So five kilos should cover my expenses."

"Unfortunately my profit is being eroded." Rashid stopped before an ornate table supporting a silver ice bucket with champagne and cut crystal flutes. A boyish slip of a girl in fitted sweater and micro denim skirt stood in attentive readiness. Rashid flicked his fingers and she withdrew the open bottle, pouring carefully into a glass flute which Bently accepted, wondering when he would get to fuck her. He preferred big tits himself, this one looked too skinny. She also looked nervous but that he didn't mind. Women should always be kept nervous.

"You ain't drinking?"

"Muslims don't."

Never trust a man who doesn't drink, Bently thought, but said, "Well, more for me then." He watched Rashid's eyes flare then turn cold, his breath escaping in a drawn out hiss.

"You want more, then you shall have it my friend. A big surprise. Salem," he shouted. "Bring your dish."

"Salem," Bently repeated, wrinkling his nose as he watched his enforcer carry in a silver platter covered by a high domed lid. Carefully he placed it by the ice bucket, pushing the girl aside before holding his hand in readiness to uncover the contents.

"What you doing here? You're supposed to be looking after my interests on the street. What's this game then?" Bently looked between them.

"You must understand Mr Bently that we Asians always stick together in business. Our alliance forms a strong brotherhood from which outsiders are excluded."

"You want Routt to take my place." Salem pointed at Bently with his free hand and lifted the lid with the other. "You make big mistake."

Bently's scream echoed across the hall, the same time his glass smashed on the floor. Turning to run he found a dozen men advancing from the doorway. All wore military fatigues, all had beards, all stared at him with hate filled eyes.

"What the fuck's going on?" He backed until two of the men grabbed him, twisting him and bending him so he stared straight into the face of Routt's severed head. Purple from heavy bruising under caked blood, one of the eyes had been gauged from its socket, the other bulging as if pressured from inside the skull. Bently began to retch on realising the bared teeth were held apart by the man's penis.

"One other thing you should understand," Rashid said. "Not only is drink forbidden to us, it is also forbidden that we steal. And you, Mr Bently have stolen five hundred kilos of my father's heroin. I am duty bound to retrieve it. So save yourself a painful death, speak."

"I stole nothing, nothing, Salem must have nicked it," Bently screamed in panic, feeling his body shake before he threw up over Routt's head.

"You lie." Salem grabbed his hair and yanked his face upwards. "Routt told me before he die that you took it. He drive one truck for you. When I receive shipment five hundred kilos missing. You tell me where, I give you quick death." He produced a knife and flicked open the blade. "Tell me or you end with bollocks in your mouth."

"I fucking never touched it, I swear." Bently felt the blade on his cheek, screaming as it sliced through.

"OK." Salem pushed him back towards his men. "He thief, string him up. You," he pointed. "Go fetch pigs."

A scream jerked Sean back from half slumber. Cursing his inability to have remained awake and vigilant he peered through one of the spy holes. Below a guy he guessed to be Bently was held by a jeering bunch of uniformed and bearded militia, most of whom were armed. All stared at some abomination in the centre of a silver platter.

Sean eased the lens of his camcorder into an adjoining spy hole, opening the viewing screen and adjusting range for the best picture. A head stared back at him with one bulging eye. Next moment Bently threw up scattering those close by. In reaction the bulbous brute of a man who had raped Sammy on the terrace began gesticulating with his arms and shouting orders.

"Fetch pigs and hang this one. Then I, Salem, will question him."

In noisy obedience the men started pushing Bently towards the pig enclosure, pulling and ripping at his clothes as they did so. When his flabby flesh became exposed their cries of abuse were suddenly mixed with the squeal of pigs outside the French windows.

Only after the bearded ones moved away did Sean realise that Sammy had been trapped amongst them. The look of terror on her face told him everything and free of restraint she fled for the door, only to be grabbed at the entrance by someone immediately outside. Two, then four uniformed men bodily lifted and brought her back. Kickboxing would not solve this problem. Held by arms and legs she twisted in helpless struggle as they lifted then placed her spread-eagled over the main table, as if readying her for ritual sacrifice. While one pushed up her skirt, two others were grabbing at her breasts, goading her to greater struggles as she thrashed against the tabletop.

Sean banged the wood panelling cursing his inability to help her. To go down he would need to first get out of the cellar which, considering the quantity of drugs inside, was probably locked. After that, confrontation in a shooting match would end with both Sammy and himself dead. To fire on them from here would give away his presence. Worse, aiming through a narrow hole at a target twenty metres distance meant he had equal chance of hitting

Sammy. He figured rape would come before murder so for the moment her situation didn't threaten life. All other attention became focussed on Bently. It gave Sean time to find a solution. He adjusted the camera lens for a wider angle feeling an absolute shit. But, as he had learnt the hard way, never go into what you can't get out of.

Men had now lifted Bently into the pig pen, tying his feet to haul him upwards so he dangled headfirst from the gallows. Shouting encouragement his torturers scrambled clear, leaving two behind who held out Bently's arms while jamming his suspended body between their own. Salem pulled the cover from the side table and lifted the chainsaw beneath. Holding it high he whirled the motor in test so the chain rattled noisily over its ratchets, then posturing as if a warrior ready to do battle, he stepped into the pen to stand one side of Bently's outstretched arms. All fell silent.

"Where you put my master's drugs? You steal from us. Tell me, or you die," Salem shouted.

"I never, never, no, no." Bently's scream sounded over the squealing pigs.

Salem looked to the head table where Rashid raised both hands in the manner of a priest officiating at some pagan ceremony. For a moment he paused, then dropped his arms.

Sean screwed up his face realising what lay ahead the same moment Salem brought the whirling chain down onto Bently's wrists. Blood jetted upwards and in straight lines back and front, the chain grinding through bone until dropping Bently's hands on the floor, his screech of pain vanishing under the cheers of watching men. As if job well done, Salem and helpers climbed from the pen leaving Bently to gently swing by the ankles, blood pouring from the stumps of each wrist, his voice now a continuous wail of pain.

Rashid again lifted palms upwards as if in prayer. "As they have fasted, so let them eat," he ordered.

Sean made sure the camera captured both his movements and voice, keeping all in view as the French doors were opened and ten large hungry sows pushed against each other in their scramble to enter. Bently's hands went first, snatched up and fought over by the four leading animals. The others went for Bently's suspended torso. To encourage their hysterical feeding, Salem lowered Bently into their midst. Snouts ripping at face, arms and rig cage. Their bloodlust vibrated the banqueting hall in a cacophony of savage greed while devouring Bently's eviscerated entrails, truly pigs at the trough.

Sean left the camera and drew out his automatic pistol, no human should suffer such a fate but trying to aim through a hole, he found a shot to kill Bently impossible. Next moment the body dropped to be immediately covered by large feasting sows. Sean put away the automatic and went back to his camera, thinking if this went before a jury Rashid and followers would never leave jail. The boss now moved to position himself next to Sammy, ignoring her protests while stroking his chin in thoughtful contemplation. Salem and his men still remained by the pig pen, congratulating themselves on what they clearly considered some kind of victory. All turned when Rashid shouted, "She is a Christian whore."

"She batcha boy," Salem shouted in response and hurried for the table, followed by the others en masse. Rashid spoke to one of the men beside him who drew out a knife, stood between Sammy's legs and with precise movements cut off her knickers, tossing the severed lace to one side. Sammy's scream of outrage briefly rose above the pigs but by then Salem has reached Rashid's side and started arguing.

Sean picked up his automatic and tried to find a firing line through the holes, better to kill her than let her suffer Bently's fate. Because of her struggles she had shifted sideways to the table so he could see her open thighs and the curve of her pubic mound, leaving the top of her body hidden. Rashid stood shaking his head, hands raised in a gesture of helplessness. Salem suddenly looked resigned and turned away leaving the knife man to reach fingers under the black triangle of the girl's pubic hair and seemingly into her vagina. Groping aggressively and shouting in triumph he tried to pull out what had been carefully tucked from sight with the root so tightly drawn under it gave a small surface indentation causing a false appearance of vaginal lips.

"Bloody hell," Sean whispered, holding his fire while watching the man yank testicles and penis from between her buttocks, allowing all to be pulled upright and taut. Knife ready, he waited on Rashid's instruction but in anticipation of further entertainment, others pushed round blocking Sean's view. Sean realised the sudden opportunity and fired into their midst, the sound filling his chamber and rebounding from the hall ceiling.

One man slumped, clutching his shoulder while others sprung back as if a scorpion had been dropped into their midst. All stared into space, clearly baffled. Sean fired again. When a second man crumpled the others scattered, including the knife man, leaving Sammy intact. Sean watched apprehensively as some unslung their rifles. The next part he figured could get dangerous. Four men bunched to the left made his third target. The shot winged one of them causing the others to blindly fire at walls and ceiling. Rashid ducked from sight beneath the table while Salem and half a dozen of his brave warriors fled through one of the French doors. Sean fired again without hitting a target but the objective was achieved.

When her last tormentor let go, Sammy wriggled off the

table with the movements of a frantic eel. Moments later she sprung into a sprint for the door. Mission accomplished, Sean jammed the camera into a pocket and let off one more shot before squeezing his way down the spiral staircase to the cellar. Behind him several rounds penetrated into his chamber as the banqueting hall filled with the sound of automatic fire. Cranby won't be please, he thought.

Sean reached the wine cellar as the frenzy of automatic rifle fire petered out. No doubt, Sean figured, because they had emptied their magazines without realising a target. Rashid and Salem might have a bloodthirsty bunch of enthusiasts but they were also untrained. Faced with a real enemy they would panic and run.

After worming past the first millstone Sean pushed the top from where it leant against the wall, enabling him to use its pressure on his palm so it rolled into place. He checked once that camera and automatic were safe then used his torch to push into the darkness. Arm in front against cobwebs he hurried to the corner, stopped to check for any sound back or front, then headed toward the exit praying Cranby had left the ladder in place.

He shouted relief on seeing it and did not falter when leaping straight up the rungs. Shoulder to covering slab he eased it aside and emerged onto the tower floor. A slit window high in the wall allowed enough light for him to remove the ladder and replace the flagstone. Only then did he peer from the partially open door to the forest beyond. No sound of rifle fire or shouting came from where roof and chimneys rose above the trees. Instead he heard birdsong and the rustle of wind through foliage. Tranquil, he thought, but had no doubt as to the danger still facing him. Salem and his men could appear anytime. Minutes later he found the track where Cranby had stopped.

"Bollocks," he said aloud on discovering no one there. Or maybe Cranby had expected him to die. He had questions for that man. He extracted his mobile, toying with it while considering who, if anyone, he could trust. He had evidence to put Rashid away forever. That would terminate any future finance for Universal Youth, certainly in this area. Probably also for National Street Security and the role of Directus Iurisdictio in SS formation and control. Still holding the phone he began to jog along the lane towards St Albans. Maybe Fox and Cranby had intended him to die in the spy chamber and later recover the film from his body. With evidence to blackmail Rashid, both would have power over his financial contributions. But would that power bring Government control via CAT into Directus Iurisdictio? Just who, if anyone, were they in league with?

CHAPTER 21

Sammy sprinted from the front entrance, saw no one and ran down steps towards a white Rolls Royce. She shouted relief when the door opened under her jerk and again on finding keys in the ignition. So trusting, she thought and slid behind the wheel. The car came to life with a gentle purr and for a second it sat in splendid readiness before Sammy put it into drive and stamped hard on the accelerator. Instantly the car lurched then executed a tight curve as she steered into a U turn, the wheels churning up grass and flowerbeds until regaining the drive where it hurtled towards the main gates. As it sped away rifle shoots shattered the rear window causing her to scream and duck, her foot still hard down. At high velocity the car smashed head on into the gates, flinging both back on their hinges while crunching up fender and bonnet. Air bags immediately blew from the front pinning her against the seat, leaving her barely able to see as the car flew over the lane and flattened a stock fence on the opposite side. Still powered by her foot on the accelerator the crunched up machine sped over open fields, through a second fence and stopped only when it embedded itself amidst undergrowth and trees. Twisting in the seat Sammy fought to release herself from behind the airbag. After unlatching the lock she pushed with both feet, straining to wedge the door open against . branches until having room to climb out. Once clear she bent, resting hands on knees while looking at the concertinaed front and gouged bodywork of her escape vehicle.

"And my first drive in a Roller," she said, thinking everything was getting beyond her. Time to call the boss.

Shouts from the gateway sent her darting amongst the trees, running full tilt for the far fields, knowing they would follow the car tracks, knowing if found they would shoot her on sight.

* * *

Sean keyed numbers into his mobile and waited.

"Sean, are you OK?"

"Battered, but living. I need immediate assistance."

"What's your location?"

"Jogging along some lane towards St Albans, about a mile or so from Cranby Hall."

"Figured you'd be in trouble which is why I'm not far away. Lucky we have Sky Angel."

"Sky Angel," Sean repeated.

"Code name for our UAV. Look above you. The Witch sanctioned collaboration with CAT. Deep Cut is now a combined operation. I'm on standby somewhere within five miles of you. Go centre of the lane, preferably where there are no trees. CAT has a Tarantula Hawk UAV which has been monitoring the house. Looks like a lot of panic and activity."

"You're never alone with a Tarantula." Sean stopped to look up at the sky. He saw nothing. Then maybe a black speck hovering and circling.

"OK, we have you. Stay where you are, I'll be there in ten minutes."

For moments Sean toyed with his mobile. Time to trust a wider field, he thought, then keyed in Coobart's number. This time the man answered.

"I hope your call is important. Not only is it Sunday but I'm just about to sit down for a late lunch."

"I need the team back; I need them to check some properties. There are people on our side being less than honest."

"You mean the Witch? We've agreed to collaborate with her."

"I mean everybody, including those who condemn me behind my back."

Sean listened to Cobbart's embarrassed silence. "I was not one of that gathering," he said finally. "At all times I remain on your side, Sean. Just understand there is more going on than you realise. As for your team, I'll do my best but they're committed to other operations, it will take time."

"We haven't got time."

"It would help if I knew where they need to search and for what."

"Drugs for one, five hundred kilos. Also human teeth in a pile of pigs shit. Teeth are the one thing pigs can't digest. Somewhere near here there are an awful lot of them."

"Are you crazy?"

"To be on this operation it helps."

Charlotte squeezed her sister's hand and stared down at the open grave. "Do we have someone who has risen from the dead, or body snatchers?"

"The grave is not deep, maybe he wasn't dead. Maybe he dug himself out." Anjali shrugged.

"He must have been unconscious when they put him in. Even with no other injuries he would have suffocated."

"Unless someone dug an air passage for him," Anjali said and knelt down to push aside soil from a cloth. "Yuck." She wrinkled her face. "You smell it? Chloroform."

"Meant for Routt no doubt, but used on someone else."

"Or both, except on one of them it didn't quite work."

"Salem wouldn't use chloroform on his own men and Routt didn't occupy this grave which means someone uninvited did. Someone snooping perhaps?"

"Who do you think?" Anjali asked.

"Fagan. He was sent here to spy, who else?"

"I think we'd better sit and plan carefully, sister. If we mess up, no one will be pleased."

Charlotte put hand to mouth as if thinking of the consequences, becoming startled when her phone rang. "Sammy, where are you?" she asked, then went silent as she listened, her eyes growing wide, her jaw dropping. "He did what? Stole five hundred kilos. Pigs. My God." She looked to Anjali. "But you're not hurt? OK, we have to do something. I'll talk with Anjali."

Sean sat on a bank where he could see the lane fifty metres in either direction, repeatedly checking his watch, realising time was vital. He just prayed Sammy had made it out. Her mother would be frantic if she realised the situation, more so if Sammy was questioned and possibly arrested for conspiracy to murder and drug smuggling. Ballet dancer, kick-boxer, some girl she turned out to be he thought, then laughed on realising he still considered her a girl.

He heard the car before seeing it and stood ready to

move back amongst bushes, sighing relief when Victoria's BMW came into view. Seconds later he sat beside her.

"My God you look a mess. Fox was right." She began to drive.

"You with him?" Sean asked.

"Going there now. Looks like you need a bit of stitching."

"No time. Rashid has two thousand kilos of heroin in his house plus five hundred of Semtex and a group of armed men. They just murdered Bently but in saving Sammy I gave away my position. If we don't move fast Rashid and his men will disappear with both drugs and explosives. I have a film of Bently's death, not pretty." Sean removed the camera. "I want you to get it into safe hands. It will put this lot away forever."

"OK," Victoria said and pulled over into the next lay-by. She took the camcorder, removed the chip and slotted it into some computer device incorporated within her dashboard. She pressed buttons. "Done, MI5 now has a copy." She passed the chip back.

"With Directus Iurisdictio in every cubbyhole can your boss be trusted?" Sean asked.

"The Witch may be an evil cow to some but totally straight and trustworthy to her job. Trust me, trust the Witch. And at this point also trust the Fox."

Sean leant back and repeated. "At this point, that means you're kind of uncertain about Foxy yourself."

"Just call it rivalry between agencies." She turned onto an A road then into a transport lay-by, stopping her car behind a long wheel based transit van. "OK." She looked around to check for anybody watching. "A quick swap."

Both left the BMW at the same time a side door on the transit slid open. Next moment they were inside.

Fox, Rottweiler, Meatball and another man sat at a monitoring bench staring into computer screens. The third man worked two joysticks before him, his screen showing an aerial view of Cranby Hall.

Sammy sat hunched in one corner, dressed in a tracksuit. Hugging knees to chest, she looked forlorn and miserable but gave him a weak smile. "Thanks, I owe you," she said.

"You saved me from Routt with a dropkick. I owe you."

"Just helping an OK guy. He would have killed me if you hadn't stopped him." She tried a second smile, her head to one side as if in question. "Can you keep a girl's secret?"

"Sure I can, no problem Sammy, and regards to your brother when you see him."

She smiled openly this time.

Colonel Fox left his screen, checked the view from the Tarantula UAV and indicated a seat against the van's bulkhead. "Sammy's one of the best and most productive undercover operators I have," he said as both men sat. "Except unfortunately for this operation her cover is now blown."

"Definitely a girl who will go beyond the call of duty." Sean leant back. "Got a drink, water, anything?"

Fox rummaged in a cupboard and passed over a bottle of mineral water. "Mind if I have the camera?" He put out his hand. "What's your assessment?"

Sean gave him the camcorder and watched him pass it to Meatball who slotted the chip into his computer. "My assessment Colonel is immediate return for immediate action. Rashid has enough heroin and Semtex stored to start and finance a protracted war. His support for Universal Youth and the SS is a sham. What he's really deploying is his own gangs in the form of the Death Heads. He's hiding and recruiting behind religious faith to start a jihad insurrection against this country. Directus Iurisdictio sanction him because of his contributions, but none of them realise what he's really up."

"Fucking hell." Meatball pushed back his chair as if trying to escape the images on screen.

"As you see, they are not pleasant people," Sean said. "But neither is Rashid stupid. He knows someone shot at his men from a hidden location, that someone witnessed Bently's death. It won't be long before he starts searching for secret passages and chambers. With that and Sammy's escape he'll take no chances and move the merchandise to a new location. If you want him, act now. Bring in the police."

"Can't do. One, I don't know who is on who's side, on DI or Rashid's and two, putting a raid together would take hours. He and his explosives will have gone by then."

"So what do you propose?"

"Do what we did in the old IRA days, get rid of the lot. Blow the whole fucking thing up."

"You can't just break the law," Sean said, sipping water and feeling the creep of exhaustion.

"What law? We're CAT. We play by the same rules

those guys do. The problem with politicians and media is they expect everything to be politically correct. They want nice wars with nice people following nice rules. These idiots live in cuckoo land. No truck has arrived yet to move this stuff but that doesn't mean they're not already shifting it from the cellar in readiness."

"What choice?" Sean asked.

"None. This is Plan A. Myself, Al and Reg here will go to the woods overlooking the house and cause a diversion by firing through the windows. That should bring Salem and his men out of the cellar to run or retaliate. Job done, providing we have one volunteer who knows how and where to place a detonating device amongst the Semtex." He looked at Sean.

"I might have guessed."

"Good man."

"That's Plan A, so what's Plan B?"

"There isn't one. OK, let's go to work."

"I'll come with you," Victoria said.

"No way." Sean sipped more water and stood.

"I want you to stay here with Rick," Fox told her, pointing to the UAV operator. "If people escape the surveillance drone can follow them. Then you call your boss and have her intervene. In fact call now, we may have casualties."

Victoria tutted but extracted her mobile.

"I'll go with you," Sammy said from her corner. "I know Salem. He's very superstitious. If he sees you he'll think you're a ghost. I've also been in the cellar, I know my way around."

"You're too young, for Christ's sake. They were going to butcher you, rape you, kill you," Sean said.

"Listen mate, I do techno raves twelve hours non-stop. I'm fitter and faster than you'll ever be. I want my mum to live a safe life, not get blown up by some religious freak wearing a suicide vest." She stood. "Yo Colonel, I'm your girl."

"Trooper Fairbright, you'll receive recognition for this." Fox grinned at her.

"Trooper," Sean repeated. "I thought you were a dancer, a ballerina no less."

"Special training for Special Services. I was also a para." She walked past him to where Rottweiler and Meatball turned away from the screen showing Bently's final demise. Both look ill.

"Timed detonating device," Rottweiler said opening one of the cupboards and taking out a mobile sized gadget. On top lay a series of buttons and a dial. "Press first button for one minute delay, second for two, third for three and so on 'til five. If you want longer, turn the dial six to thirty minutes. Press the red button on the side to arm it, place preferably out of sight between the packaging or failing that on top, then run like fuck."

"I'll take that." Sean reached out.

"But I'm the CAT operative." Sammy snatched it from Rottweiler's hand. "If I'm killed, then you take over."

Sean steadied himself as Fox drove the van from its parking place. Moments later they were heading back into country lanes. "OK, this is the brief," Fox called back over his shoulder. "We drop you near the tunnel entrance. How long to reach the main cellar?"

"With good flashlights, say five minutes."

"OK, you wait by the tunnel entrance while we move into position. The moment you hear firing you go for your target. We'll keep them occupied for ten minutes then make our retreat. By then you should have placed your detonator so do the same, and fast. If five hundred kilos of Semtex goes up it will leave a fucking great hole in the ground. Hopefully we all arrive back at the van the same time. Then we get out. With a bang that size every emergency service in the county will turn up and we don't want to be seen. All understood?"

"No problem"

CHAPTER 22

Once out of the van Sean led Sammy to the watchtower and ushered her through the door. Both rolled away the millstone and slid aside the covering before lowering the ladder. Sammy shone a flashlight inside and screwed up her face.

"Hope there're no spiders down there."

"Spiders and rats," Sean said spreading his hand in imitation of one. "Great big hairy things which crawl down your clothes."

She stared back at him, her eyes narrow. "Not true."

"'Tis. Why don't you stay here? Watch no one takes the ladder. You can't get out unless the ladder is there. You want to be trapped down there with big hairy spiders crawling in your hair and rats chasing you?"

She sniffed, folded arms and looked to the door. Sean could see she had fear also that she wouldn't give in.

"OK," he said. "But as you insist on dying with me, first tell me, are you male or female?"

"Sort of female hermaphrodite. My twin sister died during our birth. Perhaps her spirit moved into mine." She shrugged. "In result I entered this world with a gender abnormality, no womb and a willy where my vagina should be."

"You're very good at hiding it."

Again she shrugged. "Easy when you know how. With two fingers you push the testicles back up into your body where they sheltered when a child. Then you draw the willy tightly under your legs to wedge it between buttocks. Helps if you have a foreskin. And there it stays, out of sight and out of mind. Done properly I can even create a pubic mound with an indentation down the middle which suggests my correct genitalia. If the thing ever drops down through excessive movement, I feel horrified, I don't want it. Think of me as a female hermaphrodite, I love the impossible. I'm the perfect lesbian."

"Why don't you get it cut off?"

She gave a sad smile. "Maybe one day I will. But for now my girlfriend likes it. Calls it her living dildo. The breasts are real though," she said and held herself. "Aided by a little cream and exercise, but all mine."

"Fair play to you." Sean smiled for her. "Why not? You are who you are."

"My mother doesn't mind, but sometimes I become as Sam, that little boy whose spirit died when I took over his body. Sometimes I cry for him."

Sean looked to the ground unsure how to reply. "Maybe you are as one, and that one is Sammy."

"Thanks." She held out her hand to him but did not touch. "What I do is as much for him as me. He would have been a brave soldier, is a brave soldier. I maybe a girl but I also feel his spirit. He wouldn't run from spiders. My mum wasn't surprised when I joined the army. She realised it was as much for Sam as Sammy. I was a medic in the Paras, also trained as a sniper. But being a girl made it difficult. Then because I lived round here and had connections with Universal Youth I got recruited by CAT. Couldn't tell Mum though, I feel guilt about that."

"Were you by the grave last night, did you dig soil way so I could breath?"

"Didn't know what else to do." She stared at the ground.

"So you're Justitia, the Dark Angel. I heard you tell Salem and his men."

"No." She shook her head. "Not me. If they believed that they wouldn't have treated me the way they have. They're scared of Justitia, they believe she is the evil spirit of death. But she's not, she's more the While Angel."

"And who is that?" he asked.

The echo of shots through the trees broke their conversation. Sammy shook her head. "OK, let's do this," she said and slid down the ladder.

Sean followed three steps behind, their flashlights from Fox giving good illumination, showing the bend and cobwebs beyond. Sammy made no cry or protest as she ran through and leapt over scurrying rats. He felt proud of her silent courage. She bounced against the wall and fell in her effort to stop when reaching the millstone. Sean shot past her, bashing head against the tunnel roof as he skidded down on to hands and knees. Pushing back and levering the stone as previously, he partially rolled it aside until able to squeeze through. Blood trickled down his face, going into his left eye and over his lips.

"Sod it," he whispered.

"You're bleeding," she said, wriggling behind him into the wine cellar.

"It's nothing, nothing." He wiped blood from his chin and pulled out his automatic pistol. "Switch off your torch and leave it by the entrance," he told her.

Voices sounded from the cellar and Sean leant close to Sammy, his hand on her shoulder. "I have a key to the door. When I open it, I'll fire at whoever is there. Hopefully they'll run. When I indicate go plant your device, set the detonator for five minutes then jam it out of sight underneath the Semtex. After that, as Foxy said, run like fuck, OK?"

"Ride on cowboy."

Sean shook his head, squeezed her shoulder then went quickly up the steps. Through the keyhole he saw no one in the cellar beyond, but part of the heroin had already been shifted. The lock turned quietly and he swung the door wide the same moment Salem came out through the cellar archway leading up to the house.

For moments both men stared at one another, Sean levelling his automatic, Salem in total disbelief at the blood smeared apparition which had materialised from nowhere. His scream echoed through cellar and passages, trailing all the way upstairs as he fled.

"Now," Sean indicated to Sammy, moving to the cellar entrance, covering while she crossed to the Semtex and started to set her device.

Peering round the edge of the stone staircase wall he heard frantic shouting from the passage above. Two men encouraged by Rashid appeared nervously at the top and Sean fired shots, hitting one and sending the other diving back.

"Done." Sammy ran over and sheltered behind him.

"Out of here, now, now," he ordered and waited until she reached the wine cellar door before following. He had almost made it when Salem reappeared. Immediately he opened fire, spraying the door as Sean slammed it closed, fumbling and dropping the key. A flicker of light from the

tunnel showed Sammy already there and Sean leapt the steps
going to his knees as he landed, then snapping off one more
shot when light appeared in the doorway above. Salem leapt
back giving time for Sean to squeeze past the millstone. He
had no time to ease it back as a dozen rounds cracked into
the opposite side. Safer to run, he thought, and that fat slob
could never force himself into the restricted opening. By the
time Salem had pushed the millstone clear Sean figured to be
round the bend and heading for the ladder.

Along the dark passage Sammy's light flicked between
walls and floor as she ran. In haste Sean's own flashlight had
been left but automatic in one hand he held the other in
front, passing through the cobwebs. Behind he heard the
millstone thud over and Salem's triumphant shout as he
crawled into the tunnel. Sammy's light disappeared
indicating she had rounded the bend, safe he hoped.

The crash of gunfire in the confined space imploded on
Sean's ears with the whiz of a bullet passing his shoulder,
others embedded themselves or chipped chunks from the
wall. He turned once and fired back, heard Salem shout.
Next moment he hit the tunnel wall and threw himself round
the bend. Sammy's light came back into view, frantically
weaving as she ran. Seconds later she reached the ladder and
began to climb. Sean breathed relief then threw himself to
the floor as rounds from Salem's weapon pitted ceiling and
wall to his left. Up ahead Sammy's light fell from ladder to
ground, dropped he figured in her haste. Regaining his feet
he started running again until a deafening sound and the
invisible force of explosion hurled him face forward. The
very ground trembled as if gripped by vibrant spasms. Earth
fell from the roof thudding over the tunnel floor while
behind him white light flared from a fireball which hit the
wall where the tunnel bent. Heat seared over him,
evaporating air to leave him choking for breath as more rock
and earth fell from walls and roof. Standing he staggered,
trying to regain balance and mind before lurching towards

the fallen flashlight.

Sammy lay at the bottom of the ladder, her eyes closed, her body still, her tracksuit top and trousers wet with blood.

"Fuck, fuck." Sean put fingers to her neck feeling for a pulse, found none but still drew her up and over his shoulder. Standing on the ladder he edged her head, then body through the opening, pushing up her legs so she folded out on the floor above. Continuing to climb he found his ankle jerked by an iron grip which wrenched one foot from its rung. Sean dropped but managed to wedge both elbows on the flagstone floor enabling him to twist and look down before stamping a heel into Salem's face. Still the man clung on, not letting go until Sean stamped over and over. Suddenly released Sean heaved upwards, rolling on top of Sammy as he realised his automatic had fallen. In search of a weapon he saw the Semtex explosion had inwardly crumbled part of the tower wall and as Salem's head came into view Sean grabbed the largest rock to hurl it against the man's skull. He fell screaming, rolled on the tunnel floor but still tried to snatch for the ladder's lowest rung. Too quick for Salem's dazed reaction, Sean lifted the ladder and threw it aside before returning ready with another missile. Salem had regained his feet and stared up with blooded face. Hair singed, his clothes burnt, he leapt in vain effort to reach the opening.

"Put ladder back, put ladder back or I cut your balls off."

"Your butchering days are over pal," Sean said and threw aside the stone to lift the covering slab. "Rot in hell." He watched Salem unsling his rifle and heard the mechanism click on an empty chamber. "Always save the last round," he said and dropped the slab over the entrance, listening to the muted threats while rolling the milstone from the wall, staining with the effort until its weight was firmly in place.

Sammy still showed no sign of life as he stretched her out. For moments he looked down at her, uncertain whether she was dead or alive. For a moment he hesitated then opened the tower door and gathered her in his arms.

No roof or chimneys rose above the forest, instead a billowing cloud of swirling smoke blocked the sun and dropped dust particles to turn everything white. Sean skirted chunks of masonry which littered the track as he carried Sammy towards the van. He prayed and prayed it would still be there, prayed she held on to her life.

CHAPTER 23

The van remained as left, the side door open where Victoria stood anxiously staring towards the trees and rising smoke.

"Get the medical kit," Sean shouted as she came into view. The backdoors of the van opened and both Meatball and Rottweiler leapt out simultaneously. One pulled a stretcher from the back, the other took Sammy from Sean's arms and gently laid her out before both lifted her into the van.

"Where's Fox? We got to get her to a hospital," Sean said, climbing in beside Victoria.

"Wait, wait," Rottweiler shouted as he uncovered Sammy's legs to examine the torn flesh from a bullet wound. "Clean exit, but she's losing blood fast." He began to apply a tourniquet. Meatball had her top off and was stuffing bandages to wounds in her side and groin.

"What's her blood group?" he shouted.

Rottweiler finished the tourniquet and opened a lower cupboard to reveal the vehicle's emergency supplies. Briefly he checked a list. "A positive," he said and rummaged through a box full of blood sachets before selecting one. Moments later he had a drip connected to her arm and the sachet hooked on a door handle. Sean felt impressed, these guys clearly knew exactly what they were doing, down to having the blood group of CAT operatives. Victoria touched fingers to his cheek and he sat resting forehead against her hip.

"You OK?"

"Where's Fox?"

"Gone with the UAV operator to help recover it. The

blast smashed it into trees up the lane."

"Fuck that, we got to get her into hospital," Sean said, the same time the side door slammed back. The drone operator heaved in a square platform with what appeared to be a large fan blade in the centre surrounded by electronic gadgets. The van rocked as Fox also climbed into the driver's seat. Moments later they were speeding down the lane. Victoria took out her mobile and spoke rapidly before leaning over to say something to Fox. He nodded and switched on a tracking device located in the van's dashboard.

"Are there any A & E hospitals around here?" Sean asked. "One capable of dealing with bullet wounds."

"No." Victoria sat beside him and clasped his hand. "But when Foxy told me to get help from the Witch she gave authority for a full deployment. Not only has she got people out watching, when she heard what we intended with that amount of explosives she mobilised our field medical unit. That's a mobile operating theatre with doctor and medics who served in Afghanistan. The vehicle's leaving the M1 now. Foxy has linked our tracking device. We should meet up in about five minutes."

"Just pray she lives that long."

"She will, and you need some treatment yourself. Jesus, you look a mess." She squeezed his fingers.

"What am I going to tell her mother?"

"Leave that to the police," she paused. "This operation isn't over. The reason they kept the drone up so close to the explosion is that after the shooting started a car left the house, top of the range Audi 800. We got the licence plate details. It belongs to Rashid. He actually drove past this van just as the Semtex went up. Hence the drone crashed up the lane. Rashid might have other stores of arms and explosives and until the guy's in custody, he remains a threat."

Even at four miles distance the farmhouse shuddered.

"What was that?" Charlotte stood up from the kitchen table and ran to the window, Anjali behind her.

"Plane crash at Luton airport?" Anjali said and led her sister out into the courtyard.

"No way. That was some massive explosion. That's Cranby's place." Both watched the cloud plume upwards, swirling and billowing dust.

"If Rashid was in that, he's dead," Anjali said.

Charlotte nodded her head. "After what he did I hope so."

"We should have told the police."

"You are the police my sister. We may have cleaned the place up since last night but your colleagues would have asked what Rashid's Death Heads were doing here? What were we doing? My God, Cranby will go mad."

"Maybe Rashid decided to get rid of any evidence against him."

Charlotte shook her head. "Too much money involved. More likely he's switched to plan B."

"Which is?"

"Hide. Change his ID, go to ground."

"If Sammy is right." Anjali turned to her, showing a face without expression. "You certain she's trustworthy? I know

261

she's your girlfriend, but ..."

"But nothing, she's more than that. Something always worried me about Rashid and his generosity, Sammy joined the SS in an attempt to infiltrate the Death Heads and find out their motives. She did it all for me and she succeeded. Rashid is the villain and it's imperative I protect Universal Youth from his criminal activities."

"But Rashid gave us everything. The clubhouse, funds for countless good activities." Anjali shook her head.

"It's all a front and because he plays the true blue county gentleman, Cranby sees only his money and doesn't ask where it comes from."

"Serious minds are going to look at this," Anjali said. "That explosion will start a lot of investigation which will eventually arrive here. We need to act now so we can sidestep any suspicions that might occur over our activities. If we are arrested, because of our involvement and Rashid's contributions, Universal Youth will be hit by the full force of media accusation. We need to be seen as the good guys, those who stand against corruption and evil."

"Agreed. So I propose we get evidence enough to compromise Rashid and divert attention to his association with Salem and his murder of Routt. Then truly we can all play the victimised innocents."

"Question Rashid?" Again Anjali shook her head. "Charlotte, somehow I don't think a guy desperate enough to blow up his house is going to sit down over tea and tell us his future drug dealing plans. There is no simple way."

"Yes there is because Sammy told me Bently stole five hundred kilos of heroin and Rashid will want it back. If we tell him we know the location and if we somehow record our conversation we can pass proof he's a dealer. Least enough to get SOCA on his and Salem's tracks and away from us."

"More likely he'll kill us," Anjali said, still watching the swirling dust cloud.

"No. I'll set the meeting in an open place where we'll know if he has any of his thugs about."

"Sounds highly dangerous to me."

"It is, but as much for him as us. I'll phone him now on the pretence of finding out if he's OK after the blast. He'll be so shocked when he discovers I know of the drugs I'm sure he'll agree to meet me."

"Us, sister, I'm not going to let you do this alone, even if it does mean the end of my career and possible imprisonment. I'm too far involved. After all the work everyone has done for Universal Youth, its continuation and good name is more important than either of us."

"And certainly more important than the life of Rashid Bayat." Charlotte picked up the phone and dialled.

The articulated eight-wheeler medical unit met them on the main Luton to Harpenden road, blocking traffic as the two vehicles stopped one behind the other. White coated orderlies transferred Sammy between them.

"You too," a medic pointed to Sean.

"Can't, I've got things to do."

"Yeah, well do them later." He took hold of Sean's arm and half pulled, half lifted him from the seat.

Sean felt too beat to argue. Only when in the unit and moving did he realise Victoria had stayed behind. They stripped off his jacket and shirt, covered him in a white gown and started to treat his wounds. An injection put him into a half doze and he closed his eyes, not really caring anymore. When he awoke his chair had been reclined, he had stitches closing the top of his head and two more in his cheek. The vehicle stood motionless. Across the unit an orderly sat filling in forms.

"Where's Sammy?" Sean asked. "Is she OK?"

"Sammy." The guy looked perplexed. "The other casualty had an emergency operation and is now under intensive care, situation stable but dangerous. But you can leave whenever you want."

"Where are we?"

"Central London."

The taxi ride cost him twenty pounds plus a tip and he fumbled for his keys wondering if Fox would reimburse expenses. The lift carried him to the second floor of the mansion block and let him out opposite his flat. His head hurt and what he wanted most was a whisky.

Key back in pocket he entered the flat and leant against the door. Home alone, no better situation, he sighed and passed to the living room. Victoria stood holding out a large whisky.

"Isle of Islay," she said. "Your favourite."

"You're an angel." He accepted and sat down. "How did you get in?"

"You gave me a key two years ago, remember? That's how long we've been an item. Or has that bang on the head muddled your senses?"

"Forgot, cos we always go to your place." He took a large gulp of whisky. "I needed that."

"Bought you a nice lamb shank, guaranteed no horse meat, a bottle of Rioja and some Cognac. You've had a hard day, lover."

"How's Sammy?"

"They hope to save her, no guarantees. I went to see her mother. She and partner are at the hospital."

Sean finished the whisky and held out his glass for more. Once full and the bottle beside him she entered the kitchen and busied herself. The meal tasted good, the wine perfect and the brandy lulling. When Victoria again entered the kitchen to complete her domestic role, Sean retired to the bedroom with the Cognac bottle. He checked his wounds, stripped off his clothes and got under the covers. Eyes closed he heard her enter and was conscious she stood by the bed looking down at him. "So how's my brave soldier?"

"Whacked, but somehow awake." He opened one eye.

She smiled and quickly undressed. "I know the best way to get you asleep," she said, straddling her knees over his hips, clasping with both hands as she fondled him. "And bless you, you're not so dysfunctional after all." She knelt up a little, manoeuvring so he slipped deep inside to be lost in the moist pleasure of her body. "Don't worry my love, just lie back and think of England. Leave the rest to me."

"You really fancy Sean Fagan?" Charlotte asked as she lay on the bed beside Anjali. "Or just hustling for pleasure?"

"My secret," Anjali said and smiled inwardly.

"I thought we didn't keep secrets. I'd certainly give him a try."

"He wouldn't disappoint. I found him most satisfying." Anjali turned her head. "How do you find Sammy?"

"My dear sister, life is life, sex is sex. Some things are best just enjoyed and not analysed. Wish I knew where she was. I'm worried."

"She's an able girl. Let's worry about tomorrow instead. You sure he'll come?"

"Positive. 11.30 sharp. No others, just him and me."

"What do you mean," Anjali leant up on an elbow. "I'm coming too."

"No, best I do this myself."

"Under no circumstances are you going there on your own. We started together, so we'll finish together. No arguments, no ifs, no buts. It's the two of us."

Charlotte blew out breath. "If you insist, but it may not be pleasant."

"Such is life. But why the top of Rutland estate tower block?"

"Because it's open with no place he can hide men."

"Charlotte, you can hide men all over a council tower block. They probably live there. The roof maybe open but that doesn't mean he won't have men in a stairwell below ready to grab us."

"He can't harm us, not if he wants his drugs."

"Don't believe it."

Sean woke to the sound of rushing water and felt across the bed to an empty space. For moments he breathed the lingering smell of her scent and brushed fingers over the empty space still holding the indentation of her body. Briefly he lingered in the bliss of half sleep, then the water stopped and the shower door clunked as it opened. End of peace and quiet. She's going to drag me off to war, he thought.

Minutes later Victoria left the bathroom dressed in bra and pants, a towel wrapped round her hair. "I'll check Fox and the Witch for any new developments," she said, going to her bag.

Sean examined the white lace of her pants stretching a little as she bent. "I want to go check on Sammy first, then, and only then, do I take up arms," he said.

She came back and stood over him as she flicked fingers across the iPhone. "So be it." She began to talk into the phone.

Sean lifted his index finger and stroked the lace between her legs. "It's only 0800 hours, still time for you and me to plan the day over an in depth meeting."

The military hospital on the Embankment appeared state of the art with every facility; bright, clean and functional. No scruffy waiting room filled with the smell of humanity, the sick, broken and derelict. No bodies on trolleys lined the corridors, no hard pressed nurses rushing from place to place with sheaves of paper. Instead, after Sean and Victoria had shown their ID's a smiling receptionist in pristine whites and cap filled out their passes and gave one to each. "Trooper Allbright, Ward 304, third floor, lifts over there," she pointed. "The ward's intensive care so report to Matron. No visitors without her permission."

"Is it urgent?" the matron asked when they arrived on the third floor.

"Personal. I was present during the incident, just want to know how she is."

"He," she said pointedly, "has a fifty-fifty chance of survival. Only two visitors are permitted at any one time. Mother and a close friend are already there, but," she came round the counter. "I'll speak with her."

Sean followed to the ward where an armed protection officer sat looking moody and uncertain. Sammy lay propped on a bed. Tubes ran into her body from various monitors, their screens flashing whatever information they recorded. Her eyes were closed and her face still as marble. If he hadn't known otherwise he would have thought her dead. Dolores turned when the matron spoke to her, then with Berty came out into the passage.

"You," she spat the word with the venom of a striking serpent. "If you were with her then you're responsible." Her eyes flared and for a moment Sean thought she would strike him but Berty placed a restraining hand on her shoulder, calming her.

"That's not how it was," Sean said.

"They threw her out of the army because of her sex and now you get her shot. She might die."

"She never left the army because of gender difficulties, Mrs Fairbright," Victoria intervened. "Instead they seconded her to a Special Forces unit dealing with counter terrorism. Why do you think she's in a military hospital? She received these wounds while on active operation."

"What? How can that be? She never told me."

"She wasn't allowed. Sean Fagan saved her life by carrying her to safety. If it wasn't for him Sammy would certainly be dead."

"Dead," Dolores repeated and began to weep. "The other one died, Sammy can't die too. She keeps her sister alive. She is her sister."

"And a tough girl. Brave as they come. She'll pull through," Sean said and stroked Dolores's arm. "You can be proud of her."

"They said she might never dance again. She loved dancing. Taught the kids at UY. Why didn't she tell me? Said she'd been sacked on medical grounds. She could have told her mum."

Berty put an arm round Dolores's shoulders and drew her close. "Like the man said, she's Special Services, secret and all that."

"Not disturbing anything am I?" Detective Inspector Dan Reece said as he entered the corridor with two male and one female constable. "They said I'd find you here."

"No more than two visitors," the matron told him. The Met protection officer stood holding weapon to chest as he barred the way.

"This is business, lady." Reece showed both of them his warrant card. "Dolores Fairbright, Bertha Smith. You are now both under caution. I'm here to question you over the poisoning of Chief Inspector Hackett during Saturday's Timpton fete."

"What are you on about? The boss had a heart attack," Berty said.

"The man was given oysters laced with cyanide poison. I want to know who prepared those oysters."

Both looked at him, open mouthed. "We all prepared them. They were fresh, nothing wrong with them," Dolores said, eyes narrow at his accusations.

"Not those eaten by the Chief Inspector. So, who prepared them?"

"Could 'ave been anyone, Charlotte, anyone."

"Right. I want a statement from both of you." He indicated the female constable to come forward. "You too Sean Fagan, and I officially inform, you are now all suspects in a murder enquiry."

"I'm afraid you'll have to wait," Sean said. "This lady," he indicated Victoria, "is from MI5 and I am about to accompany her to Thames House where I am also to be questioned."

"What?" Reece puffed fat cheeks as Victoria showed him her ID.

"I'm afraid we take priority," she said and grasped Sean firmly by the arm.

Reece stared as if kicked in his bloated stomach. "I'll have to check on this." He took out his mobile.

"My daughter is dying, don't you have any respect?"

"For a fairy and a couple of dykes, you're joking. Take their statements," he said to the woman constable. "And don't get too close. Don't want any hanky panky."

"You're fucking shit." Dolores struck out causing Reece to duck and drop his mobile as Berty grabbed her.

"Right, all of you downstairs, now," the matron ordered.

"This way sir." Victoria led Sean away, firmly holding his arm.

"You two wait."

"Arsehole," Sean said over his shoulder as he and Victoria entered the lift and closed the doors.

"You think Dolores poisoned Hackett's oysters?" Victoria asked.

"No, least she's not Justitia. I just don't see it in her character to go round killing scumbags. Neither do I see Berty in that role."

"That leaves Charlotte."

"Or Charlotte's little helpers. Sammy's not Justitia, she told me and I believe her. But she did collect the shells and hide them. That could have been to protect her mother or Charlotte. Maybe Justitia doesn't work alone. It has to be Charlotte. She has the physical and mental strength, the social background and is not encumbered by a husband or children. But who did she want to kill, Hackett or me?"

The lift stopped in the basement and both hurried to Victoria's BMW. "I have it from on high that Hackett had become disillusioned with Directus Iurisdictio. In return for no charges against him he had agreed to talk," Victoria said as she drove up the ramp and entered into traffic. "DI also knew you were a plant, so I guess they intended to poison you both. One down, one to go. You're still a target. Rashid maybe causing diversions, but Directus Iurisdictio remain active."

"If Charlotte told Salem to bury me at her farm, then she'll think I'm dead. I'd like to see her face when she discovers I'm not. I'd know for sure then. It also makes it nearly impossibly for her to have a pop at me."

"DI have cells all over England. It won't be Charlotte creeping in on you but someone from the Midlands, Scotland, someone out of darkness you wouldn't know or suspect. Remember DI, like Street Security, are national."

"So to get off the hook I need someone else to spill the beans on DI and once that knowledge is reported there'd be no point in killing me."

"You know someone?"

"I think maybe I do," Sean said. "But first I'd like a talk with Charlotte."

Victoria did not answer as her mobile rang. She plugged it to hands-free so Sean could listen. "This is surveillance one," a voice said. "The vehicle you requested has been picked up leaving the Congestion Zone. Seems the guy spent last night at a London hotel. Now heading for the M1. We have a drone following."

"Roger, please keep me informed," Victoria answered and switched off. "Looks like Rashid's heading back to St Albans and district."

"So let's jump him and remove him from the equation."

"Carrying an unlicensed firearm can get you five years inside," Anjali said, watching Charlotte remove the Browning 9mm automatic from under the pillow.

"Being unarmed when others carry knives and guns can

get you killed. I'll risk the five years."

Anjali plonked down on the bed. "Logic I suppose, but if shooting starts the police will soon turn up. We must avoid violence at all costs."

"So we plan carefully." Charlotte sat beside her, automatic in lap. "Rashid is sly, devious and in no way to be trusted. Think of him as a venomous snake trapped in a corner. I chose the tower block roof on the Rutland council estate because it's open space. The edge has a metre high wall, low enough to be deemed unsafe. Several disagreeable hoodies have committed suicide from there." She gave a tight smile. "Sad."

"Is that why you're familiar with the place?"

"Only through my charitable work with Universal Youth. Council estates are not really my scene," Charlotte said, clasping her hands as if in prayer. "The authority have never got round to erecting a fence so the whole area is locked and out of bounds. In consequence the locks are all smashed and the place completely open. Kids play up there, gangs meet and dealers peddle crack. But at 11.30 on a Monday morning it will be deserted."

Anjali looked sideways at her sister. "I investigated two of those so called suicides in my work. I found no proof to establish them as such, or, for that matter, no proof they were accidental or murders. If Rashid has men there they could easily throw us off."

"I think not." Charlotte picked up the automatic and removed the magazine before standing and crossing to her dressing table. She looked in the mirror at the reflection of them both while continuing to talk. "Firstly, the guy will want his heroin. The street value is around forty million and he's desperate for it. So long as we don't tell him where it is, we're safe," she said while emptying the magazine rounds amongst others lay on the dressing table surface.

"Charlotte my dear, we can't tell him where it is because we don't know."

"But he thinks we do. So even if he has men there he won't kill us, not 'til he has his hands on it or knows we are lying. That gives us plenty time to weave our deceit and extract." She began to select rounds from those before her, choosing each with careful deliberation as to its functionality.

"OK, so we ensnare him by his demands and threats for knowledge of the stolen drugs, but there will be no witnesses but us. So how do we record all this?"

"Two ways," Charlotte said as she began to refill the magazine with her chosen rounds. "First, over my iPhone. I phone the landline here which has an answer phone, I then leave the call open and the machine records everything said. Plus we each carry a portable voice recorder as back up." Charlotte clipped the loaded magazine back into the pistol butt. "It will work, I know it. For the sake of nation we have to give our idle and aimless young a chance at responsible citizenship. That means no drugs coupled with strong justice and good leadership. We get rid of soft justice, those who give rights to criminals while placing victims last." Charlotte huffed breath and turned towards Anjali holding the automatic.

"After that lecture, in case you start shooting every dodgy looking layabout, I think it safer I carry the weapon." Anjali held out her hand.

"Five years inside, remember? What about your career?"

"That ended when we laid our trap for Routt. If this comes to violence the chances are we'll both end up in prison."

Charlotte handed over the Browning butt first. "Hopefully you never have to use it. The point of this whole venture is bluff. Should it get physical, we run."

"Agreed." Anjali gave a tight smile while weighing the Browning in her hand. "You scarper, I'll cover."

No." Charlotte sat beside her, hugged her then clasped her fingers. "If it comes to violence, your job is to get all our info to the right authorities. Let me deal with Rashid, I'm not without ideas and resources."

"How?"

"Sex for one, he's been trying to get inside my knickers since we first met. For that purpose he'd rather take me captive than kill me."

"But he'll kill you afterwards."

"No, once you escape that will only make his situation worse. My death would have no point. Don't worry, Anjali, I got my own plans, Rashid's done for. Primary importance is the reputation of Universal Youth and our information to destroy him. No way will I let that shithead get away."

"OK," Anjali said. "Let's do this."

Charlotte checked her watch. "One hour thirty-five minutes," she said, going to her cupboard. "I have two tracksuits, we wear them and wrap towels around underneath to appear suitably fat. We buy a couple of baby buggies, put up our hoods and approach the tower block looking like estate mothers. It will fool his men and hopefully enable us to leave the same way."

"Hopefully." Anjali began to shed her outer clothes.

* * *

When Victoria's mobile rang she slotted it to hands-free on the dashboard. "We have a drone up and following the target," Fox said over the speaker. "Rashid is approximately four miles ahead of you and still heading north. I have a two man team on standby. What is MI5 providing?"

"Me," Victoria answered as she drove. "The Witch paid for yesterday, now it's you and CAT footing the bill."

"Come on Victoria, CAT doesn't exist, neither do its resources."

"You've got drones. Just make sure there's a couple available when needed. Should we require extra bodies we'll have to call in the police."

"Not advisable," Sean interrupted. "Rashid has a small army at his disposal. If it comes to confrontation too many boots around could turn it all very messy. Let's just see what develops and play this steady. We don't want the public involved."

"Agreed," Fox said. "I'll tell my boys to keep their distance." His voice suddenly rose an octave. "Target has left the motorway at junction 6 and is now heading for St Albans south. Will keep you informed."

"Roger and out." Victoria leant to switch off her phone while manoeuvring into the inner lane. "If, as I believe, Rashid is a member of Directus Iurisdictio, they will now realise he's been using them to remove his competition. Chances are they will kill him for it. Once charged as a premier drug baron he'll turn informer in exchange for leniency. This man can be very useful to us."

"I got my SOCA team close by covertly searching suspect premises," Sean said. "If push comes to shove, I'll call them."

"Searching for what?" Victoria asked as she turned off the motorway.

"Five hundred kilos of heroin is missing from Rashid's shipment, but for now my guys can't touch it, can't be seen even looking. I have no proof of anything."

"Want to tell me about it?"

"Not 'til they have something positive," he said running his hand up her thigh. "Let's keep our focus on Rashid. If he's been placed on the list, Justitia the Dark Angel will not be far."

On Anjali's advice Charlotte parked half a mile from the Rutland estate so her car would not be associated with forthcoming events. Anjali felt it essential to make their escape before any police involvement. She figured Rashid's reactions would fall one of two ways; playing the gentleman he pretended to be or turning violent. If the latter they were finished but she felt determined to go down fighting. She'd shoot him before allowing harm to Charlotte, or perhaps better to simply kill him outright at the first opportunity. The man spread spores of evil for his own gain, he deserved to die.

Opening the car boot Anjali helped her sister remove the newly acquired baby buggies, her body encumbered by towels wrapped around her waist and hips to give girth.

"How you feeling?" Charlotte asked, patting her own extended stomach.

"Fat. Honestly, how can anyone allow themselves to get such a size?"

"Easy, just eat too much. But it allows us to blend

perfectly with the environment." She opened her buggy then fluffed a blanket up in the seat. "Got to look like you have a baby," she said handing a second blanket to Anjali.

Anjali copied, then put up her tracksuit hood. "OK, ready when you are."

Walking side by side both checked their watches, judging their pace, periodically looking to the street for signs of a Death Head gang. No one. Anjali's confidence grew.

Rutland estate had the atmosphere of a Soviet construction, built in the sixties but now in need of demolition. Faded paint and replacement windows had once tried to enliven the place but austerity measures and council cuts now left walls streaked with dirt and green mould. A few cars stood parked before low rise flats that partially surrounded the ten storey block. The smaller of these cars gleamed under proud ownership; others had flat tyres, some stood dirty and scratched with spoilers, quadraphonic sound systems and no tax discs.

Anjali kept her eyes sharp as they turned towards the tower block, Charlotte did likewise. Three hooded youths sat on a wall near the entrance, one black, one white and one Asian.

"Oy, pig face," the nearest called. "Wanna give me a blow job?" All three laughed.

Anjali heard Charlotte hiss breath between teeth, her head down as she held the swing doors allowing Anjali to push her buggy into the entrance hall.

"Leave them here," Charlotte said manoeuvring the buggy beneath the stairs.

"They'll be stolen," Anjali warned and glanced out to the youths.

"We take the chance. You have the gun handy?"

"Under the zip, cocked with safety on." Anjali patted her shoulder bag as Charlotte pressed for the lift.

"Out of order, shit." She looked to the stairs.

"Let's jettison these first." Anjali pulled at the towels round her waist. "If Rashid sees us like this he'll small a rat."

"OK," Charlotte said and began to divest herself of the padding.

Once more slender, Anjali ran hands over body, waist and hips looking at the re-emergence of Charlotte's statuesque and athletic form.

"We'll switch on our voice recorders and connect my mobile at top of the stairs," Charlotte told her, then for a moment breathed deeply as if in preparation. "OK, let's go," she said, swinging up the stairs, Anjali close behind.

Anjali heard no sounds other than the scuffing of their trainers on concrete, neither did she see anyone in the corridors they passed. It seemed to her the whole building stood deserted, as if the residents had fled to a better life. When they reached the tenth floor she stood conscious of her breathlessness whereas Charlotte seemed unaffected. Ahead of them a single staircase led to a door and companionway giving access to the roof.

"Well, no men as yet. Switch on your voice recorder," Charlotte said, extracting the digital device and setting it to play before using her mobile to phone Halsham Manor's voice recorder. She returned both to her pockets. "I'll go first, you cover me. If Rashid is alone, fine. If he has Death Heads there we retreat and re-plot."

Anjali unzipped her bag and extracted the Browning

9mm. "OK sister, once again into the breech," she said rubbing Charlotte's arm. Both turned and mounted the stairs, Anjali aware that beyond the roof lay a long drop to the hard concrete ground below.

"The Rutland council estate." Freddy Fox's voice sounded over the speaker. "Target met up with a dozen guys then all entered the tower block. Few other people around. He's now alone on the roof. What's your location?"

"Still driving." Victoria pressed keys on the satnav. "Close, maybe five minutes. Why didn't you tell us earlier?"

"Because I had to change drones and needed to know the situation. My guys are also closing in but won't make contact unless you request. Target is now sitting on the roof as if waiting, which means his men are hiding on the floors below."

"We're on our way," Victoria said. "Watch out for my blue BMW."

"Roger, out."

"Do we go in or do we wait?" Victoria asked Sean.

"Wait and watch. The guy's lost all his shipment, he's desperate so it's my guess he'll do something desperate to reverse the situation. What I want to know is whether certain members of Directus Iurisdictio come to his aid in the hope he'll continue to supply money, or send the Dark Angel to kill him. I reason that's what the heavies are for, in case Justitia turns up. If so, when she does, we go in."

When Charlotte pressed the handle downwards, metal

scrapped on metal, the sound accentuated in the confined stairwell before the door swung open. Locking over her sister's shoulder, Anjali saw no one. For a moment she felt relief, hoping against hope Rashid had failed to keep the appointment. Charlotte edged forward until her shadow cast a feminine silhouette on the tarmac roof covering. She looked both ways, then her shoulders squared.

"He's here, alone, we have him," she whispered to Anjali before stepping out to have a clear view of the surrounding roof. "Good of you to come," she called, indicating for Anjali to follow. Anjali put away the Browning, zipped up her bag and pushed the activated voice recorder into her tracksuit.

"Two of you." Rashid stood from the parapet wall as Anjali came into view. "It's not often I get to be alone with two beautiful women. How can I help you?"

"Sorry to hear about your house," Charlotte said, moving closer.

"Cranby's house. Nothing left but a large hole. I thought maybe you could tell me about it."

"We weren't involved."

"Then why are we here?" Rashid said, stepping several paces away from the edge, his arms folded.

"Someone stole five hundred kilos of your heroin. I can tell you where it is." Charlotte also stopped so at least ten metres separated them.

"A socialite and a police officer telling me how to acquire heroin, most interesting."

Standing at Charlotte's shoulder Anjali realised Rashid played his own game with them. Clearly he would not trip up easily. "Universal Youth is our priority," she said. "It's why we're here. OK, drug pedalling is a somewhat unorthodox means of raising charitable funds but the end results justify the means."

"We tell you were the heroin is, you donate twenty percent to Universal Youth."

One arm across his waist, Rashid put fingers to his chin in mock contemplation. "My dear ladies, DI has no further purpose for me. I have recruited the men I need, and you, Justitia, with your colleagues, have removed all those little people who traded for the likes of Bently and Grogan," he said, looking between them. "So I think we'll just find out what devious game you two are really playing. Farid," he shouted.

Anjali turned as a brutish man stepped from the doorway. Of Asian appearance he moved with a roll of his shoulders, his teeth black and ragged, his face pockmarked. Behind him came other men, all with the Death Head logo on their T-shirts. Anjali unzipped her shoulder bag and extracted the Browning immediately causing the new arrivals to charge. Knocked off balance she heard the weapon fire, heard one of her assailants scream. Next moment she was held firmly as hands ripped off her tracksuit bottoms.

"We have a situation," Fox's voice came over the speaker as Victoria drove onto the Rutland estate. "Two women came out onto the roof and approached Rashid. We can't confirm ID but it looks like Robson and Osborne. Now there are other guys pushing out behind them. Both women are being attacked, their clothes pulled off. Looks like rape. We need immediate action."

Victoria halted under the block while Sean leapt from the

car at a run, leaving the door wide open. Impatiently he pressed for the lift, realised it didn't function, then went for the stairs.

"Are you armed?" he yelled to Victoria who threw off her heels to follow barefoot.

"Yes, are you?"

"The weapon you gave me."

"Don't use it unless desperate. It's illegal."

"One of those women is Justitia. Be very careful, she's more than illegal, she's extremely dangerous."

Anjali screamed, lashing out with one free arm as they pulled off her shirt. Left in bra and knickers her legs were pulled apart, one brute with his erect penis out getting down on his knees, shuffling in readiness between her open thighs. She heard Charlotte's scream of rage mingle with her own, then Rashid shouted a word of command in Urdu. Immediately she was hauled to her feet, allowing brief freedom to kick one bare heel into the face of her would be assailant. Held by two men with a third encircling their lower thighs, both women were turned to face Rashid. As if time held no importance he returned to the parapet wall where he sat toying with the Browning 9mm automatic pistol, the voice recorders in his other hand. He grimaced then threw them both into space.

"You are foolish women. But I am kind." He looked between them. "Give me the information I require and in a few days when I have my heroin, both of you will be released, never to see or hear of me again. The alternative is you get gang raped, then sold into sex slavery and taken to somewhere in Africa. Meanwhile I will expose the members of Directus Iurisdictio of whom I know many in high places. Secondly I shall destroy and expose Universal Youth as a recruiting ground for drug dealers and violent fascist street gangs. So first, which one of you is Justitia, the Dark Angel?"

"I am," Charlotte said immediately.

"No, I am," Anjali followed after hesitating.

Rashid stood up and levelled the automatic, waving the aim back and forth between them. "Before the explosion, Salem told me Justitia had stolen my heroin. And I believe it was her who blew up the rest. So Justitia, tell me where my shipment is or I kill your sister now." He pointed the Browning at Anjali.

"My pig farm," Charlotte said.

"Then I don't need you." He swung the barrel back. The men holding Charlotte shouted and ducked the same time Anjali heard the distinct click of the automatic's firing pin striking a dud round. Next moment two shots cracked the air causing men to crouch and turn towards the metal door. Anjali screamed her relief on seeing Sean and a woman, both of them waving automatic pistols, both shouting for everyone to lie face down. Now, loosely held, Charlotte had kicked one man aside and with a free hand punched another in the throat. Anjali also started to fight, biting the face of the man at her shoulder before throwing herself backwards over the one who held her thighs. The first screamed and clutched the torn tip of his nose, while the one on her left arm went down with her fall. Legs free she kicked out with her feet the same time digging nails into the eyes of the face beside her. His scream and the shouts of panic amidst more warning shots caused total confusion, allowing her to roll free and onto her knees before regaining her feet. Lashing out with fists and nails she ran to assist

Charlotte who fought with her knickers half down, her teeth bared while she kicked and punched anyone in range.

"Die, you murdering whore," Rashid shouted, waving the automatic as he tried for a clear aim the same moment as Charlotte launched herself towards him. The impact of Rashid's shot to her breast caused her whole body to judder. Anjali screamed as the bullet burst from Charlotte's naked back in a spray of blood, bone and flesh but the impact did nothing to stop her forward momentum. Shoulder down she drove hard into Rashid's chest, pushing him backwards until his lower legs hit the parapet wall. Anjali heard her own scream as Charlotte's weight carried both over the edge. For seconds her world seemed locked in a void without sound or movement, as if time and existence within had frozen. Then both fell, , leaving Anjali listening to her sister's last word, the syllables turning to a drawn out scream. " Justitia ... a ... a ...a ... a."

CHAPTER 24

St Albans police station vibrated with the noise of voices and activity. Police officers dragged from mundane routine found themselves suddenly part of a major incident where senior officers and high ranking strangers from other agencies mingled in the corridors, passing from meeting to interview rooms, each with their own theories and set of ambitions. In the foyer and outside, the Press had gathered in force, clamouring for statements or making up their own interpretation of events.

No one had asked Sean if he was armed, only why he had been there and what, if any, connection he had with yesterday's explosion. Both he and Victoria had agreed only to say they had arrived as part of an undercover operation into drug trafficking, all else was restricted information between SOCA and MI5. He revealed nothing of his own beliefs and conclusions.

DI Reece seemed totally enthralled. He had already given three press interviews and changed his suit twice, not noticing the stain on his wide silk tie. Finally he issued a statement that arrests were imminent. Sean despaired, he wanted out, to pick up his car and get back to London. He needed to talk with Cobbart and his team. He needed to refocus on his own operation which he felt was rapidly coming to an explosive head. He found Victoria sitting on a bench in the corridor, her elbow on the wooden arm, her palm against chin. "Ready for off?" he asked.

"Reece wants one more interview. The man's a pain in the backside. I think he's got it in for your friend Anjali." She looked pointedly at him but never asked the question he feared. Perhaps she guessed the truth and chose not to have it confirmed. After all, both pretended to be free agents.

"Two of my team have been searching Charlotte's farm,

digging in pig shit to be precise."

"And?"

"They found human teeth. The one part of a person's body pigs can't digest. Not a few teeth but hundreds and hundreds. One of the reasons she kept them free-range was so any evidence of such would be widespread and difficult to locate. When I lay in the field that morning the pigs chased me. Not normal behaviour for pigs unless they were hungry and used to eating human flesh. My guess is all the yobs who disappeared round this area probably ended as pork pies or bacon. Charlotte, or someone known to her, must have fed them body after body. No wonder so many criminals disappeared never to be found."

"So Charlotte was Justitia, the Dark Angel?"

"It would appear so, but the person or persons I want are those who controlled her, the local inner circle of Directus Iurisdictio."

"So, next step?"

"Dangerous."

"There you are." DI Reece came down the corridor, weaving round people as he approached. "We've arrested ten members of the Death Heads, another in hospital. All plead they only went there for a gang meeting, that Osborne and Robson tried to sell them sexual favours. Hard one to swallow that, but my mind is open. Just need the three of you to clarify a couple of points, then you can go."

Sean ground his teeth but followed the detective with Victoria. Anjali sat in the interview room, her eyes and expression without emotion or light. Sometimes her lips moved as if in silent prayer or unspoken conversation. A policewoman constable sat in one corner, notebook and pencil at the ready. Sean occupied a seat between Anjali and Victoria and folded his arms.

"OK, this interview 14.02 hours starts now." Reece pressed buttons on the recorder. "I am trying to ascertain why Detective Sergeant Robson and Ms Osborne were on the roof," he paused and looked between them. "A weapon has been recovered, though we have no firm forensics as yet, I believe it's the one which shot Ms Osborne. Can you explain why your fingerprints were on it, Sergeant?"

"When we were attacked one of them produced a gun. I struggled, grabbing it by both barrel and butt, but I never secured it," Anjali said in a flat, deadpan voice.

"Did either of you see this?" He turned to Sean and Victoria.

"Bodies were everywhere, punching, fighting, diving for cover. We, I mean Miss Lawless," he corrected himself on remembering his weapon was illegal. "She fired warning shots which caused more confusion. People scattered. During that mayhem Sergeant Robson grabbled with the automatic trying to disarm her attacker."

"I agree," Victoria said and crossed her legs, distracting the detective's attention.

"Why were you on the roof?" he said directly to Anjali.

"As a police witness. Charlotte had suspected Rashid of being a drug baron so went there to confront him. He suggested the meeting place. After we arrived men came and attacked us."

"Why didn't you first report to your superiors?"

"I had to be sure of the facts. In the past my information has been dismissed as pure speculation," she said, staring straight at him.

Reece shrugged and looked to Sean. "So why were you there, Mr Fagan?"

"As an ongoing part of a separate operation, one currently classified. Detective Sergeant Robson is also part of that operation so as from here further information is out of your jurisdiction."

For the first time Anjali turned and looked at him, but still without expression.

"MI5 confirms that," Victoria said.

Reece's fat jaw dropped and for a moment he stayed speechless. "I must warn you that Sergeant Robson has been suspended from further duty."

"That means SOCA pays her instead of you. Now we must go." Sean stood and Victoria followed. Anjali returned to staring at the wall. "This young lady has suffered a lot of trauma and grief, I suggest you allow her to go home and rest."

Reece wobbled his chins as he nodded.

Victoria dropped Sean by his car, kissed his cheek and told him to call that evening. An hour plus later he sat with Cobbart and his team in SOCA headquarters, Pimlico. Heidi waited to one side, pencil poised to scribble notes of proceedings.

"No more pig shit," Jan said crossing legs and folding her arms.

Sean considered her one of his most capable officers.

Tall and willowy with a neat, curvaceous bottom that men drooled over. She dismissed their licentious advances with contempt, preferring instead the comfort of her own gender. Sean considered her close cropped blonde hair and lack of makeup, thinking she would partner up well with Sammy.

For the moment we have teeth enough to make our case. More important, did anyone get evidence of the missing heroin?" He looked across the faces.

"Nothing on the Osborne site," Diane said. "And at Cranby Hall police were everywhere. We had plenty sniffer dogs to help and looked in most of the pig houses. Nothing." She shook her head. The opposite of Jan, Diane sat with buttons stretched over a full bust, makeup carefully applied to all parts of her face. As always her eyes held open invitation whenever they met with Sean's. On that count Sean stayed faithful to his bond with Victoria.

"I had to be certain," Sean said. "Which leaves one other player in the field. So we spring the trap I talked of." He looked to Chad's thoughtful Afro face, then to Simmy, Bob, Pete, Steve and Ahmid, the youngest of his operatives. All stared back, intent and unsmiling.

"You sure about this?" Chad asked.

"I trust you guys. When have you let me down?"

"When we're asked to work miracles," Jan said and shook her head.

"With luck an angel will help in that department." Sean gave no more, just watched them frown. "Also CAT and MI5 are involved."

"And would that be Victoria Lawless?" Diane asked, her face deadpan.

Sean pressed lips together. He never took umbrage. All of them ribbed him over Victoria, all of them had long guessed at the secret affair no one spoke of. "MI5 have been very co-operative in Operation Deep Cut, with Ms Lawless being closely involved. She's on the team."

"CAT, they're a bit dodgy," Simmy said.

"It's my belief that CAT are principal players here. I've only met four of them, all totally unorthodox and without consideration for rules. I also have the feeling they're playing games over our heads while working for a higher office within the Secret Intelligence Service. Their main asset is use of Tarantula Hawk surveillance drones. For our part we follow our sole objective, the dismantling of Directus Iurisdictio."

"So when do we start?" Simmy asked.

"As of now. Mike will brief you on your individual roles. When I leave here I go straight to lay the bait. I expect action to commence tomorrow so consider yourselves on standby. Mike."

Mike stood and came to the front. "OK. Simmy, Jan and Chad, you're firearms team with backup from CAT. Diane, you're co-ordination. Carole, Bob, Pete and Ahmid, you make arrests and secure prisoners. But remember we don't go in until moments before start of execution, and that will come via CAT who have a mole implanted amongst DI security." He looked to Sean. "Split second timing is essential to secure incriminating evidence."

Cobbart followed Sean from the room. "You sure about this?" Cobbart asked, shaking his head. "It's not at all conventional. Health and Safety would seriously disapprove."

"These people believe they are untouchable, because of it

they assume superiority. Their downfall will be arrogance coupled with belief they are above the law."

"Sean," Cobbart said with slow deliberation. "Your suspicions of CAT and higher dealings may not be without some foundation, in which case there maybe trading. Only the threat of law and retaliation may enter into this operation, not justice."

"What's your position boss?" Sean stared at him, he was placing more than trust in this man, he placed his life.

"Cranby," the voice answered, sharp and officious over Sean's mobile.

"We need to meet," Sean said.

"Concerning?"

"You and Directus Iurisdictio."

"The abbey, main entrance in one hour." Cranby rang off.

Sean made it with minutes to spare. Cranby watched his approach then entered the interior, moving up the aisle to sit amongst empty pews. Sean followed and sat beside him.

"I trust this is extremely urgent," Cranby said.

"You told me five hundred kilos of heroin were carried through that tunnel, yet there were cobwebs between walls and no footprints."

Cranby shrugged. "A dry floor wouldn't leave foot prints and spiders spin a web in hours."

"Spiders only spin webs where there is light to attract

their prey. Those cobwebs had been hanging for years and years, probably from when flaming torches had lit the walls. The floor is wet from rain which had soaked down through the earth. I left footprints."

"Are you calling me a liar?"

"You never saw anyone in that tunnel, which means the heroin was stolen before it reached Cranby Hall. How did you know that?"

"Have you told anyone of this?" Cranby looked sideways, eyebrows furrowed.

"No," Sean shook his head while staring up at the high vaulted ceiling. "I'm not one to spread rumours. I wanted you to confirm it."

"I saw men go in and out of the tunnel. That's all I have to say. I suggest you think about this and tomorrow report it to your seniors."

"Did you steal Rashid's heroin?"

"What a preposterous accusation. I am terminating this conversation forthwith." Cranby got up and left. Sean remained staring at his ancient surroundings, wondering how many other bloody plots had been forged within these holy walls.

"Peppered steak and red Rioja, your favourite," Victoria said. Draped in a cream silk slip of a dress that hung backless to her buttocks and moulded over the exquisite form beneath, she appeared at her most seductive.

Sean let his imagination fly, guessing she wore little if anything else. He looked forward to finding out. "Is this the condemned man's last meal?" he asked, showing a small, enquiring smile.

"You forget you have a band of able warriors riding to your rescue."

"If they get the timing right."

"The way you've planned it we won't know of that 'til after," Victoria said pouring his wine.

"Everything's down to CAT's hidden mole and more, the morality of Justitia. One has to have faith."

"You more than anyone." She watched him eat.

At the end of the meal, at the end of the wine, she led him to her bedroom and undressed him with tender fingers before allowing him to discover her nakedness beneath the dress. When he entered into the soft velvet of her body she closed her eyes, gently murmuring as if in ecstasy. He prayed she was, prayed she did not fake the paradise of love only to gratify his pride. He wanted it to be real. This could be the last time. It had to be real, it felt real, felt like absolute heaven.

At 7 am the alarm rang and jolted him into the sharp morning light. He dressed quickly and made coffee.

"You want breakfast?" Victoria asked, coming from the bedroom, this time in jeans and shirt, clothes suitable for action.

"Toast." He pressed buttons on his mobile. "Diane," he said when she answered. "All ready your end?"

"Two cars outside and waiting. Colonel Fox has a drone

on standby plus what he calls an extraction team. These guys are getting more and more involved."

"Safer for my part. OK, I leave the premises at 0745 hours. Stay vigilant."

"Roger that."

Sean switched off and ran his hand over Victoria's hips as she stood by the toaster. "What are you offering tonight?"

"Champagne, then all my love." She touched his cheek. "I'm scared, Sean."

"Don't be, you only die once."

CHAPTER 25

Sean drove to his flat constantly checking his rear mirror and reporting his position. Morning rush hour traffic had already slowed everything to a crawl, adding frustration to his anxiety. After finally parking in his reserved slot at the back of the mansion block he walked round to the front and gained access via a keycode. Instead of using the lift he ran up the stairs as customary, almost barging into a uniformed constable standing sentinel outside his flat.

"What the hell are you doing here?" he asked, seeing a totally unexpected disruption to his plan.

"You the resident of these premises, sir?" the constable asked, ringing the doorbell.

"So what?" Sean showed his ID. "I'm with SOCA."

"Best speak to the sergeant," he said as the door opened.

"Mr Fagan?" the sergeant queried, looking at Sean's ID. "You'd better come inside."

A third officer in a suit sat at the kitchen table, rising when Sean entered. "I'm Detective Inspector Willet," he said. "Sean Fagan, I'm placing you under arrest for possession of an illegal substance, namely one kilo of heroin. Anything you say will be taken down and maybe used in evidence against you. You will be removed to a police station and there make a statement."

"This is crap."

"Evidence says otherwise. You will come with us."

"I need to make phone calls," Sean started to protest, then suddenly realised the situation might not be as seen. More uniformed officers came into the room, too many he figured for a routine arrest unless they expected violent protest. One of them patted him down and removed his mobile, leaving him grateful he had returned Victoria's 9mm pistol. "Hey, you can't take that," he said, watching the phone placed in an evidence bag. Two of the largest uniformed men proceeded to cuff him.

"It will be returned," the sergeant said, gripping his arm as he was led from the flat. No one spoke in the lift and the bunch of men around him held up pedestrians as he was hustled to an unmarked police car. One of the escorts placed a hand over his head as they manoeuvred him into the backseat, all very health and safety. Two of the largest squeezed in either side, the inspector sat in front. Each remained stoic and rigid while the driver fixed a magnetic blue flashing light to the roof, then drove the car out into traffic.

Still uncertain if events were all part of an elaborate hoax, Sean stayed silent hoping against hope that his team followed and a drone hovered unseen somewhere overhead. Eventually he asked, "So where are you taking me, Paddington?"

"St Albans," the inspector said. "That's where your arrest warrant was issued. They'll answer your questions."

Reece, Sean thought. That arsehole with his interference was messing the whole operation. Why hand't Cobbart found out and informed the team? Unless, unless, just maybe these guys were not working to Metropolitan Police orders. At Junction 6 they turned off the M1 motorway and headed for the station until cutting round the back of the abbey to open country. Sean realised then and tried to sit forward, the same time the guy on his left fumbled something from his pocket and twisted sideways.

"Where're you going?" Sean said and winced when a

needle jabbed his neck with the sting of a wasp. "What the fuck?" He hunched shoulders attempting to dislodge the hypodermic syringe stuck in his flesh but jammed between solid walls of muscle and with his wrists cuffed he found it impossible to move. The more he struggled the weaker he grew.

"Do not resist, Mr Fagan. You are going nowhere. Your arrest is not under the laws of modern ineffective justice but under the ancient laws of Direct Justice, Directus Iurisdictio. You will be fairly tried and executed."

Sean listened to the words but instead of panic a sense of inner calm prevailed. He felt the needle removed from his neck but no pain. The faces either side now appeared to float in a haze, the bodies as if grey shadows. A voice spoke to him from nowhere.

"That's good, Mr Fagan, you relax. It will be over before you know it, you'll feel nothing."

"Relax," Sean murmured to himself. "Maybe sleep." His limbs seemed incapable of movement. Down here in the warm cosseted depth of somewhere he felt safe, he'd stay here a while, no need to move. People looked down at him, faces from above who lifted him to his feet and walked him somewhere, he didn't know where, didn't care. The handcuffs were removed then his arms tied behind his back, his ankles shackled by rope so he could only hobble. He felt a sting in his forearm and the mist started to clear. Someone blindfolded his eyes and he was led forward, the only sound being the fall of his footsteps on flagstones. Consciousness began to return with startling clarity. He became aware of the grip on his arms, the only indication of another's presence. A door opened and closed behind him. He sensed himself manoeuvred between wooden bars which enclosed at waist height. The escorts removed their hands leaving silence and darkness to enshroud him. He heard the murmur of voices as if a gathering judged him. A male voice spoke out, cultured and authoritative, one he immediately recognised. "Remove his blindfold," Cranby instructed.

Sean found himself in a single shaft of light, his surroundings left in semi-darkness which shrouded the five figures who sat before him, maybe one a woman. Bigger shadows loomed against the stonewall, large men, still and silent. He stood on some sort of platform enclosed by a stout wooden frame which rendered him immobile. Immediately in front, a singular wooden lever protruded a metre high while above rope which then formed a noose, ran through a metal eye secured to an oak beam. Realisation came with swift horror. He stood on a gallows.

"Sean Fagan, you are charged and found guilty of betraying your high office in the administration of justice. The Metropolitan Police searched your flat and found one kilo of heroin from which no doubt you planned to make evil profit. You were in liaison with Rashid and threatened to corrupt the youth of this country with vile drugs and crime. For this, the court of Directus Iuriscictio sentences you to be hung by the neck until dead. Justitia, carry out the sentence." Cranby sat down again.

Justitia emerged from an alcove with the silent flow of a ghost draped in a long dark cloak, the hood hiding her face so Sean saw only the white glisten of one cheek. In silence she loosened the knotted rope from the wooden rail, so allowing a length to slide through the metal eye until able to place the noose over his head. This close he stared directly into her face and the steady, unblinking determination which glowed within her eyes.

"Anjali," he whispered.

"The Dark Angel, no less," she whispered back and tightened the noose around his neck. "Now the time has come, Sean Fagan, prepare yourself for the unexpected." She stood away, allowing enough slack for the fatal drop before retying the remaining rope to the wooden rail in some secretive slip knot known only to her calling. "We are ready," she spoke aloud and caressed her hands over the polished shaft of wood as if stroking some ritual phallic symbol.

Sean opened his mouth to shout. This was not as planned, this was not meant to happen. Anjali stared back at him, her eyes wide so the whites seemed huge, her jaw revealing the slightest tremor as the small hands which had caressed him in their lovemaking tightened white knuckles around the lever.

"Now," Cranby ordered.

Sean sensed the floor beneath his feet fall away. Shouting a last protest, he saw flashes of light, felt the noose tighten and jerk his neck, felt his head yanked to one side, his breath choked before hard flagstones on the floor below buckled his legs, painfully crashing him down on his knees. Next moment splayed legs landed across his shoulders, forcing him face down before a soft body rolled on top of him. Nose squashed against the ground, the rope was loosened from around his neck and his head jerked upwards allowing the noose to be pulled over his face.

"Just do as I tell you," Anjali said while producing a penknife to cut the rope hobbling his legs. "Run, we have seconds." She hauled him upwards, threw aside the noose and rushed him through the darkness until they hit a wall.

Sean heard shouting from above and a light flashed down through the gallows trapdoor. From somewhere within the pockets of her cloak Anjali produced her own torch and dragged him along the wall to a door. For moments she fumbled with keys, then opened the lock and pushed him to a passage beyond, the same time someone lowered themselves through the trap. On the other side she re-locked the door, threw aside the key and hurried him towards steps and daylight. "Bloody run, run," she yelled. "If they catch us they'll kill us both."

In the long corridor above, chairs lined the walls between high sash windows which gave onto a cloister and ornamental gardens beyond.

"Free my hands," he said offering them up as he turned his back. More shouting sounded from somewhere in the house as he waited, feeling her sawing at the ropes, straining against the knots until suddenly his wrists flew free. Three men came into the corridor from the far end, shouting as they raced towards him. Sean grabbed one of the chairs and raising it above his head, crashed it down against a wooden window to smash glazing beads and glass. The second swing completely destroyed the lower frame allowing Anjali to climb through while he battered one of the men with a third swing, then threw the chair at the remaining two. Next second he was also out the window, following Anjali's speeding figure down the cloister and into the garden via an arch in the enclosure wall. On the other side two men in military fatigues stood with automatic rifles at the ready. Anjali had stopped, clearly not knowing which way to run.

"Mr Fagan, we've been waiting," one of the men said and lowered his weapon. "Boss is round the front."

"Who the fuck are you?" He held Anjali's arm, as much for his own reassurance as her protection.

"Combined Agency Task Force, Special Ops. This way please."

Five Land Rovers stood on the manor house driveway, the manicured lawns spreading to distant walls and gates.

Freddy Fox leant against one of the vehicles in his customary wax jacket, cords and cloth cap.

"You OK Fagan?" he asked as Sean and Anjali were led to him.

"Where's my team?" Sean looked as more armed militia led handcuffed prisoners from the house, Lord Cranby amongst them.

"Well, as this is all kind of off record, we felt it best if officialdom with its rules were kept to one side. In consequence they're probably in some café drinking tea. Cobbart's around but I don't want him too involved." He looked at Anjali. "So Ms Robson, how are you?"

"Still somewhat bewildered." She looked at Sean as if wanting to say more, her lips trembling. "I phoned you three times telling you to get out. I warned you but you took no notice."

"Oh yes I did, that warning was from someone with a conscience. I didn't know it was you but I put my faith in it," Sean said. "Faith I knew would not be misplaced. Faith in a Dark Angel who stood for justice, not self-righteousness. One who refused to kill an innocent man. Which is why you left Hackett's death to your sister, your shadow Dark Angel, but one who was a stalwart of Directus Iurisdictio." He rubbed his neck. "Though I must admit, for moments I really believed you were going to hang me."

"For moments so did I," Anjali said. I was so worried about the knot I tied on the gallows. I thought it might not pull lose. Then you would have hung. I think Colonel Fox will explain. You will excuse me." Tears streaked her cheeks. "Hope to see you at the funeral. Glad we made it." She touched Sean's arm and walked away.

* * *

The debriefing took place at some disused RAF barracks, as unknown to Sean as the manor house where his execution nearly took place. Individual interviews with lower and senior members of Directus Iurisdictio were conducted in secrecy while Sean sat brooding in an office overlooking a weed infested runway. The justice of humanity had been placed above the justice of law, justice into which he had become embroiled.

Victoria joined him after two hours and hugged him for a full minute before he spoke.

"Did you know about all this?" he asked.

"Not until after you left. All arranged between the Witch and Fox. Anjali was so distraught over her sister's death, followed by Cranby's demand for your execution, she went to Fox and confessed. In the true tradition of CAT, Fox gave her sanctuary within their ranks, which meant exoneration from any possible charges. She in turn told them all she knew. She's now one of their covert operatives. That aside, they're proclaiming you a hero who went beyond the call of duty. They now have more information and more insight into Directus Iurisdictio than they dared dream of."

"Members talked that easy, I'm surprised. They'll probably get at least five years apiece."

She took his hand, leaning to him as she might a child. "You don't understand, Sean. No one is going to prison. The whole objective was to get informants at the heart of Directus Iurisdictio. Because of your bravery they have achieved that. In return for no charges, all of them are talking non-stop. They're even signing the Official Secrets Act. Most of them are low rank, but Cranby has already mentioned names which reached to the highest levels of Government, banking, law and civil service. Within a year, MI5 and CAT will have DI's complete infrastructure. The

Witch is so pleased she's even given me time off. Come on," she stood. "I'm taking you home for champagne and love."

In the corridor outside Sean came face to face with Mrs Gosling being led from one interview to another. She looked at him with nervous eyes, her face pale, her lips compressed.

"I'm ... I'm sorry," she said. "I voted against but Cranby held the deciding vote and said you must hang. You understand my reasons for joining DI, I explained. No one else did anything. Criminals were treated better than victims. The people had to do something. Directus Iurisdictio offered the solution. Don't you ever seek revenge through retribution?"

Sean thought of spiders in a tunnel. "Yes," he answered and moved on. Before entering Victoria's car he borrowed her phone to call Cobbart.

"Got something interesting to tell the team. If you can have them assembled at HQ, say in one hour fifteen, then I think you could salvage a result from this op."

"Will do," Cobbart answered.

"We were pushed right out of it," Simmy said, looking to the team now crowded into the briefing room. "We weren't even allowed into the grounds."

"Bloody MI5 had the place full of CAT operatives." Jan puffed out her cheeks. "Completely wasted our time."

"I can't tell you the details," Sean looked over their faces and read their frustration. "I can only say between various agencies a lot of trade and double-dealing is afoot. However, a central figure to all this is Cranby," he paused, knowing these guys would go the official route which would probably do him no good. "On Cranby's estate there is a wood to the side of where his house once stood. Beyond the trees you'll find an old stone tower. A heavy slab in the centre of the floor covers a hole leading to a tunnel that goes back several hundred metres to what was once the cellar. That end is unquestionably blocked by rubble, but if you look into the hole you'll find one hungry, thirsty and by now very co-operative man called Salem. Ask what he knows about five hundred kilos of missing heroin. I think he'll tell you enough to make your day."

Anjali hated the smell of hospitals, had hated them since she was twelve and sat by the bedside watching her mother die of injuries sustained in the car crash. Her father already lay dead, his skull and body crushed by the car's impact against the motorway bridge. Anjali had felt joy at that but utterly engulfed by guilt over her mother's death. She should never have told of her father's abuse. Perhaps then her mother would not have killed him, would not have driven their car along the motorway at one hundred and twenty miles an hour. Now guilt over Charlotte's death also savaged her mind, tearing her apart as if the jaws of some angry beast screamed for vengeance. It was she who had brought Charlotte in when they were both in their late teens. It was she who had taught her to kill, to feed bodies to pigs or bury them in some lonely wood. Guilt over her death consumed her and only in the continuation of their work by destruction of evil did she believe lay forgiveness for their deeds. She had to go on.

Sammy gave a tight smile and reached out slim fingers. "She protected us and destroyed Rashid," the girl said. "Without his money the Death Heads will fall apart. I loved Charlotte, she looked after me. I miss her like I would miss my mother, sister, lover, all rolled into one. But I never betrayed her; I never knew she helped you. Even if I did, I would have stayed silent. My job with CAT was to infiltrate the SS and the Death Heads. I met Charlotte through Universal Youth, we both worked hard to support it. Love between us just grew. She never, ever mentioned Justitia or what she did for her. If I had known I would have helped too. She was, is, an angel and angels never die. I feel her spirit as I feel Sam's spirit and because of that I can help you. Don't think of yourself as the Dark Angel, but the White Angel, one who protects the good and the just."

Anjali squeezed the hands between her own. "They've let them all go, pardoned them in exchange for information and secrecy. I don't know what will happen now."

"I'm being let out this afternoon," Sammy said. "Fox is my boss, but he's OK and now we're sisters at war against a common enemy, we can work together. Charlotte would have wanted that."

For a moment Anjali bit her lip. "The police have released her body, the funeral is in three days. To honour her memory I believe there is something we can do. Are you able to walk?"

"On crutches, yes. They operated and cut away the damaged bits. I'll never have babies," she shrugged. "So I've arranged to complete my gender re-assignment. The wounds are still healing, I can't run or jump, but I can do most other things."

"Colonel Fox tells me you were in the army, the Paras no less, a trained sniper."

"That and more. I did it for my brother, the sibling I enshrouded. But I couldn't maintain the pretence, they wouldn't let me into the women's side, so told me to leave."

"I'll talk with Fox. I think Justitia has one last mission."

CHAPTER 26

Sean rested his elbows on the table, feeling the ache in his neck more irritating than the bruising to his ribs inflicted by countless kicks. Opposite, Victoria and Alice Sibree sat in moody contemplation, Victoria's feminine aura contrasting with the Witch's short razor cut hair, her drawn expressionless features, her skinny frame draped in a straight grey suit. Others present were Fox and Cobbart. Sean surveyed their disgruntled faces. The Witch and Fox looked to him with hard eyes. Victoria and Cobbart stared at the tabletop.

"You should never have told anyone about that heroin without my say so," Fox said.

"You wanted me to let Salem die?"

"He would have lain there for years; no one would have blamed you."

"Colonel Fox, five hundred kilos of heroin out amongst the populace would have caused extensive violence and crime," Cobbart said. "Sean had no choice but to report his suspicions of Cranby and Salem's whereabouts. We stood aside while you raided the manor house and secured your DI prisoners. We have made no comment on that or the lack of charges which followed. But there is a limit to what we close our eyes on. And that limit is five hundred kilos of heroin."

Sean nodded to his boss, glad of the man's support. "Cranby will sell the whole consignment to a drug wholesaler and with a percentage of profit build himself a splendid new house. He might be a member of the Security Services with influence in Government and Whitehall, but his sole objective is self. He is one of the controlling influences within the National Street Security gangs, a fascist organisation that will eventually attempt to bring him and others to power in the same way such gangs brought Hitler to power."

"You don't understand," Alice said. "I arranged immunity from prosecution in return for high ranking names within Directus Iurisdictio. Likewise with lesser members for their information. If Cranby is arrested for possession of drugs he will see it as a betrayal. He might well start talking to the Press. If he reveals the same names given to me then Directus Iurisdictio will become world news. Accusations levelled against certain ministers and MPs would bring down the Government and do enormous damage to our economy. We are just climbing out of the worst recession in years. Serious incriminations against our banks and financial system via the criminal activities of some leading members, no matter how well meaning or misguided, will not be welcome. In the national interest we must prevent this."

Fox pursed his lips and stroked his chin while looking between them. "One of the negatives in allowing Cranby free of prosecution is that it places him in a position where he has opportunity to blackmail us. First over our deal with him and secondly by release of more names to the Press. Under the circumstances, I think it prudent to prevent this, the same time moving against any threats of neo-Nazi insurrection. Additionally it will help keep other informants mindful of their secrecy."

"So what do you propose?" Cobbart asked.

"Considering the moral high ground of some who are present that will remain classified and strictly confidential." Fox folded his arms and the Witch gave a distorted smile.

Outside in the corridor Cobbart drew Sean to one side. "Fox is going to try and recruit you," he said in whisper.

"From that little meeting I think not, though working

without the confines of rules and regulations is tempting."

"Then be tempted. For Fox, you know too much for one on the outside. You're also clearly a very able man. Fox will judge your recruitment as a major asset for CAT. The same time I know your loyalty to SOCA and nation. We need someone just to keep an eye on things in case he oversteps his brief. When he approaches, say yes. Good man."

Anjali shifted papers in Charlotte's office. Most were farm related; feed bills, sales, wages, invoices for goods in and out; all very tedious. With no one to care for them and with the lawyers' agreement, the livestock had gone to auction. It left Anjali with a sense of closing the place down and abandoning her sister's home. She rested her head against the desktop and wiped tears from her eyes. Money, money, Charlotte had left her everything. She was rich, richer than she wanted or needed. That, she figured, was why Charlotte had shown such trust. Instead of leaving it to Universal Youth she wanted Anjali to do so for both of them, to show them as two sisters. She would sell the farm, the house, the contents, whatever lay in the bank. All would go to Universal Youth, then perhaps Charlotte might rest in peace.

The sound of pigs squealing on the near hillside lifted her head, pigs where no pigs should be held only one meaning. Looking from an upstairs window she saw the feeding pen contained at least a dozen sows, floppy eared British Lops. She knew exactly who they belonged to, his horsebox and Land Rover stood to one side. She took out her mobile, keyed numbers and spoke. "Stand to."

Out of the garden she strode up the hill with unhurried ease, seeing the pen had been divided in half. Cranby stood in the empty one, while two men remained outside by the gate which divided them. Anjali figured this might be her end but didn't really care. She deserved to die. Her will had been made, a little to Sammy, the rest to UY. Perhaps she'd meet Charlotte again, or maybe both would be cast into hell.

"We've been waiting for you," Cranby said, above noise from the quarrelling pigs. "Thought our hungry friends might attract you. They become so agitated when starved."

Anjali stopped by the railings and watched Cranby reach into his jacket to produce a small, shiny automatic. "It used to be Rashid's," he said. "Don't worry, I won't let them eat you alive."

"How kind of you." She looked to his minders. She recognised both as constables from her own station. Large able bodied men with not much brain. Both had an expression of nervous uncertainty. "Don't worry boys, if Justitia dies, no one will be left to hang you."

"You betrayed us," Cranby said. "You betrayed your oath and our sacred laws. The penalty is your life."

"No, my lord, you betrayed our laws by stealing heroin, by condemning an innocent man to hang. You put greed and prestige before honour, truth and justice. You are the one who should die."

"I am the Lord High Justice of this area. I, and no other, decree laws and penalties. Now get into the pen." He levelled the pistol.

Anjali climbed in beside him. "Aren't you scared your friends will open the gate, that the pigs will eat us both?"

"These men have sworn allegiance to the laws of Directus Iurisdictio and unlike you, Justitia, they will honour their oath."

"I wonder." She raised her arm, then dropped it. Seconds later Cranby's head exploded with the impact of a soft headed bullet. Brain, blood and bone sprayed sideways towards the pigs who scrambled in noisy confusion while the faint echo of a rifle shot rebounded from the trees. Anjali winced and both men screamed in shock and disbelief. "Don't move," she shouted at them and snatched the fallen automatic. "One of your heads is in the crosshairs of a sniper's telescopic sights. Do exactly as I tell you, or die." She vaulted out of the pen and glanced back at Cranby's fallen body. Both men continued to stare at her with gaping mouths. "Open the gate," she ordered over the pigs' agitated squealing.

"No, for fuck's sake, they'll eat him."

"You would have them eat me, so now have them eat him. I am Justitia, the Dark Angel. Open the gate or you will both die."

"Look, you can't do this."

"You came here to murder me, there is a witness to everything that has happened. Open the gate, let the pigs devour the body, then go away. I will talk with you later. Directus Iurisdictio is finished, betrayed by this man. Now a new order takes over and we have much to do." She turned and started back towards the house, hearing the pigs go crazy with blood lust. She turned once to see them fighting each other in their rush, pushing round the body as they fell to eating. Without turning again she continued walking, knowing Sammy would be packing up the long range sniper rifle provided by Fox. Later they would meet, maybe they would get drunk together, cry together, even sleep together. They were united now both by Charlotte's death and the resurrection of Justitia in another form. They had struck a bond that bound them forever in unholy union.

* * *

In dark suit and tie and with Victoria by his side, Sean walked up the driveway to the 12th century church of Timpton village. On either verge stood members of National Street Security in light khaki uniforms and berets, gold lanyards hanging from their right epilates, silver flashes of the SS on their arms and chests. To Sean only the swastikas were missing. The curate welcomed them at the door and they entered to the sounds of Bach's Mass in B minor. Sean recognised senior members of Universal Youth and police amongst the mourners. Others by their dress and bearing were clearly from high places and positioned at the front. Behind were local farmers, villagers and social friends. Sean saw no one other than Anjali who might be family.

Seated in isolation with Sammy, each held the other's hand, seemingly oblivious to the gathering behind them. Occasionally Sean heard whispers as to the whereabouts of Cranby, brought to the fore by his absence. He made a fair guess of where the man might be but felt it best left to the consciences of others.

Throughout the service a group of young men and women in tight black suits occasionally stood and sang solemn and oppressive Gregorian chants which reduced both Anjali and Sammy to silent tears, their faces gaunt with grief. Praise for the deceased came from the low and the noble. Then all followed the coffin out to the graveyard and a hole in the ground.

Standing a few rows back Victoria linked Sean's arm. "Come what may, in body or in ashes, this is where we all end," she whispered.

Sean shook his head. "No, some end as bacon or a pile of pig shit. We'll never know how many but I bet Cranby is amongst them."

"Anjali knows, I'm sure."

"But Anjali's not saying – and no one will ask her because no one wants the truth."

Earth fell on the coffin, then flowers were placed on the earth. Birds sang in nearby trees and a plane heading for Luton Airport droned overhead. "All as normal," Sean said as people dispersed. "One world on top, another hidden below, all controlled by the few."

"You're getting to be a cynic." Victoria tugged his arm and led him to the grave.

He shook hands with Anjali and kissed her cheeks. "Will we be hearing from you?" he asked.

"I've resigned from the police and joined CAT. So in some silent, secret way, I suppose you will." She clasped Sammy's hand and gave the youngster a tight encouraging smile. "Guess that makes us all brothers and sisters in arms."

Sean touched her shoulder and walked away. Fox waited by the churchyard gate. Victoria let go of Sean's hand. "Say yes. You'll not regret it. Out there the world is big and bad and there is much for you to do. I'll be by the car."

"So, what's your decision?" Fox asked.

"Will pension and salary be the same?" Sean thrust hands in pockets and looked to Fox with eyebrows raised.

"Pension, yes. You'll remain officially with SOCA so they provide salary. But with CAT you also get additional bonuses and expenses after each operation."

"You mean I'll be able to afford a new car and still pay my girl's school fees?"

Fox laughed. "Plus holidays in the Seychelles, but don't tell anyone."

"When do I start?"

"Soon as you sign the papers, pass selection and complete the training. A CAT operative needs more than police skills. You will be drafted to our Secret Operations Executive. Your assignments will be covert, undercover and mainly alongside MI5. Other times in far away places with MI6. You will need the field ability of an SAS member, the inquisitive searching mind of a detective, the invisibility of a spy and the tenacity of one who never lets go. The demands on you will sometimes be disagreeable and frequently formidable. On the up side you make your own rules and decisions, you whack the bad guys the best way you can and do a lot of good for humanity and nation. You also get a plenty of leave. You'll need it."

"OK," Sean offered his hand and felt the firm grip of Freddy Fox's fingers. "Let's go to war."

THE UNWANTED

People who bought this book also bought

The Unseen

Sean Fagan of SOCA investigates the ritual murder of three young women and finds links between each victim and the world's most popular computer game, Princess Kay-ling. When police high-tech units examine hard drives taken from the murder victims' PCs, traces of subliminal psychotic induction are found. This induces victims to trust and obey characters from the game. These characters then order the women to remote places or use this trust to gain entry into their homes.

When a fourth woman is murdered in Ireland, Sean realises he hunts a serial killer capable of global influence. He also discovers the Government is aware and observing. When his young daughters become involved, nightmare encircles him.

NEXT TIME YOU SWITCH ON YOU COMPUTER
ARE THE UNSEEN WAITING TO ENTER YOUR
MIND, OR ARE THEY ALREADY THERE?

The Uncounted

Sean investigates the Agency, a criminal fraternity trafficking illegal immigrants. Trapped in a wretched world of modern slavery and barbaric killings, Jelena, an illegal from Kosovo, dreams of freedom but violent forces which shaped her adolescence still dominate her life. Jelena is given to an Islamic terror cell as a disposable chattel and finds herself locked in a luxury flat with millions of virus contaminated bank notes. Death seems certain until events reunite her with Gavrilo, the boy she had known and loved when both were adolescents. As Fagan closes, a bomb containing enough Anthrax to kill thousands is unwittingly carried by Gavrilo into Central London. Fagan and team desperately search as the timing device ticks to detonation.

IS THE GIRL ON THE TRAIN BESIDE YOU A FREE CITIZEN OR TRAPPED BY DEBT BONDAGE, ONE OF MANY THOUSANDS ILLEGALLY TRAFFICKED INTO BRITAIN FROM EASTERN EUROPE?

THE SLAVE TRADE IS ALIVE AND FLOURISHING.